THE REAPER'S SEED

THE SWORD AND THE PROMISE

Jaffrey Clark

ISBN: 0975469037
ISBN-13: 978-0975469033

DEDICATION

To the ones who hope for redemption.

ACKNOWLEDGMENTS

Many thanks to friends and family who have read bits and pieces of this story and shared their thoughts. A lot of people fall into that group as this story is ten years in the making, and only halfway done. Special thanks to Graham Osborne, Nic Imfeld, Colin Scull, Philip Gemmell, and most of all, my parents and my precious wife.

CHAPTER 1

"Hurry! We can't be late."

Sometime after the sun had set, the voice of a boy no more than twelve years of age, urged the progress of one still younger. As two dark figures, they made their way on foot along a winding trail. The forest floor was already coated with the first leaves of fall, filling the moist air with their earthy scent. Though the trail was well worn and easily followed, underbrush from both sides threatened to grow it over.

With a waning moon and only a few bright stars shining through the dark forest, each step needed careful placement. A steady breeze blew through the trees from the north, causing shadows to cross the path with the sway of the branches above.

As was common with these two, and quite natural among siblings, the older and taller led the way. Their thin hooded coats and tightly woven slacks afforded as much camouflage as a deer or rabbit would need to avoid unwanted attention. With similar awareness as such creatures the two boys watched the way closely, peering into the dark to detect any movement. At a point where the trail passed between two monstrous oaks and into a clearing, the older of the two broke into a trot. His right hand never left the hilt of a short sword he kept tucked in his belt. His younger brother, who had no such defense, kept close at his heels.

Each had their own way of moving through the forest. A fallen tree provided the first with an obstacle to climb over while the second slipped under with remarkable agility. A large stone in the path was both for jumping over and jumping off. Before long the woods grew thin, allowing a little more light through the thick canopy above. The underbrush gave way to the long grass that filled the fields ahead of them but the trail continued, only now against a softer terrain.

Breaking from the edge of the trees, the boys entered a vast field with a lone hill at its center. Leaving the shadows of the forest behind, they cast shadows of their own as they followed the trail toward the hill before them. On the crest of this hill a fire flickered in the night like a beacon, quietly calling for an audience.

Upon seeing it, the older of the two pointed with great anticipation. "There it is! They are beginning!" he cried under his breath.

With a laugh they both took off running, racing each other to the top. Their hoods swung behind them, wrapping over one shoulder, then the other. The older had the clear advantage in length of stride and pulled away, though not by much, for his little brother was determined not only to keep up, but keep from being left behind. As they neared the top, the silhouettes of people sitting around the fire could be seen, with several more still arriving.

"We haven't missed a thing," the older brother exclaimed through labored breath.

"We made it," the younger sighed, wiping his forehead with his arm.

The boys slowed their pace as they arrived at the small gathering, catching their breath as they began to observe all who were present. The group consisted of a range of ages. Though it was mostly men, the women and children there were given the seats closest to the fire. Quietly the boys made their way around to a long, flat rock set at the base of a tree where an old man sat at the head of the group. There beside him, they took their place on a log at either side.

In a soft voice he welcomed them. "I am pleased to see you both here. I trust your uncle's directions served you well. Did you have any trouble finding your way through the woods?"

"No, sir," the older of the two responded quickly. "We did quite well along the path. It wasn't hard at all." He beamed at the chance to give a good report of himself.

His younger brother made sure to join in the response, though it was an echo of what had already been said. "No, sir, we had no trouble at all." He was still out of breath as he pulled his hood up over his head tightly and shifted in his seat. In the light of the fire, an unsightly scar on his neck became visible. Having worn it since birth, he had made a habit of wrapping his hood a little tighter than was necessary to hide it from view.

"Bravery begins in the small things," the old man said. "Not many boys your age come to these meetings." His long gray hair swayed in the breeze, which was stronger up on the hill, and his beard moved in rhythm with his words. "Very well.

I am proud of you both."

"Thank you, grandfather," the older of the two replied. "We just can't wait to hear you tell the Story. We have never heard it told at Hill Top before."

"Well, Corred, tonight you will. The Story makes us who we are and gives us direction for the future." Turning to his other grandson, he placed his large, calloused hand on his head. "Androcles, it is also time you learned what all men must know."

Androcles smiled widely, content just to stare up into his grandfathers eyes for as long as he could.

Waiting for the group to continue gathering, the old man sat with his arms resting on his knees, patiently warming his hands by the fire. His broad shoulders hung low in such a position but it was clear by their width that he was not lacking in physical strength. The cloak he wore was one of distinction, set apart from his ordinary dress, for he was a wise man, once a warrior. Less remarkable were his shoes, made of animal skins and wearing thin near the toes. A long sword lay at his feet. Its leather and metal scabbard was adorned with various carvings, and the butt and hilt were bright silver. The handle was fashioned from a type of dark, grainless wood that appeared timeless, not at all worn by use.

As he sat observing the crowd fondly, his heavy brow shaded his eyes, which were only revealed by the flicker of the flames before him. His whole appearance spoke of old age, except his eyes. Though the face surrounding them was weathered, wrinkled and scarred, his eyes were young and bright, as if the years he'd lived had only deepened their color.

The light of the fire danced also among the branches of the tree that hung over the group. Its twisted form marked the landscape, standing alone, scarred by lightning, abandoned to the sun. Apart from the vines that climbed the base of its trunk, it had not a single leaf to rustle in the wind, but its roots were as firm as rock, part of the hill it stood upon.

The old man called the group to attention. "Thank you all for coming," he said with a nod. Trying to make eye contact with as many as possible, he greeted them, some by name, but all with, "Peace, be with you."

He was greeted in turn. "Peace, be with you, Creedus Corred."

Corred took it all in, crossing his arms over his knees. Pulling his hood up onto his head where it hung loosely, the light of the fire revealed the whole of his face. He not only shared his grandfather's name, but his features, and most of all, his deep blue eyes.

Looking around at the group and then back at his grandfather, his mouth half open, Androcles, on the other hand, looked very little like his grandfather. With green eyes and curly blonde locks, he was short, even for his age. Brushing some hair from his eyes he leaned forward to get a better look at his grandfather's face.

When the group had fallen silent again, and all eyes were on Creedus, he began . . . . .

"The City of Amilum stands abreast the highest mountain in the West." Pointing there with the full length of his arm, he looked into the distance, fixed on the far horizon. "It is a beautiful city, unlike any other, a city of life and love, with light like the sun and perfect peace. There is no pain and no death in the City of Amilum. Plants do not die or wither. Weeds are not to be found. And eagles, the most beautiful creatures, grace the skies with their flight. Every citizen of Amilum has one as a companion and the first eagle, Nestor, dwells in the highest tower as the companion, of the King of Amilum." Having set the stage, Creedus paused a moment before continuing, as if to leave time for everyone to see the great city in their minds' eye.

"In the courts of the King there once dwelt two servants: Fidus and Philus. They served the King with their lives, and in this devoted service they found their meaning and joy. It was a high place of honor that they held, where they communed with the King daily, receiving his favor and care. The King loved his servants dearly.

Fidus was trustworthy with his work and faithful to finish what he started. His attention to detail was unrivaled. Philus on the other hand, was not always as careful and seldom as productive, though he worked just as hard. He did everything with an evident love for the King and the desire to make him great. They both had different talents that served the King well.

Also in the courts with Fidus and Philus lived a young woman named Elene. She was the fairest maiden in the city. Though Fidus desired her affections and he was worthy of her, she gave her heart to Philus. They fell in love, never to be separated, a bond stronger than any other between servants. The three of them remained friends and prospered in the courts of the king.

But, as time passed, something took hold of Fidus' heart and mind that began to lead him astray: he thought more highly of himself than of those around him. This single prideful thought, a seed of evil, took root in his heart and began to grow. His eagle knew it and ceased frequenting Fidus' quarters, or following him from the skies when he walked the city. Only the King took notice right away that his servant was changing, and so he watched silently to see what would come of it. He sensed Fidus' pride.

Undiscerning of the change that was taking place in his friend, Philus continued in his tasks with joy, confiding in Fidus as he always had. As the seed of evil grew in Fidus' heart, and he became increasingly proud, Philus was influenced by his friend's words and actions. Fidus' influence took root in Philus' own heart and he began to think more about himself than about the King. A discord was felt and Philus' eagle as well frequented less, disturbed by what it sensed was the presence of something other than love.

The King saw what was taking place and his concern grew. Expressing this to the other servants within his palace courts, he set a watch on Fidus, but determined to believe that his servant was true.

One evening after his tasks were finished, Fidus approached Elene in the palace garden. There the pride in Fidus' heart reaped a harvest. He laid before Elene a plan to overthrow the King and become ruler of Amilum himself. Fidus assured her that if she would leave Philus and love him, he would give her everything she had ever desired. Elene was frightened and pained to hear him speak of such things and she fled to find Philus. Hearing the report of Fidus' treasonous plans, Philus feared for his own life and remained silent, agreeing with Elene not to speak of it. Though refusing to join the rebellion, Philus and Elene became traitors through their silence. Their own fellowship became fragile and shaken. Not only that, but like Fidus, they became the first citizens of Amilum to lose the friendship of the eagles.

For the first time, servants of the King served themselves.

It was the first time that love had not governed the actions of his servants, and the King knew of it. His spirit was disturbed and his anger warmed towards Fidus. He again told the other servants of his palace courts to be on guard.

The following day, with the pride in his heart now on his tongue, Fidus beguiled five other servants to join with him in his plot. The seed of pride in his heart had begun to bloom. Like poison, his evil intentions influenced these five servants, bending their minds and darkening their hearts; they became his servants instead of the King's.

That evening, too fearful to sleep, Philus and Elene watched in horror from their window at the result of their silence.

Fidus and his five servants climbed the highest tower of the palace to where the King was resting. Reaching the window of the King, Fidus raised his hand to strike down the ruler of Amilum. But, evil could not live in Amilum, and Fidus was seized and bound before he could carry out his treachery. When Fidus' five servants tried to flee, they were surrounded by Nestor and their own eagles and captured.

When the morning came the King brought his prisoners to the Center Square of Amilum in the presence of all its citizens. Because of Fidus' treason the King took from him his name and gave him a new one. From that day forward he became known as Mornoc, for his rebellion had brought darkness to Amilum and death to himself. The King also took from the other five servants their names, but he did not give them new ones. Instead he called them the Children of Death, and they became faceless and disgraced. He condemned Mornoc and his servants for their crimes and foretold a day when he would send a final punishment upon them. Under the weight of this curse, they fled Amilum and wondered into the wilderness below.

Philus and Elene were present to witness the fate of their former friend. And when the King saw Philus, he wept, for he knew of his beloved servant's treasonous silence. Because the King was just, he set to punish Philus for his disobedience, escorting him to the city limits. The King took from Philus his name and gave him another, calling him Homsoloc, for he would be a man in a lonely place. The King then declared a sentence of exile. But Homsoloc was not left without hope. There, at the city gate as they stood alone, the King gave him two gifts. The first was the Sword, fashioned by the best metal worker in Amilum, with the city's name engraved on the base of the blade. Imperishable, it had a blade than would never grow dull, could never be damaged, and would remain loyal to him. The King charged Homsoloc to hold to it tightly, warning him of the enmity that would arise with his former friend. The King knew that Mornoc would not rest until Homsoloc also became his servant, as was the fruit of his pride.

The second and greater gift was the Promise, that one day the King would redeem Homsoloc, and provide a way of return from exile. He spoke of one that would come from the City of Amilum to lead Homsoloc to final victory over his enemy, Mornoc, and end the exile, making a way back to Amilum and the courts of the King.

Before the King left Homsoloc's side, Elene ran to him, unable to hide, for her heart belonged to him and she shared his shame. Seeing this, the King wept all the more, for he knew that their hearts were one and that together they had dishonored him. Their beautiful love, once treasured in his courts, was now weakened by their pride and fear. The King turned his back on them and they were shut out from the city. Together, Homsoloc and Elene descended the mountain into the Lowlands, which stretched into the East as far as the eye could see. They would no longer enjoy the provision of the city or the friendship of the eagles. They were forced to find shelter and a way of life apart from the King's favor.

Meanwhile, Mornoc and his servants hid themselves from the light of Amilum because of the severity of their shame. Still lamenting their disgrace, they wanted only to return to the city and rule it themselves; they became embittered, hating the King and all that he loved. From their haunts Mornoc and his servants saw Homsoloc and Elene descend from the mountain, and together they planned to make them both slaves. They were no longer in the presence of the King and could do as they saw fit.

Surprising Homsoloc and Elene, Mornoc and his servants surrounded them. When one of the servants took hold of Elene, Homsoloc raised his sword and slew him in jealous rage, spilling his blood on the ground. The place became known as Mortfen, for it was the first murder and the beginning of war between Homsoloc and Mornoc. Homsoloc drove Mornoc and the remaining four servants before him, leading Elene into the East, far from the City of Amilum. And no matter where they went, always blocking the way behind them, driving them on was a phantom beast, more terrible even than Mornoc. Like a matchless predator, it hunted them, for though Mornoc and his servants were cursed to await a final judgment, Homsoloc and Elene had become mortals.

Through pain and toil, Homsoloc and Elene raised up offspring, who, like their father, were easily led astray. There was a weakness in their hearts toward selfish pride, a soft soil for the working of evil. Mornoc knew this, and though he could not enslave Homsoloc and rule over him as long as he wielded the Sword from Amilum, he devised ways to beguile his sons, the pride of Elene. He was able to lead some of them astray as he had the five servants of the King, by appealing to their pride. These sons of Homsoloc became traitors, serving Mornoc, who never relinquished his desire for the throne of Amilum. Most of Homsoloc's sons resisted Mornoc, some to the point of death rather than forsaking the Promise of the King.

In this way the Lowlands were inhabited. Homsoloc and Elene became fruitful through hard work and pain, and Mornoc undermined them, building his own kingdom, an army of traitors. And so the Lowlands became a world of division. One side held fast to the Sword and the Promise and the other raged against all that the King loved."

Creedus paused, sobered by his own words as he stared into the flames. A gust of wind tossed some of his gray hair across his face, hiding it from his audience.

The air felt colder, even the fire seemed to grow dim.

With both hands the old man pulled the hair away from his eyes and looked up at the stars as if searching for something. "But . . ." he said, with longing in his voice. Pointing the full length of his arm and forefinger into the air, he continued, ". . . there was yet the promise of one to come. There *is* the promise of one to come, as surely as the brightest star still shines in the sky." A tear welled up in the corner of his eye and rolled down his wrinkled cheek, leaving a trail of moistened skin. "There is one that will come, who is able to deliver."

Looking down again he recited something from memory. "From the hills, from the very shadows of these lands will come a light, one man, unlike any man . . ." his voice strengthened as he heard his own words, ". . . a deliverer from the West to bring an end to exile, for the hope of every heart and the life of every soul. He will come swiftly to crush our enemies and to make a way of return to the home of our father . . . the City of Amilum."

Many in the crowd nodded in witness, as familiar with this oracle as they were the ground beneath their feet. Others looked at the old man as if they had heard of this promise for the first time.

Corred looked into the flames, deep in thought, agreeing with the very idea of such a hope, for his heart embraced it; he knew it had to be true.

Androcles hid a tear after seeing his grandfather cry. He was still too young to fully comprehend why it had all happened.

The fire was growing low by the time Creedus had finished, so several of the men in the group fed it with the last of the wood that they themselves had brought for the gathering. The night was well advanced and it was near time for everyone to return to their homes, but a last word from their leader was awaited.

"But for today, my friends, we have the Sword and the Promise," Creedus said. With the fire again rising, he bent low to the ground and grabbed the sword that had been lying at his feet. As he pulled it slowly from its scabbard, it sang softly. With a light all of its own, an emblem at the base of the blade shone most brilliantly of all: Amilum.

Everyone present beheld it with awe. Corred and

Androcles, with their mouths gaping, wondered at the weapon that had come from a place they could only imagine.

"First, the Sword," Creedus said, ceremonially, "whose blade is ever ready to cut, and will not fail the faithful who wield it." Slipping it right back into its scabbard, he placed it back at his feet. "Second, the Promise, which is greater. Because only in its fulfillment can we be saved."

Only the crackling of the fire filled the air for a moment. The image of the Sword still burned in their minds, making the Story of their heritage more alive.

"As for *your* swords, and our hope in the coming redemption . . ." Creedus addressed them all again, "the first you must keep ready, and to both we must all hold fast, with all our strength. What you fix your eyes upon, you will become, even if it is the very thing you fear." He searched all those gathered. "We are still at war with the host of Mornoc. If you lose sight of the Promise and your sword collects dust, your very identity will be weakened." He held up his finger and leaned forward as the light of the fire danced in his eyes. "Keep your swords sharp."

CHAPTER 2

8 Years Later

A waning moon, dimmed by thinning clouds, cast its faint glow on the wooded landscape below. The leaves of the trees were once again falling, coloring the forest floor in shades of orange, red, and brown, permeating the air with their scent. The changing temperatures gave rise to a mist from the earth's warm surface that hung suspended, still as stone. The crack of a stick was as good as a shout.

Through such a scene a young man swiftly made his way on foot along a well-used path. His steps were sure and he traveled the path with a seeming knowledge of every twist, dip and turn to the very texture of its surface.

Steadying the sword at his side with his left hand, Corred swung the other to match his gate. Little could be heard of his travel apart from the sound of his breathing and the occasional crunch of leaves. The color of his clothes matched the season in drab shades of brown and olive. The hood of his shirt hung loosely, allowing for better vision. His dark brown hair fell to his shoulders, and though his features were not distinguishable in the dark, the length of his stride spoke of his youthful strength. And though he traveled without a companion, Corred was not alone.

From a higher point in the woods, against a thicket, a silent figure bent low to the ground to hide his outline. He was carefully watching Corred's path. His dress was black, matching dark eyes and on his back hung a pouch full of short spears. His hair was just as dark except for a few blond tips still clinging to black roots. Crouched motionless, he looked ahead, seeking a point of ambush. Once located, he quickly turned back into the thicket to carry out his attack.

As Corred made a turn in the path, he heard the snapping of a twig in the distance. His attention was drawn to the hill on his left, but there was no motion to accompany the sound. His pulse quickened and his senses grew more alert with each step.

Moving with the agility of a predator, the dark figure exited the opposite side of the thicket and stood behind a tree to wait. As he slowly raised his hand to the pouch on his back, his long fingers felt one of the spears, and stayed there. For a brief moment the light of the moon revealed the hunter's features: hollow eyes, gaunt cheeks, and a sinister glare. His wide, black eyes absorbed all of the light available, shifting to and fro in search of his quarry. He walked his grip down the shaft of the spear when he heard the crunch of leaves to his right. Several seconds passed. Then, from his periphery, he spotted Corred running through the brush fifty yards out of range. Cursing behind clenched teeth, the hunter flew down the hill and pursued his target along the very path he had been watching. The spear was now in his hand, held at shoulder height, ready for release.

His pursuer now flushed from hiding, Corred fully realized the source of his alarm. Pulling his sword, he hit the full length of his stride. Fear threatened to take over, but he fought the panic and searched for a possible advantage. Ducking under the lower branches of an evergreen, Corred picked up a rock in his left hand. As the gap between he and his attacker lessened, Corred gripped his sword all the tighter. In the darkest part of the woods, he stopped on the face of a leaf. Rolling the stone ahead of him, he slipped behind a tree.

The hunter quickly released his spear in the direction of the sound, burying it in the stump of a fallen tree. Slowing to a standstill, he listened quietly while pulling a second spear from his pouch. After a moment of silence, he backtracked toward the place he had last seen his prey, stepping lightly. A low, angry growl escaped his throat.

Every muscle tensed and ready, Corred waited for the opportune time to either attack, or run. As the burning in his chest subsided, and he began to catch his breath, he listened carefully for his enemy's movements. A minute passed before he again heard the crunch of leaves. At the snapping of a twig, now further away, he drew a deep breath and took off at a full sprint, aiming for the main path out of the woods. Within a few steps another spear flew just behind him, skipping across the forest floor.

Pushing so hard that he barely touched the ground, the hunter attempted once more to catch his prey. But this time, the intensity of his pursuit seemed to be well matched by his target's flight. Unable to keep pace, the hunter hurled a second spear down the path with the full force of his body behind it. It found its mark.

The spear tore through Corred's shirt and cut his shoulder

before lodging in a tree just beyond him. Without slowing, he soon broke from the trees and passed into a field of long grass; he was almost there.

On the other end of the field was a cabin, set on the outskirts of a small village. The light from a lantern on the doorstep of this cabin brought back his shadow as he neared the end of his flight. Corred's legs were screaming, but he didn't stop. The windows of several of the cabins ahead of him lit up the night. Not everyone in Oak Knoll was yet asleep.

Slowing his pace just a little, he kept going until he reached the third cabin on his right. Made of wood plank and logs, it rested several feet above the ground on a foundation made of mortar and stone. The chimney, rising from the foundation along the front wall, smoked lightly.

After carefully returning his sword to its sheath with trembling hands, Corred reached for his wound gently. The thick plumes of his breath matched the rise and fall of his chest as he ascended the short set of stairs. Sweat trickled down his forehead as he cast sideways glances into the dark.

Knock, knock, knock. Corred's knuckles left a few spots of blood on the door before he returned to holding his wound. The sound of shuffling feet inside could immediately be heard. A young lady in a white gown opened the door a few inches and looked out to see who was calling at such an hour. Her eyes grew wide when she saw who it was.

"Corred!?" She opened the door and let him in.

Taking a last look back to where the glow of Oak Knoll faded, Corred stepped inside. Some of his hair clung to his face as he took a seat in a chair just inside the door. In a breath of relief, he spoke: "Tell aunt and uncle I've been wounded by a spear."

The young girl's lip quivered with fright as she hurried into the next room. "Aunt, uncle! Corred has been hurt!"

The light of a fire flickered throughout the room, revealing its thick rafters and simple design. But its warmth was lost on Corred. He remained motionless against the wall, catching his breath, still listening for the sound of footsteps outside the door.

From the bedroom rushed a middle-aged man and his wife, each carrying a candle.

"Where were you hit, son?" the gentleman asked.

"In the shoulder. It's just a cut," Corred responded. His face, initially flushed from the chase, was now growing pale.

"Oh my," his aunt exclaimed as she drew near to observe the wound. "I'll get my things to clean it up. Galena, get some herbs, dear." With that she hurried back through the door she had come from while Corred's younger sister ran into the kitchen.

"Returning from Hill Top?" Corred's uncle asked with high eyebrows. There was little shock in his voice as he observed his nephew with a calm concern.

"Yes. He knew the path well. I barely escaped." Corred looked out the window. The light on the steps of the first cabin he had passed still flickered peacefully. With a sigh, he lowered his head and closed his eyes.

His uncle placed his candle on a stand next to Corred's chair. With his hands on his plump waist, he inquired further. "Were there any others from Renken that you could have traveled with?"

With his eyes still closed he took a long breath. "No." When he opened his eyes, he glared at the opposite wall angrily. With a curled lip he added, "It was a scout."

Corred's uncle scowled slightly at his nephew's bitterness. "Have no part of hate." Stepping nearer, he bent over and placed his hand on Corred's good shoulder. Ignoring his wound he looked him in the eye. "You are a son of the Promise. Stop clinging to things of the past, all they have left to do is fade, like your enemies. Even those who were once our friends will pass, like the leaves of Fall. Pray mercy for those who have forsaken hope."

Corred struggled to believe what his uncle said. He took another deep breath and shivered, hanging his head. He knew it was true.

"I am sorry. I forget myself," his uncle said. "Come, sit in front of the fire and warm yourself." Corred's uncle moved his chair as Corred repositioned himself in front of the fire.

"Thank you, uncle." Corred fell back into the chair leaning over a little in the direction of the flames.

Galena rushed into the room with some crushed herbs and a bowl of soup. With loving care she placed the bowl in Corred's hands. She swept her long blonde braids over her shoulders, and stood back to give her aunt room.

Corred's aunt returned with an old wooden tray that carried two earthen bowls, several rags, thread and a short, curved needle. "Logen, dear, fetch my table from the kitchen?"

Uncle Logen quickly grabbed the table and placed it to Corred's right, just under his wounded shoulder. "Shae, you'll be wanting your stool as well?" Uncle Logen asked loudly, returning to the kitchen.

"Yes, please," Aunt Shae answered as she set her tray on the table.

Corred pulled his arm out of his shirt and Aunt Shae went to work immediately, dabbing his cut with a rag and cool water. He winced at the first touch, but then sat silently sipping his soup with his left hand. The sweat on his face was beginning to dry, plastering some of his hair to his forehead. His handsome features became more distinguishable in the light of the fire.

Corred turned to Galena and asked, "May I have some bread?"

Without answering she hurried back to the kitchen and returned with part of a loaf.

"What happened?" Aunt Shae asked anxiously.

Corred finished drinking a mouthful of soup. "I was returning from Hill Top where grandfather and the others were meeting. I took the path I have taken a hundred times, but this time a scout was waiting for me, not long after I entered the woods." His voice became animated as he described the encounter.

"Did you have a chance to confront him?" Uncle Logen asked. He stood behind Corred's chair observing his wife's work.

"Yes, once. But it was too dangerous. He would have certainly run me through before I had been able to strike a blow. The pursuit was nearly the full length of the wood. I was only able to escape after fooling him with a diversion." He was still a little tense, trying hard to relax as his aunt threaded her needle.

There was a moment of silence as his aunt began sewing the wound. Focusing on his food, Corred blocked out the pain and continued. "His attack was so intense; I have never felt such hate from a man." He shivered just thinking about it.

"Scouts are hardly men," Uncle Logen said objectively. "They don't have a loving sinew in their bodies. Anyone who despairs to the point of becoming the very thing they once feared, is . . . lost."

Corred handed his empty soup bowl to his sister and nodded passively, taking the bread. "Thank you, Galena." He quickly changed the subject. "Tomorrow I am going to see Einar. He will want news from Hill Top, and he will certainly want to know about this."

Uncle Logen nodded and looked at his wife knowingly. Like parents to Corred and his sister, they knew how much he had suffered at his enemy's hands, and the hurt ran deep. It lay in a place where Corred still tried his hardest to disown it, deny it. Only his sister was left.

Galena had not held on to her pain the same way. She had allowed it to break her, and now she was healing.

"You're not going anywhere unless you get a good night's rest," Aunt Shae proclaimed. "You can sleep here in front of the fire. I want you warm. I know it's only a good scratch, but don't you take it for granted." As she finished applying the crushed herbs, which she mixed with water to make a sort of paste, she looked to Galena. "Bring some blankets, dear."

"Thank you, aunt." Corred kissed her forehead.

*   *   *   *   *

A strong wind howled outside, sending a burst of air down the chimney. It swept across the floor, into Corred's face. Awakening with a start, he rolled onto his wounded shoulder and groaned. He instinctively reached for his sword, which lay next to him. The sound of rushing feet echoed from his dreams.

Several large coals glowed faintly still, providing a little light. Corred leaned on his elbow and listened carefully, disoriented. Heart pounding, eyes bulging, he waited for a knock at the door, a voice, or a bump on the wall . . . something. Nothing came. It was silent.

Sitting up completely, he looked out the window toward the first cabin in the village. It was pitch black. The lantern had gone out. Returning to his back, he wrapped himself in his blankets and drifted again into a restless slumber.

CHAPTER 3

When Corred arose, the clouds of the night before had moved on. Before anyone else had stirred, he dressed himself and stoked the fire, adding wood from the pile that sat in the corner under the window. The thick pane had a slight frost in the corners where moisture had gathered. It had grown quite cold over night, whitening the grass with one of the first frosts of the year.

While the fire slowly came back to life, filling the room with its sweet smell, Corred unsheathed his sword. With the flat side of the blade resting on his knee, he sat down and looked it over carefully. The sword was commonplace, nothing special about it, but it was well kept and its edge was visibly sharp. Corred drew a small, flat stone from his pocket, spat on it and diligently sharpened a section of the sword that had lost its shine.

Pulling some of his hair, he ran it lightly over the blade; it cut with ease. Next he held the sword out with a straight arm, looking down its shaft. Pleased with its appearance in all regards he returned it to its sheath and leaned it against the stone of the fireplace.

As he stood in front of the fire Uncle Logen emerged from his bedroom rubbing his hands together. "Quite the crisp morning, eh?"

"Quite," Corred responded dryly.

"Your aunt and sister are in the kitchen as we speak, preparing breakfast," he said, grabbing an armful of wood for the cooking fire. "Or, at least once they have these," he added with a smile in the corner of his mouth. "Hungry?" he paused to ask the obvious.

"Very," Corred replied, unable to keep from smiling at his uncle's simplicity. "Is there anything to be done?" he asked.

"Not with your right arm, there isn't," Uncle Logen answered over his shoulder.

"Did he ask if he could work?" Aunt Shae inquired from the other room.

"Yes, he did. He has the nerve of a resilient young man much in need of knowing his limits," his uncle replied as he stoked and fed the fire.

Corred followed his uncle into the kitchen. Along the right side of the room was a large fireplace, a great deal larger than the other and surrounded by an array of cooking utensils. Aunt Shae was at the center sitting on her well-worn stool.

"Good morning, brother." Galena greeted him with bright eyes and a smile.

"Corred, take a seat at the table with your sister and rest," Aunt Shae commanded.

"Yes, ma'am," Corred responded respectfully. There were already four plates placed in front of four chairs with a fork at each.

"Aunt, aren't we having barley cakes and eggs, Corred's favorite?" Galena asked as she braided her hair.

"Not only that, we have molasses," she replied, turning around and winking at her niece. "How is your shoulder, Corred?"

"I don't feel a thing, aunt. It is so well bandaged you'd never know I was wounded." Corred leaned into his chair.

"Hah," his aunt replied, pleased with his flattery. "As long as you don't try to save the day you'll heal up quickly." She spoke loudly with her back to the table, leaning over the fire. With a familiar precision she poured four cakes into a large pan and placed it over a grate that sat above a pile of coals. From a basket that sat on the stool she pulled several brown eggs. Everyone watched as she cracked them and poured the contents into a second pan of sizzling butter.

"What a heavenly sound," Corred exclaimed, smiling widely.

"I'm glad to see you still smile, Corred," Galena remarked playfully. Finished with one braid she began the next. "How is grandfather?" she asked.

"He is well. Not as strong as he once was," Corred said, feeling the stubble on his chin. "But still capable of commanding respect."

His aunt tended to the cakes, flipping them carefully. "I wish he'd not place himself in harm's way like he does," she said softly. Out of the corner of her eye she saw her husband standing over her. "Sit down with your nephew, Logen. Please don't hover over me when I'm at the fire."

"Your father has never been one to slow down or let up, my dear." Uncle Logen chimed in. He slowly seated himself, obeying his wife's wish. "We need men like him." Looking at

Corred he added. "Did many attend last night?"

"Not as many as a year ago," Corred replied. "The lack of interest is rather disturbing, actually. No one takes any serious alarm when one man disappears, or someone is killed when hunting. It's assumed to be thieves with the obvious motive of plunder, and no more is said of it."

"Complacency, son. It's been around forever. A lack of resistance makes a man comfortable," Uncle Logen replied.

After a pause for thought, the cook gave some directions. "Galena dear, can you get milk and molasses. The cakes are almost ready." Aunt Shae nodded in the general direction of what she requested.

Lining one side of the room from floor to ceiling, thick planks of wood were fastened to the wall at a slight slant inward to ensure that items could not easily fall. They were filled with goods ranging from cured meats to baskets of apples and other dried fruits and vegetables. Herbs, flour, corn meal and the like were kept in earthen jars, all in a row.

Galena returned to the table and poured four tin cups of milk to the brim. Retrieving the molasses next, she was sure to handle the jar with care.

"Here they come," Aunt Shae announced. "Don't even think about biting in until your uncle has blessed the food," she instructed as she dished one to each plate from the pan.

"I say, it is blessed," Uncle Logen teased. When his wife ignored his poor humor he quickly followed with a short prayer. "May this food bring nourishment to our bodies and may we be truly grateful for its provision, the provision of the Promise and its fulfillment to come. Amen."

"Amen." Everyone agreed and turned their attention to their food while it was still hot.

"After you, sister," Corred said, pushing the molasses across the table toward her.

"Thank you," she replied.

The whole of the cabin filled with the aroma of breakfast as they enjoyed a meal together. They ate until the barley cakes were gone, and the rising sun shone brightly through the eastern windows, filling the whole room with light. No more was said of the prior night's events, especially of Corred's attacker. The absence of the topic was pronounced but as the meal concluded Corred's countenance grew serious once again. Aware of the time he at last stood.

"I must go. I need to speak with Einar about the events of last night, among other things." Kissing his aunt and sister, he grabbed two apples, a loaf of bread, and a canteen.

"Travel safely, son," Uncle Logen said, with a firm handshake. "Let us know what comes of it."

"Yes, uncle." He withdrew from the kitchen, strapped on his sword, pulled on his coat and promptly walked out the door.

A clear sky overhead covered the land with an endless sheet of blue. The sunlight reflected brightly on melting frost, brightening things even more. From the top step Corred shielded his eyes for a moment as he looked to the cabin on the outskirts of the village. The lantern was not sitting on the front step. *Interesting.* He walked up the street to see if it had just been blown over.

Not only was the lantern missing, there was something on the front step in its place. Cautiously approaching he watched the edge of the woods in the distance. Standing upright and driven into the first plank of the step was a short black spear. *I'm glad I stayed the night with Uncle Logen.* Corred looked around for the lantern, expecting to see it broken in the grass, but it was nowhere to be found. He knelt down to observe the weapon. The black blade was driven well into the wood with dried blood along one side of the blade. Corred felt his shoulder. It was the same spear. Pulling it out of the step with one quick jerk, he broke it over his knee. Looking toward the woods angrily, he threw the broken spear into the grass.

Corred turned sharply and headed back into the village. *What could have sent a scout after me? What could it mean? Why now, all of a sudden?* The questions made every breath seem a little more precious. He had cheated death. It made everything seem more precious.

Occasionally he would raise his head from his musings to greet a neighbor by name as he walked past their cabin. Corred was well known in a village where neighbors were like family, if not actually related. Surrounded by oak forests to the north, west and south, Oak Knoll was appropriately named.

Upon nearing the other end of the main road, Corred turned east, cutting between two cabins and into a field of recently harvested crops. There was much less green left in the landscape, but for now it was giving way to the colors of fall, and the birds were singing just the same. Before he had made his way through the field Corred started to run, hoping to traverse the eight miles of rolling hills between himself and Renken by mid-morning. With the passing of each crop row he would flush some animal from its hiding place: a few doves, a hedgehog, or a rabbit. Passing by a few rows of fruit trees, he startled a deer that had been feeding on what remained of the apple crop. The young buck took a few bounds away, but then stopped sharply, comforted to see that Corred's direction suggested he was not a threat. Corred kept running and the buck returned to eating.

Once on the other side of the fields that stretched away from Oak Knoll to the east, Corred picked up a well-worn wagon trail and headed south, toward Renken. The road was half stone from the wear of horses and wagon wheels with rising banks on either side, carved out by years of use. With well-placed steps, he steadied his sword with his left hand and measured his pace with his right.

Corred enjoyed the run, as it was one he had done many times before. If anything was out of place since the last time he had passed by, it caught his eye. They were his hills, his home, and that brought a bit of peace to his restless thoughts.

After nearly two hours of running and walking, he paused at the top of a hill to take a drink from his canteen. Spread before him a large plain of tall grass, now turning brown, ended on the shores of a great lake by the name of Tormalyn. It was a wide, cold lake, fed from the north by the Beryl River. Swelling significantly in the spring from the melting snows in the north, it was presently receded after a long hot summer.

In the center of that plain, several hundred yards from Lake Tormalyn sat the town of Renken. Easily the size of ten Oak Knolls, it was the largest in the region, surrounded by farms and smaller clusters of cabins along the shores of the lake.

The collection of each chimney's smoke hovered over the town in a thin cloud. With the array of different structures and rooftops slanting one way and another it was quite the puzzle of humanity. Rising up from the middle of this maze was a flagpole, bearing the flag of Renken: a raven in flight.

On the trail below him a horse-drawn wagon full of split wood made its way toward the heart of town. Corred instantly recognized it and smiled, mischievously. *Oh, this is going to be fun.* He steadied his sword with his left hand and ran down the hill with a grin on his face. At the bottom of the hill he carried his speed into the flat, chasing down the wagon. Without slowing, he bent over and picked up a rock. Closing in on the wagon, he waited until he was at the back wheels before lobbing the rock onto the driver's lap from behind.

"Huh!" the driver startled and spun around. "Who was that!?" He leaned this way and that, looking all over for the cause of his alarm.

Corred slowed quickly and ducked behind the enormous pile of wood to avoid being seen, stifling a laugh.

"What's this foolishness?" the driver asked loudly.

Corred ran around to the right side of the wagon and flew by the driver giving him a tap on the shoulder.

"Huh!" he started again. "Corred, I knew it was you!" the driver yelled after him. Loosening the reins, he urged his team of horses to pick up their pace and they broke into a trot. The wagon driver began gaining on Corred, who at this point was quite winded.

"You really ought to get yourself another horse, Corred. It's a lot faster, you know." The driver mocked his prankster as he pulled alongside of him.

Corred jumped up with him for the last stretch. "I won't disagree with you, Garrin. But I can always bum a ride while you're heading my way." Corred slapped him on the back and knelt next to him.

Garrin was Corred's cousin, several years older, and the only son of Uncle Logen and Aunt Shae. He was a muscular man, thick in the arms and chest, an imposing figure. His square jaw and patchy stubble stood out from the rest of his features, giving the impression that he was not to be bothered, though he was a very amiable man.

"What are you up to, cousin? Certainly you didn't run all this way to play tricks on a man hard at work," Garrin said with a smirk. He moved a piece of straw around his mouth to accommodate his speech.

"Sure I did. I haven't got any hard work of my own to do." Corred poked his cousin in the side. Straightening his face he said, "I am going to see Einar."

Garrin looked back at the road and rolled his eyes slightly. "What business do you have with vigilantes? Corred, in case you missed it, there hasn't been any fighting to do in nearly fifty years. Why don't you drop the swordplay, work the fields, and sell your goods in the markets like the rest of us?" His tone revealed his disappointment.

"I do work the fields. I also watch the fields, Garrin. There may have been a lack of conflict now for twice my years, but that doesn't change anything." Pulling away his shirt, Corred turned slightly to reveal his wound.

Garrin leaned over get a better look. "What's that all about?" he asked raising his eyebrows. "That's quite a knick."

Corred replaced his shirt and coat, and focused on the town ahead. "I was attacked by a scout."

Garrin returned to watching the horses. "A scout?" he asked quietly, thinking it over.

"Without a doubt," Corred responded. "These were not the actions of a thief; whoever it was meant to take my life."

"When?" Garrin inquired without taking his gaze from the road.

"Last night, on my return home from Hill Top." He said it very plainly, letting it sink in with his skeptical cousin. "Just like a thrilling hunt, only I was the prey. He knew the path I was taking. I barely escaped."

Garrin gave no response, choosing simply to chew on his straw and appear unmoved.

As they came to the entrance of town, Corred slapped Garrin on the back again. "Good to see you, cousin." With that he jumped off of the wagon and cut between two houses as Garrin drove on, watching him slip away. Corred hoped such news would convince his cousin of the truth, but he didn't hold his breath; Garrin was stubborn.

A large town of nearly ten thousand, Renken was divided into two sections, one for the well-to-do and a tighter section for those who had to cook their own meals. It was for the later that Corred headed. These streets were smaller and more worn, allowing just enough room for two mid-sized wagons to pass. The air was stale, trapped by houses and only moved with stronger winds. Sections reeked of human waste, which was not as well managed as the east side of town where there were one fourth as many people and almost twice as much space. There were many meager shops and market stands on the front steps of shacks that housed upwards of six. Most homes were made out of plank with a thin stone foundation, a step down from the cabins of Oak Knoll, but much more familiar to Corred than the inns and homes of wealthy merchants.

Renken was much like the other cities of the Lowlands in that it too was full of men who were living for the present. If you had the right sum of money, permission for almost any venture could be granted, whether it was in the interest of neighbors or not. Where there was no king, men did as they pleased.

Corred kept to himself while he worked his way through

the muddy streets. Though he knew the town well, the town did not know him in quite the same way as Oak Knoll. The only folk interested in his presence were those selling feed, food, and supplies; but Corred was not there to make any purchases.

At one corner, a gaunt old man with his feet wrapped in rags and a staff under his right arm sat against the wall of a shack with a blank stare on his face. His eyes were hollow and devoid of emotion, and his face was worn and thin; he was at best, unlovely. Corred paused to look at him. The beggar gave no response but simply stared into the street, moving his lips a little.

Corred reached into his bag and retrieved an apple. Approaching the man he leaned over and offered it to him. This grabbed the beggar's attention enough that he ceased speaking to himself; his mouth fell open. Corred saw that he only had a few teeth left to show, so he quickly exchanged the apple for part of his loaf of bread. Placing it in the beggar's open hands, he rested his right hand on his shoulder and smiled at him. A tear welled up in the beggar's eye as he mouthed a few words of thanks. The gesture went unnoticed by those hurrying about their business, and Corred continued on.

The west side of town was laid out in a very haphazard way, with winding streets and no real rhyme to its design. Every row of homes held a new surprise in architecture; scarcely a single home was the same size as the next. In the middle of the western district of Renken lay the villager's market place. Between two long rows of houses pointing toward the lake, a wider-than-average street was filled with stands, walk-in shops, penned up animals and every sellable item a man could want. The houses were taller than the rest in the western district simply for capacity's sake and the wealth that they brought from their trade. Business was in full swing for the day, with folk coming and going by wagon, on horseback, and on foot. The eastern side of town bought a majority of its goods from the villager's market place, but made profits more exclusively from trade with the region at large and with less available commodities such as metal, delicate clothing, and furs and spices.

Corred passed by the market place quickly with his head half down. His business was in the southern corner of town, the bottom-most edge of the village.

In a line of cabins that faced southeast, toward the lake, one particular house stood out from the rest. It was oblong, like a sort of shell or boat that had been turned over, with one long chimney at the center along one wall. Though similar to the cabins of Oak Knoll, in that it was made of layered logs from the surrounding forests, it looked nothing like them. The stone foundation was higher than its neighboring structures and the wall of the house facing the street was only a little wider than the front door. The steps that ascended to it were also made from the trunks of several trees, split in halves and fitted together.

It was at this house that Corred pulled up and gave a quick rhythmic knock. Initially, there was no recognition from within. Corred waited patiently before raising his hand to knock again, but before his knuckles could fall on the door, it opened. As it did, the heat from inside rushed past Corred's face.

A short, muscular man appeared in the doorway with a smile. "Corred, come in. What brings you down my way?" He extended his meaty arm. "Come in, come in."

"Einar, I have news from Hill Top," he replied. Corred grabbed Einar's arm above the wrist in a familiar and purposeful greeting.

Closing out the world, they walked to the middle of the room where the fire was burning brightly. Corred's host grabbed two chairs from around a small table and placed them in front of the fire.

"So, what kind of news do you bring from Hill Top? I would have liked to be there myself," Einar said as he took a seat. His dark blue shirt hung loosely from his thick arms and broad shoulders while his pants wrapped around his much thicker legs. He looked to be at least twenty years older than Corred by the maturity of his frame and graying temples. His features were rounded, marked by a big nose and tiny, piercing green eyes. Sliding his chair closer to the flames, he stoked the fire with a metal rod that was leaning against the hearth.

Einar was the closest thing to a best friend that Corred had. Formerly a fellow wood-worker and friend of his father's when Corred was a child, Einar had become like an adopted uncle, having never started a family of his own. Like Corred's aunt and uncle, Einar had tried to fill the gap when Corred lost his parents. He had continued teaching Corred the carpenter's trade that his father had begun when he was a boy, and for years Corred had joined him off and on for different jobs in Renken. Ten years later Einar was still reaching out.

Corred shifted in his seat and began. "More of the same; most have grown too comfortable. It was poorly attended." Corred tucked some of his hair behind his ear and leaned on his knees toward the fire. "A man from the Northern Villages was there. He was coming to Wellman to see my grandfather and others of the Véran to voice concerns of scout attacks. At Hill Top he spoke of three men killed in an ambush along the Rundum River, east of the villages, not far from some of the trading posts. The signs were obvious. Apparently, there are very few attending the gatherings in the north as well."

Einar listened quietly. He leaned the stirring rod against the wall, sat up straight, clasped his hands and rested them on his lap. "What has been the response to these attacks?" he asked.

"Naturally the town officials from those villages attribute it to roving thieves, but it is clearly untrue. These men had been hunting for meat, not furs. They had no boat full of goods for trade, no money bags."

Einar took a deep breath. "Even if the town officials don't honestly believe their own explanation, they don't want it to be a scout attack. They know that they are not ready for any kind of conflict and they don't want to have to prepare for one. Trust me, the lack of vigilance in Wellman, Oak Knoll, and here are not exceptions to the rule. Every town, village and settlement in between has become lax. And do not underestimate the ability of people to explain away the occurrence of evil. It's in our nature, Corred. History repeats itself because people forget the past. The records of our fathers are a testament to it." Einar knit his brow. "I know I preach to a preacher; it's the people out there that need to hear the truth, though they won't listen. I have tried. There is a stubborn resistance even here in Renken that continues to grow." He sighed deeply. "When it comes, and someday soon it may, I fear there will have to be great loss to awaken the Lowlands to the enemy that still lives among us, an enemy that has always lived among us. I just pray that there will be enough strength to answer if such a thing ever happens."

Corred turned to look his friend in the eye. "It is indeed alarming, but that's not where it ends. On the way home from Hill Top last night I was attacked." He watched Einar's reaction. "I barely escaped with my life, and my attacker left the same spear that cut my shoulder driven into the step of my cabin." He pulled his shirt back to show his bandage. "He also took the lantern, as if to claim my life."

Einar raised an eyebrow. "I am glad you are okay." After a pause he continued. "Did you confront him or was it simply a foot race for Oak Knoll?"

"I had the chance, but I didn't risk it. I never would have reached him in time to fight hand to hand." Corred shook his head, recounting the fear he had felt.

"Who else knows?" Einar asked.

"I spent the night with my aunt and uncle, and Galena. Aunt Shae stitched me up. I also told Garrin when I met him on the way into Renken, but he brushed me off as usual."

"I know how you feel. Though we are respected by some, they are becoming fewer. There is even an official here in Renken that has begun to think little of us, and not out of ignorance."

"Who might that be?" Corred asked.

"Lord Raven, himself," Einar answered quietly.

Corred started at these words. "Lord Raven? Since when has he become hard of heart?"

"Only recently," Einar answered. "Though I am familiar to Lord Raven, he has coldly declined my latest requests to visit him."

"That is certainly unfortunate for us," Corred said with hurt in his voice.

"Our enemy is cunning, Corred. We have not had peace for nearly fifty years because Mornoc has abandoned his purpose in existence. He is at least at work in politics, weakening men from the inside out. That's where our weakness is, on the inside. I worry that Lord Raven has some ill advisor poisoning his good sense. In the meantime, it would appear some of us are being marked for death."

"Yeah, like me." Corred ran his hands through his hair. He was visibly distraught.

Einar watched his movements. Leaning over to join Corred, he looked into the flames and spoke under his breath, as if the very words were fragile. "A deliverer from the West, . . . to bring an end to exile and the beginning of renewal, for the hope of every heart and the life of every soul."

For a long moment they both contemplated these words. The whole weight of their hope depended on them: the old Promise yet to be fulfilled.

Einar slapped Corred on the back. "Let's have something to eat; we're going to need it."

Corred looked at his friend inquiringly.

Einar smiled widely. "Your grandfather has called me to join him in Wellman. Come with me."

"I'd love to. I haven't been there in weeks and would very much like to be back." Corred responded quickly. "What did he say it was about?"

Einar stood up. "I don't know, but I don't need a lot of reason to visit your grandfather."

CHAPTER 4

Several miles south of Oak Knoll, a lone traveler ran through the woods carrying a lantern. The glass bowl covering the wick was blackened at the top from the night before. His dress was black and on his back was a pouch full of short spears.

Moving swiftly, he made his way along a subtle trail, through thick woods at the base of a rocky hill. His gaunt face betrayed some of its youthfulness, but it spoke also of an unnatural strain. He followed the trail to the lowest point of the woods and there entered a cave. In the entrance he lit the lantern he'd been carrying with one that hung from the cave wall. Crouching slightly, he followed the cave into the heart of the hill.

At thirty yards, the tunnel gradually began to open up, heading into the earth. As he continued, the jagged walls began to grow moist and the air grew warmer. In sections there was a steady trickle of water along the floor at the base of the walls. Deeper and deeper he went, leaving the sun behind. Taking one last turn, he hung his lantern on a nail in the rock, the beginning of a long row of lanterns of all shapes and sizes. From there he followed the lights to a place where the cave opened up into a large chamber.

In the middle of the cave a long stone table was lined with men of a similar dress, feasting. It was an underground banquet hall lacking all of the fineries expected at a banquet. The square room was well lit by a massive candle chandelier that hung above the table and several lanterns that hung at each doorway and along the walls. The air was filled with the smell of meat, ale, and burning oil.

At each of four entrances, one on each side, a guard stood at attention. Above one of these doors, etched in stone, was the name *"Casimir."* Ignoring the guards, the returning scout walked up to the table and joined the feasting.

Every man at the table wore a pouch of short spears on his back, black clothing, and had dark hair and eyes. The only things that set them apart were their facial features, length of hair, and height. They were all thin and haggard, like men near death, but there was an apparent ferocity about them all.

The scout took his place at an empty spot on one of the wooden benches and immediately tore into the first piece of meat within reach. All of the meat was in the form of whole carcasses, just cooked, but quite rare. Lining the table were pitchers of cold ale, earthen cups, and tin plates. The sounds of feasting permeated the atmosphere.

"Did you bring his lantern, Selcor?" a scout asked the new arrival in a guttural voice.

"Yes," Selcor replied over a mouthful of meat.

They both focused on their food for a minute or so longer before Selcor added, "I made him bleed, but he escaped."

His companion paused to contemplate the words then washed down his food with some ale. His bushy hair hung over his forehead in wavy strands. Wiping his face with his sleeve, he opened his mouth to speak again, but was cut off.

"Hail, your Mallith!" A voice cried from the other end of the table. The command echoed loudly through the chamber, ringing into the tunnels.

All in attendance rose to their feet on the outside of their benches and turned to face the entrance at the far end of the table, the one with the name *"Casimir"* carved above it. Some spit food out of their mouths onto their plates, or swallowed what was left to more quickly assume a position of attention. Once there was complete silence and every one of them was on their feet, a great gangly figure walked through the stone doorway and paused just under the light of the lanterns to his left and right.

A black robe covered the form of a man no less than eight feet tall. He stood slightly bent over but with square shoulders. In his right hand he carried a long club with a heavy metal sphere on the end, adorned with five large spikes. His long black hair was lined with thick strands of gray and his beard was kept short, appearing just as dark against his pale skin. There were scars on his cheeks running down from his eyes like tears, and his hands and forearms were scarred in a similar manner, as if burned. Like all of those present, he too carried a pouch of spears on his back.

There was an uncomfortable moment of silence. The giant slowly extended his right arm, holding the club out in front of him. In unison all of the men at the table pulled a spear from their pouches, saluting him with the point of their weapons.

"Casimir!" they all bellowed in one voice.

Casimir lowered the club to his side.

The scouts all returned their spears to their pouches in unison.

Casimir proceeded to walk with long, slow strides around the table, observing each of his soldiers carefully. No one dared to return his gaze, but kept their eyes on the door that their captain had entered, all except for Selcor. He shifted his weight slightly, peering at his captain out of the corner of his eye. It did not go unnoticed.

Casimir stopped mid-stride. Turning to face his scout, he tossed aside his club. Removing his pouch of spears also, he laid them on the stone floor. Two of the guards quickly ran to pick up his weapons and move them far out of the way; one of them labored under the weight of the club.

Pointing the full length of his arm at Selcor, he spoke. "Turn and face your captain." His voice was deep and raspy and his teeth shone white as he sneered.

Without a second's hesitation Selcor grabbed a spear from his pouch and hurled it at Casimir, running toward him with a second spear already in the other hand. His movements were swift and there was no reservation in his aggression.

Everyone present turned to watch the fight.

Casimir caught the first spear by the shaft and snapped it. He dodged the second, which was aimed at his head, while taking a step toward Selcor.

They met each other as Selcor released a third spear with all his might. Casimir dodged even this last attempt, though very narrowly, and it hit the back wall.

Moving in close, Selcor threw a quick punch, which Casimir easily blocked with his left forearm. Lunging at his captain, Selcor landed a second blow on the outside of

Casimir's leg. His third jab, meant for the captain's stomach was blocked as well, and Casimir knocked him off of his feet with a single punch to the chest. Selcor slid back toward his bench head first, reeling.

Casimir followed quickly and grabbed Selcor by the shirt as he gasped for breath. Lifting him off of the ground Casimir placed him in a strangle hold from behind. Allowing Selcor to draw one last breath he applied pressure.

Selcor grew red, then pale, pulling viciously at the long arm around his neck, kicking wildly to free himself. Even a few well placed blows to Casimir's ribs with his elbows, Selcor could not lessen the monster's grip on his neck. The room began to swim around him.

Casimir whispered in his ear, "You're learning, youngster." There was pleasure in his voice as he inflicted pain. He turned toward the group with a hard stare. They quickly returned to form, unwilling to bring the same wrath upon themselves.

Selcor's resistance began to lessen and his grip on Casimir's arm became weak. Just before he went limp, Casimir dropped him.

Slumping over, Selcor gasped for air, and rolled onto his back.

The two guards that had been tending Casimir's weapons hurried over to return them to him. Without looking at them he held out a hand for them to stop. Standing at full height he addressed the table. "Never half-kill your enemies; annihilate them. Never leave them wounded to strike back." He continued pacing the length of the table as he had before with Selcor still doubled over on the floor. "Do you think that they will spare you, who once walked among their villages and ate their food!?" He paused to look over a few of his men before continuing. "We will show no mercy. This is Mornoc's world. Those who will not honor him and serve him are our enemies, and for that they must die!" His voice shook with anger.

Selcor slowly rose to his feet, and returned to attention with a scowl.

Casimir looked at him proudly. "Give him more spears and more ale. He is a good soldier of Mornoc." He held out his hand for his weapons. "Soon, he'll be a better one."

The guard that had been holding the club released the weight of it into Casimir's hand where it rested lightly. Slinging his spears over his shoulder Casimir walked toward the door he had entered and paused to address the hall again. "Prepare yourselves. Our time is approaching."

Once he had disappeared into the tunnel and out of sight, the hall returned to feasting, as if nothing had happened.

One of the guards poured Selcor a full glass of ale while a second placed more spears in his pouch. Slamming his fist on the table, he took his cup of ale and drained it. With cursing, he ripped at his meat. Even before he had swallowed, the remaining blonde tips of his hair turned to black.

*　　*　　*　　*　　*

When the sun had reached its highest point in the sky, Einar and Corred left Renken on foot and headed for Oak Knoll. They walked around, rather than through the town, passing instead through the fields that surrounded Renken.

It had grown much warmer since that morning, providing for very comfortable travel. The warmth had a similar effect on the birds, which were now actively flying about in the fields and among the trees that scattered the land to the south of town. The air was filled with their songs.

Corred made the return home carrying the same supplies as when he had left. Einar brought with him a pack full of necessary provisions, a roll for his bed, and a sword. His sword had a wide blade and heavy oak handle, braided with leather, long enough for a double grip. It hung from a weathered leather belt along with a hunting knife of similar design.

As they walked they spoke freely about anything and everything that came to mind. The latest hunts they'd been on, trees they'd felled, people they'd met. For Einar there were always the different pieces of woodwork he'd done, mostly for the wealthy of Renken's eastern district. But, it wasn't long before the conversation turned back to Corred's dangerous encounter from the night before.

"I am still amazed at his ferocity. I could hear him cursing under his breath as he searched me out." Corred felt better the more he talked about it.

"It is a fearful thing to know that another living being wants only to take your life. Battle alone is fierce enough before facing an enemy like ours." Einar paused to gather his thoughts. "Mornoc and his soldiers have never been interested in preserving their own lives. War for them has only ever been about the destruction of their enemies. As you know, Mornoc has commonly destroyed whole villages, towns, killing every living thing, unless the inhabitants swore allegiance to him."

After walking for a while longer, Corred wondered aloud, "If he was just a scout that had followed me in the woods, I cannot imagine facing a captain of Mornoc." Corred shook his head attempting to imagine it.

"I only know one man still living who has seen a Mallith in battle," Einar said, leaning toward Corred, "and that is your grandfather."

"Yes, he has told me a little about it, but no more than I would learn from the tales that everyone has heard: heart of stone, hundreds of years old, giants among men."

"I am sure your grandfather could tell you more. Such an experience would not readily leave one's memory, and what I heard as a boy was plenty to give me nightmares," Einar said with a lighthearted laugh.

"Well, they have become the objects of nighttime tales," Corred said. "It would be quite another story to face one in its wrath, even with the Sword."

Einar nodded long and hard. "Corred, I am so very grateful that we have both lived during a time of peace such as this, but I have an uneasy feeling it may be coming at an unseen price," Einar said. His tone was serious, and he seemed burdened by his admission. "The lack of interest in recounting and celebrating the Promise is proof that Mornoc's silence is not working against him, and I am certain he knows it. An unsuspecting victim makes the hunter that much more bold to attack."

Corred thought about it for a moment, certainly not willing to disagree after his experience from the night before. The thought sobered him.

"A gathering of the Heads of Véran would be very much in order if we are to address the people's complacency," Einar thought aloud.

"Is there really enough cause for such a thing?" The answers had been given the night before, but his curiosity was speaking for him.

"You're the one with bandages," Einar said with a smirk. "It has been a long time since members of the Véran from the

Northern Villages, Shole, Renken, and Wellman have gathered together for any event. Another ill effect of the peace we all so greatly enjoy."

"What about Port?" Corred asked.

"I only know of a few members of the Véran left in that city. Most care for nothing but money." Einar said sharply. "There will be far more from Shole and the Northern Villages," he continued. "The very roots of the Véran come from Shole, reaching back to Homsoloc's last days, and his call for his sons to remember their past. He chronicled his life and everything he could remember from Amilum and those records remain in Shole. Certainly such a city cannot become as comfortable as Renken. If their heritage is not enough to stir them, Mornoc's lair lies before them to the west."

"I have not heard word from Shole in years of any movements of the enemy. Are there still patrols in the west? They would know for sure whether Mornoc is preparing for battle." Corred tossed his thoroughly chewed grass aside and grabbed some more.

Einar shrugged his shoulders. "There have been no attacks, so there have been no expeditions." Einar said, shrugging his shoulders. "Why go looking for trouble?"

Corred looked into the distance. "I understand that, but isn't it the job of their militia to watch Mornoc's movements?"

Einar shook his head. "Yes, I agree. It is disturbing how much can be surrendered in the name of peace, but I do understand their thinking."

Once they were through the fields they picked up the same wagon trail as Corred had traveled that morning. It was now busy with all sorts of people coming and going to Renken's market place. A pair of young men tended a herd of sheep and another followed with a set of yoked oxen, the sound of confused and stressed animals filling the air. Einar and Corred walked just off the road to avoid the tangle.

At the top of the hill overlooking Renken, Einar and Corred met a well-adorned carriage. They slowed a little in anticipation of its arrival, watching the small escort of guards that accompanied it.

"Lord Raven's carriage?" Corred asked Einar under his breath.

"It is," Einar said, watching closely. Leaning Corred's direction, he continued. "But I do not know the man on horseback that follows," Einar responded, nodding toward a man dressed unlike the others in the escort. "I saw him last night speaking with a gentleman in the street when I passed Lord Raven's estate."

A short man with sharp features, dark hair, and less distinguished dress than the others accompanied the carriage. He wore no hide cap as the others did, and his robe was dark green instead of the scarlet and black of Renken's guard. He watched Einar and Corred with a disapproving eye as they stood aside and bowed, paying their respects to Renken's lord. Once the carriage had passed, Einar stared at the man unabashed. But the man in green ignored Einar completely. Instead, he looked at Corred and smiled ever so slightly. Slowing his horse to a stop, he leaned over to address him.

"Young man, what is your name?" He looked him up and down intently.

"Why would a man of your importance inquire after someone like me?" Corred asked respectfully.

Einar watched on, silently.

"I recognize your face," he answered. Lowering his voice,

he asked, "Don't you have a brother?" His inquiry was gentle, but something about it was sinister.

Corred felt the heat of embarrassment and anger rise from his chest into his head. The inquiry was unexpected. "No, sir, you are mistaken," he replied, trying to hide his emotion.

The man sat up and nodded, knowingly. "I must be. My apologies," he said. "I thought perhaps you were someone else." He continued on without another word, casting a few glances over his shoulder with the same piercing gaze.

"I knew I didn't like him," Einar muttered.

Corred gripped his belt hard with both hands to conceal his anger. Unable to keep from scowling, he returned to walking at a faster pace than before. His thoughts swam with rage. *I don't have a brother!* A deep wound, still unhealed had been perfectly prodded. *I don't have a father. I don't have a mother . . .* Corred let out a long sigh to relieve the pressure building in his chest.

Einar kept at his side, casting sideways glances at his younger friend. "Anger is a foothold for bitterness, Corred. I don't pretend to know your hurt, and I never have, but I must speak truth to you," Einar said.

Corred remained silent, knowing that his voice would betray his feelings, and he would no doubt say something he'd regret. He just kept gripping his belt instead, until his knuckles turned white. *Bitterness already has a foothold.*

"What separates us from our enemy most is our hope. When we fight, it is *for* something, for peace, not out of hate, or a desire for revenge." After a pause Einar added, "You are a son of the Promise, an heir to the Sword. Nothing can change that."

Corred knew Einar was right, but it was harder to believe

these things when he was confronted with his past. Corred sighed again, trying to let go. A chill ran down his spine as he fought with his emotions, disgusted with his own vulnerability.

Though there was evidence to support that Corred's father had left his family and joined the forces of Mornoc as a traitor, Corred had refused to believe it. Ever since the day his father had disappeared, Corred had insisted that it was because he had been ambushed, and that he had died fighting, even though his father's body was never found. Only Einar had chosen to believe the best with him; even Corred's grandfather, Creedus, doubted that his son had somehow died honorably. When his younger brother, Androcles had disappeared in much the same way, Corred closed up; it had been more than he could handle.

They walked on in silence for a while as Corred wrestled with himself, unaware of the beautiful countryside around him. There was a slight breeze moving over the hills and through the grass, which swayed according to its flow. A flock of starlings flew here and there, resting in one tree, then flying to the next with a burst of sound. Several times they flew just over the trail as if headed in the same direction as Einar and Corred. The intense flutter of their wings could be heard like a quickly passing wave.

Einar broke the silence. "How is your grandfather? I haven't spoken to him in a while."

"He is quite well," Corred answered dryly. "I am sure you heard that he hunted and killed a bear armed only with the Sword last month. It would seem that sparring and sword play are not enough for him. Even though many men are stronger than him, he always beats whoever he faces, with any weapon."

Einar let out a laugh. "A lack of enemies has never

stopped him from picking a fight, has it? A warrior whether there is peace or not."

"That is my grandfather." Corred's mood lightened. "I believe he looks to appoint another in his stead, and pass on the Sword before he is too weak to wield it well. I am sure my father would have been that man." Corred fell silent again and returned to watching the path.

Einar looked away into the hills, as if searching for something. "He truly would have been," he agreed quietly. Einar again sought to change the subject. "When was the last time you were in Wellman?" he asked.

"Maybe, two months. Galena and I went to the summer festival with my aunt and uncle, as we do every year." This change of focus finally brought peace to Corred's confused and pained thoughts.

He knew exactly how long it had been: two months and four days exactly. That week he had become captivated by a certain young lady. It hadn't been the first time he'd seen her, or even his first time speaking with her, but something had changed. He couldn't quite explain the feeling, and he didn't feel the need to understand it.

"It feels like an age ago," he added, staring into the distance. *I wonder what she's doing right now.* The streets of Wellman replaced the road he walked, and a graceful figure walked beside him. He longed to talk to her again, but he knew it was not his place; she was a child of royalty. But the hope lived on in his imagination.

For some time they continued on, running for a portion to shorten the journey. By mid afternoon they left the wagon trail behind and cut into the farm fields to the east of Oak Knoll.

*　　*　　*　　*　　*

On the eastern side of Renken, Lord Raven stood on the balcony of his three story mansion. His closely trimmed beard and dark hair spotted with gray fit his dark complexion. Sharp green eyes and chiseled features added to his stately appearance. He wore no crown or adorning jewelry to mark his office, but rather a flowing scarlet robe attached to his shoulders and a gold signet ring, which he spun on his finger incessantly. Apart from these ornaments, he was dressed like any rich merchant in the Lowlands.

Overlooking the estate, his study was the highest point of the mansion where the flag of Renken flew from its peak. With a careful eye he observed the courtyard below as a young boy walked a colt around the center. A second servant attended to the two men who had brought the horse to show Lord Raven. They all watched the animal, admiring its graceful gait and the rich color of its hide. Tossing his head playfully, the colt seemed to know quite well that he was being watched.

Lord Raven's mansion wrapped completely around the courtyard allowing only two exits for the traffic of supplies, visitors, and those who came to call on the lord for such an occasion as this. There were several stables, storage rooms, and a covered walkway around its circumference. The house itself was made of stone except for in a few sections, such as the stables, which were built from the largest trees in the region. Just one of these stables would have been an enviable house among the citizens in the western part of town.

After a number of circles, the tradesmen below eagerly awaited Lord Raven's response. Withholding his reaction a little while longer, if only to cause them discomfort and make them desperate for a sale, Lord Raven finally waved to an older servant attending them below. Immediately the servant spoke with the two men. Their reactions were favorable as they were then led to the door below the balcony.

As Lord Raven retreated within his study, a short man with sharp features and a shrewd eye stood just inside the door. Though waiting on the lord as every other servant, he dressed as he pleased.

"Lowell, what did you think of the field we looked at earlier today? You have been quiet on the subject, but I know you have thoughts to share. Please, speak up, that is why I have you in my council." Lord Raven addressed him while taking a seat in his chair just inside the balcony. "Quickly, before the tradesmen come to argue."

"My lord, I have very little to say about the field, or the colt for that matter. They are very desirable in my eyes and you have the means to purchase them if it is your interest. I wish only to speak to you about something else, something that worries me."

Lord Raven gave him an inquiring look.

"After you purchase the animal, sir," Lowell said respectfully, backing away from the door. The sound of approaching steps could be heard on the wood floors.

Upon entering, the servant who had been with the tradesmen in the courtyard showed them in. His old face wrinkled slightly as he smiled. "Gentlemen, Lord Raven."

"Thank you, Orlin," Lord Raven said to his master servant, ignoring the introduction. "You may go."

With a bow Orlin left the room.

Turning his attention to his guests, Lord Raven spoke plainly, "State your price."

The two tradesmen looked at each other to decide who would give the news. After a few seconds, the one spoke up to fill the silence, "200 coins, sir. Not a coin less for a colt like this."

Lord Raven scowled ever so slightly. "I rarely pay more than 175 coins," he said dryly. "This horse is to be for a servant when he is fit for service. I will not be riding him."

The second tradesman grasped at the opportunity to press their case. "Sir, this animal was captured from the foothills in the north but three weeks ago, broken only enough to be controlled for travel. A horse like this can be well trained by someone in your house to do whatever you wish. He is a magnificent animal and quite capable of being fit even with my lord's saddle in due time."

"I've seen many horses, sir, and I assure you he is not worth 200 coins." Lord Raven put on the façade of losing interest and stood up to turn away and look out his balcony.

The second tradesman continued, "My lord, if you would take a look at my own mount just outside your window here, you will see his dignified air." Approaching the window as he spoke he pushed on to close the sale. "Do you approve of his stature?"

Pleased with the man's efforts to persuade him, Lord Raven entertained the question. "Yes, I do. I find him a magnificent creature. What is your point?" He remained with his back to the tradesman.

"Well this colt was taken from the same herd that my mount was. He is an offspring of the dominant male with one of the largest herds of the north." The man's voice was growing animated, as it was apparent that he took great pride in his work.

Lord Raven turned around and looked him in the eye. "I'll buy him for 180 coins, if what you say is true."

"By the skin on my back, my lord, it is true," the man said.

"Done. Go and see my servant, Orlin. He will manage the money with you. Thank you, gentlemen."

The tradesmen nodded their heads with a smile and turned to go.

"I will let you know if this colt disappoints me," Lord Raven called after them. "Or if you are given to exaggerations."

The tradesman who had closed the sale turned and gave a prompt response. "I assure you, my lord, he will not disappoint you." He nodded again and left.

Lowell closed the door after them. "My lord made a wise purchase," he said with a smile.

"Yes, I know. That horse was worth at least 200 coins," he replied, finally releasing a smile. "Now, what is it you wanted to talk to me about?" he added returning to their previous discussion.

Lowell paused, gathered his thoughts, and then walked over toward the balcony to join in observing the activity below. "My lord, I have been wondering . . ." He paused slightly, changing his tone to one more serious. "Is it wise to ignore the stubborn ways of these men we refer to as the Véran?" There was a slight scorn in his voice. "They walk around the town armed, claiming to be vigilant guards of the people, yet they contribute very little to the welfare of the people with mere words. There is no war for them to fight. There has not been one in almost fifty years, and there will likely not be one in the foreseeable future."

"Lowell, the Véran are a stubborn kind, you are right, and

I know there has been no war for quite some time, but they are at least true people. I have decided after our many conversations on the subject to pay them no mind at all. Traditionally, I have been patronizing, but as you say, they do contribute very little to the public good." Lord Raven paused thinking it through for a moment.

Lowell stared hard at him, searching him out.

"On the other hand, Lowell, they contribute no less to the welfare than many in the western district." Lord Raven's emotions were clearly divided. "I would loathe doing such a thing as punish devotion. Regardless of whether they are understood, they are revered. What would you suggest?"

"I do not suggest punishment or ill treatment. I only question the usefulness of what could be beneficial talent, my lord. They could become part of your guard, loyal to you, or to some other city guard. Has not their duty always been to the people, for their protection, and the keeping of peace?" Lowell said.

Lord Raven listened carefully but did not respond.

Lowell continued, "Even if they are truly devout, would it be wise to ignore them simply because they have not yet done any harm?" Lowell cast his doubt well, and the effect could be seen in the Lord Raven's face.

Lord Raven nodded. "I see what you are saying, Lowell. I will think about it, but no more talk of this for now." Turning to Lowell he addressed him directly, "I am ready for supper. Go and inquire of the maidservants as to its progress." With that he continued observing the courtyard below as the sale of the colt was finalized and the animal was placed in one of his stables.

"Yes, my lord." Lowell exited the room, leaving the door

open behind him. With a glance back at the lord he contorted his face with displeasure. Under his breath he muttered a few words of contempt as his eyes grew menacing. Saving face for the approach of a young maidservant he bid her "Good afternoon," and continued on his way through the mansion.

CHAPTER 5

The Croic River was the largest river in all of the Lowlands. Cutting through the Altus Mountains in the north, it forked into the Beryl River, which led to Renken and the southern parts, and the Rundum River, which flowed all the way through the Northern Villages to the west. The Northern Villages were made up of as many as a hundred small towns and outposts that covered a vast expanse of the northern Lowlands.

Like the rest of the Lowlands there were lines of royalty in the North, but they exercised their privilege more as servants of the people, as recognized men of councel, than as men of wealth or control. Most villages were self sustaining, relying little on trade from other regions. What one village lacked, the next one had. Farmers, hunters, and specialized tradesmen, they were a rugged people.

It was in this region that wild horses were plentiful and, in turn, a breed of men that made a living of catching and taming them for use by men. They were an independent lot, even among the Northern Villages, traveling in groups of four or five, facing all kinds of danger, every moment of their lives spent for the purpose of rounding up these wild horses to tame and sell. Where the horses went, they followed. They were well known as the Horsemen.

Despite their independence, the Horsemen, since the very beginnings of the Lowlands, had been faithful believers in the Promise. Some would say it was culture for a Horseman to believe in the Promise, but it was far more than that. Nights under the stars, days in the heat of the sun, and the hardships of their trade did not allow them to grow comfortable with living in the Lowlands. And so, they were also less apt to grow passive toward their enemies. If there was an enemy, then the Story was true, and so was the Promise. It was all the reasoning that they needed; they were simple men. They knew too much and saw too much to doubt.

Daily they left behind their wives and children, vowing to care for each other's families should they not safely return home. In this way, they were not so independent from one another, but rather from the rest of men. One might certainly say however, that the rest of men were dependent upon them.

Throughout the years, leaders would rise from among their kind, warriors to lead the children of Homsoloc in the war against Mornoc and the evil that he spread. But this was a dying trend, for there had not been war for many years and men had grown comfortable with it; the rule of money and influence had taken center stage. Those with a smooth tongue and persuasive speech were the leaders now. Valiance in battle was no longer needed, or so it seemed and many believed.

But still some things remained true. In the foothills of the Altus Mountains, the Horsemen continued watching, catching, and taming wild horses as they had for hundreds of years. The majority of them remained honest, hard-working men of the northern frontiers.

On the side of a small hill, three particular Horsemen prepared their evening meal. The horses they rode were tied loosely to the lower branches of a nearby tree. Two jackrabbits roasted over a fire as they began their meal with some bread from their packs. The fire did not burn exceptionally high, for wood was scarce and they couldn't afford a short, hot blaze.

Waiting patiently, they reclined against their saddle packs. Each contained some heavier clothing for colder conditions, a roll for their bed, rope, gloves, and meager rations to survive should they be unable to find game. With their every breath a light plume of steam could be seen in the light of the fire, as the cold of night continued its descent over the land.

It was clear by their dirty blonde hair and similar features that the three of them were brothers. One kept his hair short while another let it grow to his shoulders, but all three had the same eyes. Their thick hide pants were still covered with dust from riding throughout the day, and the sleeves of their thick shirts were rolled up in anticipation of the task at hand.

The middle of the three looked at his bread with a longing in his eye before taking another bite. "I should have brought more. I'm hungry enough to eat a leg of venison," he said.

The youngest shook his head with a smile. "Gernod, you're hungry enough to eat a leg of venison at every meal."

Gernod was a hefty fellow and certainly appeared able to eat as much as he longed for. He chewed his bread slowly, as if that would make it last longer, watching the main meal cook over the flames.

"Well, until we return home with a few catches, no one is

going to have a leg of venison," said the oldest. As he meticulously checked the rabbits with his knife, he asked, "Lanhard, did you bring many apples?"

"Yes, Bernd," he responded, not exactly pleased with making such a statement in front of Gernod. "I will share them as always, if we can't find enough to eat along the way."

Once he determined that the meat was cooked well enough for eating, Bernd evenly divided it among them.

The only utensils in use for the meal were knives, as delivery was really the only main concern, not the manner in which it was done. Each of them sat against his saddle with his lap as a table to ensure that not a single scrap was lost.

Making fast work of his meal, Bernd turned to watching the sky, cleaning his teeth with a bone.

Lanhard leaned back against his saddle, satisfied with his meal, once again ready to talk. "We're fortunate I'm such a good shot. I wouldn't have wanted to eat dried venison for the fourth night in a row."

"Agreed. I wish I were as great an archer as you," Gernod responded, now in a better mood, having satisfied his hunger. "Honestly, wouldn't you say we truly have one of the greatest archers in all the North sitting here in our midst, Bernd?"

Slowly lowering his gaze, Bernd responded with a smile, "I don't know, Gernod. A few of the young ladies back home could give him a run for his money." He tossed the bone into the hot coals.

Lanhard laughed, fond of the teasing. He seldom took himself seriously, but then again he seldom lacked confidence either. "If only the two of them had been running together, I would have only needed one arrow."

"Well, I'm glad you didn't wait for that opportunity or we

really would have had dried venison," Gernod replied. He finished his tin cup of water with a gulp and proceeded to wash his hands with a little water from his canteen.

"Go easy on the water. We are going to need it tomorrow. We're a ways away from the streams at this point." Bernd said, observing his younger brother.

Gernod nodded.

Bernd was the quiet thinker and the voice of reason among the three while Gernod and Lanhard tended to enjoy the challenges of life for their danger. Bernd was not shy by any means but he did prefer using his head when his back was not needed. They were the perfect mix for the job. Bernd always had a plan, Gernod had the strength to handle most anything, and Lanhard had a talent that money couldn't buy.

Gernod looked around as if for something else to eat. "Lanhard, do you have many carrots?"

"A few. But I want to make them last. I'd rather not run out before the return home." He went ahead and tossed one to his brother.

After adding a few of the last sticks to the fire, Bernd returned to stargazing. He folded his hands over his stomach and leaned a little farther into his saddle, stretching out his legs on the moss that covered the ground. The sky was clear and the stars were out in full as far as the eye could see. "I never tire of the night sky," he said quietly to anyone who would listen.

Gernod and Lanhard joined him in his admiration, agreeing in their silence. They all looked to the same places in the sky for familiar formations of stars. For a while they lay quietly recounting all the ones they'd been taught as children, and now knew so well from years and nights just like this one.

"I am thankful for the reminders that lay up there," Bernd said. "Not that I would forget the stories, but . . . it does me good to be reminded."

After a lengthy pause, Lanhard observed, "The Sword is especially clear tonight."

"It's that time of year," Gernod agreed.

A line of several large stars extended from a cluster of smaller ones, like the hand of a warrior gripping the hilt of a long sword, low in the western sky. Something of an arm followed and it faded from there. But, depending upon how you saw it, there was more to it than just that. The extent of the formation lay with the beholder. There was traced throughout the whole of the sky, the outline of a rider. He had a helmet and shield, a robe flowing behind him. Not everyone saw the same thing, but regardless of what he looked like, he was there, riding fast, coming in strength to strike his foe.

"Speaking of swords . . ." Bernd sat up quickly, added the last of the wood to the fire and drew a short sword from under his saddle. It was sheathed in thick hide with a molded wooden grip. The cross of the handle was tarnished but not rusting and wider on the ends than at the middle. Pulling it from its sheath, he leaned in toward the fire to bring it into the light. It shined like metal just polished. Satisfied that the edge was visibly sharp he left it alone, returned it to its sheath, and slipped it back under his saddle.

Lanhard and Gernod took little notice of this practice, accustomed to it to the point of apathy. They too carried a similar blade, though Lanhard was more of an archer.

"Boys, I'm getting my rest. Tomorrow we cross the Rundum and ride to the streams at the base of Mount Elm. I expect we'll see more than a few horses to our liking. Bless the women and children. Good night." Bernd pulled out his blanket and rolled onto his side.

"Agreed on all terms," Gernod replied, and followed suit.

Lanhard remained awake for a while longer, watching the sky, thinking through a day now passed. Only once he could hear his brothers breathing soundly did he pull out his blanket. As he made his bed, he listened for the sounds of night. It was too cold for crickets, but the hoots of an owl coming from the opposite hill more than made up for them.

As he looked in that general direction, Lanhard thought he caught a glimpse of a shape against the starlit sky moving along the edge of the hill. He instinctively reached for his knife, which he kept sheathed and strapped to his saddle. Watching until he was convinced it had been a trick on his eyes, he relaxed and let sleep overcome him.

*   *   *   *   *

Hundreds of miles south of the Altus Mountains, the enemy was not sleeping. All through the night more scouts arrived, some carrying lanterns, others empty-handed. Entering the mouths of caves at the roots of wooded hills, they followed long dark tunnels to one of four doorways to the Hall of Casimir. As their numbers grew, so did the number of lanterns lining the tunnels, bringing their operations to light. They came from miles around, traveling on foot. Some came from the east, others from the west, and a few from the south. They were an army in motion, secretly preparing for war.

The stone banquet table swarmed with activity as more scouts arrived than were leaving. Guards and cooks rushed back and forth to supply the table with enough meat and ale to match the need. The candle chandelier above burned continuously in a place where the sun did not rise. The sound of feasting was accompanied by the occasional scuffle over a choice piece of meat. If there was conversation it was coarse and dark, like everything else.

After a day's rest Selcor exited the hall through the door he had entered the night before. He went alone without a word to anyone, rubbing his chest, sore from his fight with Casimir. With his pouch packed full of spears, he quickened his step the higher he went, up toward the surface, called on by the evil that controlled his heart. He had a mission, and it was not yet complete; there were lives to claim.

The slightest bit of moonlight shone across the doorway as he ran out of the cave and headed north. Selcor passed a few more scouts in the woods while the sunrise was still hours away. Offering a quick salute with the tip of a spear, he ran on, pressing the pace.

*   *   *   *   *

The town of Wellman, several miles farther west of Oak Knoll and nearly ten times its size, lay in the shape of a circle. Its cabins and huts of all different sizes surrounded Lord Wellman's mansion and the town hall in a series of expanding rings. Wellman sat in a valley of sorts, surrounded by thickly wooded hills to the west and south known as the Bryn Mountains. To the north the landscape was much more open, dotted with crops and barns here and there, separated east and west by one main road that cut due north and forked out to the surrounding region.

Since the town's establishment, the family of Wellman had

been in control of its affairs, filling the seat of lord with its finest young men. Wellman was also home to many of the Véran. The effect of their presence had been very beneficial, and their constant interaction with Lord Wellman had provided an influence that countered that of the times. Though not heralded in Wellman at large, the Promise was at least revered, which was more than could be said of many places in the Lowlands.

Just as the light of a new day began gathering on the horizon, Corred awoke to the sound of the town bell ringing loudly. Leaping from his bed, he joined Einar in quickly getting dressed and strapping on his sword.

"What's going on?" Corred gasped, working hard to focus in the low light.

"I know of no good reason for the town bell to sound at such an early hour," Einar responded with an equal tension in his voice.

When they opened their door, Creedus was already awake and standing on his front step. The Sword already hung from his belt, and his left hand was resting on the hilt. His long, now completely white hair and beard hung loosely about his shoulders and chest, but for an old man, he stood tall.

"What is the alarm?" Einar asked, wiping his eyes.

"I cannot tell," Creedus responded without looking their direction. "We rarely hear the bell ring. Something ill is afoot."

Before he finished speaking a rider could be seen fast approaching from the center of town. The sound of his gallop filled the still air with an intensity that was out of place for the time of day.

Einar and Corred looked at each other with concern as the answer quickly approached. Creedus waited calmly for the rider's arrival.

He pulled his horse to a halt in front of their cabins. "Creedus, you are needed in Lord Wellman's house." The horse was as agitated as the man's voice, twitching and turning this way and that.

"What news do you bring?" Creedus asked.

"A man was killed last night on the western side of town. Some others are missing. Please, hurry." With that, the rider turned tail and rode as fast as he could back to the center of town.

"Get yourselves together and meet me at Lord Wellman's mansion," Creedus said loudly. There was a just anger in his voice as he pulled his coat from a peg inside the door and slung it over his shoulders. "A foul fiend will give account!" he half-yelled as he walked away.

Several heads looked out of their doors to seek an answer for the commotion.

Corred and Einar threw on their coats and quickly grabbed a piece of bread, a meager meal, but fitting for the occasion.

Wellman's chimneys smoked lightly, not yet stoked for breakfast. A light frost covered the rooftops waiting to be touched by the warmth of the sun. All was quiet; the streets were empty apart from a few people going house to house to either inquire of or to spread the news of what had happened.

Corred stopped a young woman to ask her the details.

"An enemy soldier has been seen, three men are dead, and three are missing." She was no more than fifteen herself and visibly shaken by the news.

"A soldier you say?" Einar asked.

"Yes, sir. A scout, as they call them." Not sparing another moment, she hurried on to the next house, holding back tears.

Einar and Corred jogged the rest of the way, taking one of the many streets that ran straight into the center of town. The closer they came to the town hall the more the town came alive; the dreadful news worked its way to the edges of Wellman like ripples on a pond. Husbands and fathers were taking stock of their own loved ones and their most precious belongings. All but a few houses still had the nighttime lamp burning on the front step. From among the houses, a few other members of the Véran were also jogging toward Lord Wellman's mansion, coming out of the woodwork.

At the center of town the mansion stood taller than any of the other buildings, only slightly taller than the town hall next to it. The hall doors were closed and its chimney was cold. In contrast, the chimney of Lord Wellman's mansion was billowing smoke heavily.

As Einar and Corred arrived, with a few others trailing behind them, several messengers ran out of the front door with letter pouches over their shoulders. One of them carried a short sword, the others a bow and arrow. Without a single thought to further preparation they mounted their horses, which were waiting by the town hall, and took off. The only farewell they gave was the sound of their gallop and flying clods of dirt. They took the main road headed north.

"I suppose we will learn the meaning of their haste inside," Einar said as he ascended the stair with Corred.

Opening the front doors, they were greeted by the heat of the fire in the front hall; it had been burning for some time. Creedus recognized their entry with a sober nod. He stood before Lord Wellman, who sat in a large wooden chair at the end of the hall. His eyes were red with crying and rage as he gripped the arms of his chair. He was not wearing his customary robe, but rather the dress of a common man, unprepared for the arrival of guests. His shoulder length gray hair was messy and un-kept from running his hands over his head. Known to all as a strong leader, it was staggering to see him so completely undone. On his right was a small gathering of women by the hearth weeping, some of them loudly. They too were not appropriately dressed for a public showing, one of them being his wife. Her younger daughter and her servants tried in vain to console her.

Corred's heart sank into his chest. *Where is she!? Certainly she would be here with all the others.* His mind began to race as he thought of explanations for her absence, not wanting to believe what he feared was the case.

"Is this your Véran?" Lord Wellman asked of Creedus with disdain. His lips quivered with emotion.

Eight more men filed in behind Einar and Corred.

"Yes, my lord, and well able to serve you." Creedus did not take Lord Wellman's anger and grief personally. "Many more will be arriving within days."

Lord Wellman glared at them all. "Determine who has done this thing and kill them." Looking now at the Sword that hung from Creedus' belt, he added. "Perhaps that sword will finally be of some good among men. Find my children, and bring them back." Trembling, he shook his fist in the air. "I will be avenged!" With that he rushed out of the greeting hall and back into the rooms of his house.

The women who had been weeping made no such move. A few of them were curled up on their knees on the floor by the fire, overwhelmed with grief. One of them looked at Creedus with teary eyes, searching for hope. She was Lord Wellman's youngest child.

"Your brother and sister will be found," Creedus said with authority. Addressing Lord Wellman's wife, though she did not look at him, he added, "Do not despair, they will be found." Creedus walked out of the house signaling the others to follow.

Corred felt the weight of the words. He tried to hide his concern, but it was in vain. The calm he had initially maintained slowly left his face as he began to imagine the worst. *Where could they have taken her!? Why would they have taken her?* He fell in with the rest of the group outside.

Once the doors were closed behind him, Creedus remained atop the stairs and looked over the group. With a deep breath he relayed the brunt of the news. "Lord Wellman's eldest son, Pedrig, has been slain. Several of our enemy's scouts slew him and his servants as he returned from a hunting trip earlier this morning." Without looking he pointed his right hand upward.

Ten feet above his head, stuck in one of the main crossbeams of the house was a short black spear. It had almost blended in with the shadows of the eave above it. Something from its blade had stained the wood around it; it was blood.

Creedus continued, "This wasn't enough for our enemy. He has kidnapped Lord Wellman's daughter, Olwen, her maidservant Gwen, and his younger son, Tristan. Tristan is now his only son." The strength of his youth still flashed in his eyes as he recounted the injustice.

The fear that had gripped Corred's thoughts was quickly replaced by anger. *They can hunt me all they want, even wound me, but they cannot harm the innocent and get away with it!* The very thought that the girl he loved had been mistreated set in him a resolve he had never felt before.

One of the men present asked in disbelief, "Why was the

alarm not sounded in time to stop them?"

"Our enemy is sly," Creedus replied. "Lord Wellman knew nothing of it until he heard the sound of hooves outside his house."

"What of the guard?" another asked.

"What man needs a guard when his enemies are silent?" There was a cutting sarcasm in Creedus' voice. He paused even as he said it, disappointed with himself for having shown it. "We can trifle with such questions when our enemy lies dead at our feet," he huffed. Drawing the Sword quickly from its scabbard, he let it ring as he pointed its tip at the horizon. With a light all of its own, the inscription at the base of the blade shined brightest. Creedus raised his voice, excitedly, "Get your horses and what provisions you must. We ride from the southern edge of town when the sun clears those trees in the east."

Without a word they dispersed, running back to their homes to prepare for a rescue party, and a fight.

Creedus sheathed his sword and descended the stairs. "I have horses for the both of you," he said addressing Einar and Corred.

Together they ran back to Creedus' cabin.

The chimneys were now smoking well as the news had spread quickly and brought an end to a peaceful night's rest. People watched them from their steps with wide eyes, looking for explanation; they would receive none from Creedus. His eyes were fixed on the road ahead of him. There was no time.

As they neared their cabins, Creedus was breathing heavily, but not too heavily to give a few more orders. "Pack light. Only one of them is on horseback, but if we are to catch them we must ride swiftly. I have seen a scout run like a deer."

Corred and Einar quickly packed two days rations of bread, dried meat and water in their shoulder packs, and grabbed a roll for a bed. When they stepped outside Creedus was rounding his cabin with three beautiful horses, saddled and ready. He had a pack of provisions already tied to his horse.

"The sun will not wait." He mounted his horse and dug in. "Yah!"

Corred was right behind him.

Riding around the perimeter of the town from the east side where Creedus lived, they met up with two others that had arrived before them. Brothers, and both archers, Beathan and Boyd were not much older than Corred. Neither of them had seen any more conflict than could be provided by a bear hunt. But they had a stern and settled countenance behind their light, curly hair and clean-shaven faces; they would not be denied the chance to prove themselves.

Corred met them with a firm handshake, having become familiar with them both and their love of the Promise from meetings at Hill Top.

Reed, one of Creedus' most loyal friends, was the last to arrive. Only six had answered the call when action was required.

Creedus took charge. "The scouts will be taking them south into the woods and through the Bryn Mountains. We must not let them reach the other side. In this pursuit we have two things on our side: most scouts will have nothing to do with horses, and they will only run trails because of their captives. Pray they have reason enough to keep their captives alive. When we catch them . . . ? " He paused to look each man in the eye. "Expect the fight of your lives."

Creedus addressed the archers. "Beathan, ride in the front

with me. Boyd, ride behind with Einar. We will need your eyes to track and your arrows to strike first."

"Yah!" Creedus gave his horse a kick and set the pace with his white hair flying. Corred urged his horse to stay close to his grandfather as they raced through the fields. With no crops through which to navigate they rode straight for the woods.

A farmer preparing a set of oxen next to his barn on the outskirts of Wellman watched curiously as they passed by. Pondering their hurry, for he had not yet heard the news, he scratched his head and muttered a few words to his oxen as he yoked them together.

Slowing the pace only a little, the party picked up a main trail headed for the heart of the Bryn Mountains just as the sun cleared the trees to the east. Its arrival was not as bright as the day before, as a low cloud cover was beginning to fill the sky.

For a while the woods remained open with grassy floors rather than the thick underbrush that characterized most of the area. In single file the eight of them picked their way through the trees a little faster than a trot. They quickly picked out the deep tracks of a horse that had run due south several hours before. Everyone looked to the sides of the trail for any sign left by travelers on foot.

"Over there. That is not from a wild animal." Beathan pointed to a cluster of taller grass that had been freshly trampled. Leaving the path he checked it closely. "These tracks are too wide for a deer, or even a horse. They must have come this way." He spoke over his shoulder, keeping his eyes on the ground.

"I see it on the other side as well," Corred said. "The leaves have been pressed into the grass."

"They're staying off the trail in hopes of hiding their

tracks," Reed said. "We should fan out while the woods remain open. To have any hope of catching them, we must first find their way in."

"Good, good. This will slow them down," Creedus said under his breath. "We may overtake them by nightfall."

As they followed one sign to another, the path grew increasingly narrow, headed for thicker woods. The Bryn Mountains were more accurately hills when compared to the Altus Mountains in the north, but they were very tight, and not at all easily passed. The air hardly moved and grass gradually gave way to thicket and thistle the farther in they went.

"They've moved back onto the path." Beathan alerted them to this change just as they were beginning to reach a point where the brush was no longer passable on horseback.

"With good reason," Einar remarked as he wrestled with a thistle bush that had caught his pants.

"Keep together," Creedus said loudly. "These woods are perfect for an ambush. Let us ensure we are not the ones surprised for a fight."

CHAPTER 6

At the base of a large tree, a young woman no older than fifteen collapsed to the ground. Through heavy breathing, mixed with sobs, she struggled to again raise herself to her feet. Her once white blouse was soiled and ripped along the bottom, and her blonde braids were coming undone. Both wrists were bruised and bleeding under the rope that bound them tightly, held at the other end by her captor.

A man dressed in black leaned over her and grabbed the back of her neck. "This will be the last time you fall," he growled. "Get on your feet and walk. If you do not I will quicken our pace by ending your miserable life." He pressed his words through bared teeth. Standing up he pulled her to her feet with the rope. "Walk."

Just ahead of him two more scouts were playing a similar role, following a young man and woman with spears. With their hands bound tightly in front of them, their ropes were held by a fourth scout, Selcor, who led them all from the front. He was attentively watching the events at the rear. Turning to his other two captives, he spoke coldly. "If we are caught because of your little friend, she will be the first to die. Tell her to keep going." His black eyes looked back and forth from one to the other expecting an answer. "Shall I kill her now and spare you the trouble?"

Olwen quickly turned to encourage her maidservant. "Gwen, come, walk with us. We will help you." Her face was no cleaner than Gwen's but the tears that had once covered her cheeks were drying, and though her soft green eyes were filled with fear there was courage in her voice. Strings of her auburn hair clung to the dried blood on her forehead where she had been pulled hard through thistles.

"Lean on me if you must," Olwen said, coming along side her maidservant.

Tristan offered his support silently, clenching his jaw. He was in far worse shape than his sister. His nose was battered and bloody and his right eye was almost swollen shut. He had not been as easily captured and was inclined even now to fight and die. His restraint was due only to his concern for the safety of Olwen and Gwen.

All three of them had cloth hanging around their necks, which had earlier been used to gag them, ensuring a quiet escape from Wellman. From the moment they had been taken until the present, they had been running, marching, and at times been dragged to keep up with their captors. Now in the heart of the Bryn Mountains they had slowed the pace because of the landscape.

As they made their way up yet another steep embankment, a light mist began falling on the leaves above them.

The scouts paid no mind, leading their captives deeper and deeper into the wilderness with one evident mission. They all had a pouch completely full of spears except Selcor, who had used a few earlier that morning. Periodically he looked over his shoulder, beyond his captives and into the trees, as if expecting something.

Tristan watched his eyes, trying to discern his intent. Their progress had gradually slowed to where they were merely walking through the woods. Every time he expected the pace to quicken, it only grew more relaxed. It was becoming clear that he, his sister, and Gwen were bait. It was more than he could bear.

Watching the path closely, Tristan waited for the opportune moment. As he followed Selcor around a bend in the path, he tripped and fell on his face. Fumbling in the dirt he crawled a few feet as if unable to get up.

The scout following him slapped him on the arm with his spear. "Get up. Watch your feet, you fool."

Feigning fear of more abuse, Tristan quickly rose to his feet with the help of a violent tug at his rope from Selcor. Once his captor returned to leading the way as before, Tristan went to work on his cords with the sharp rock he had picked up through his fall. If there was to be a fight, he would not be tied down to watch.

*   *   *   *   *

Hours later, with the sun's position hidden behind the clouds, Creedus continued leading the way along a winding trail. The tracks of the rider on horseback had long since vanished, but the sign of several persons on foot called them on.

They too were now on foot, leading their horses through

the steep, short climbs on an increasingly rocky path. After finding a drop of blood on a leaf and other fresh signs along the path, it was clear that they were catching up, and that their enemy might hear them coming. A decision was made quickly.

"We will be at a disadvantage for a fight, but unless we run from here, we may never catch them." Creedus left his horse untied and started jogging, his eyes to the ground.

The rest of the party was quick to follow, with Corred first in line. They loosely tied their horses to a sapling or branch, trusting that they would stay put, or at least not wander too far.

As they pressed on, the light rain that was now falling through the trees moistened their hair where sweat didn't. No one wore their hoods, concerned that they might miss the slightest sound. With darting looks this way and that, they searched for a sign, movement, anything. A broken twig, a disturbance in the lay of the leaves along the path, or an overturned stone showed them the way through the wooded hills. And it was quiet. Not a bird was singing, not a squirrel stirred. An occasional leaf would fall in the distance and catch the attention of the group, their senses sharpened by urgency.

Each man had his hand on his weapon, ready to draw. Beathan and Boyd had their bows in hand, ready to pull an arrow in the blink of an eye. Added to the sound of their steps was that of their breath, and the beating of their hearts, pounding in their heads.

Creedus slowed his pace along the top of a ridge. From behind the base of a tree at the highest point he stopped to survey their surroundings. Waiting for Reed and Beathan to join him, he calmed his heavy breathing, held his breath and listened, watching.

The six of them knelt low, hugging the ground, waiting for

a sign from Creedus to continue.

On the opposite hill, his eye caught some movement among the trees.

Turning to Reed, he made eye contact and pointed his friend in the direction of his discovery. In a hushed voice he asked, "Do you see that?"

Beathan nodded as Reed still searched.

Passing over the mountain ridge just ahead of them and to the south was a small party on foot. Weaving in and among the trees, they were spread out along the trail. Two of the members of the party wore white.

"We've caught up with them," Creedus pointed. "If we play our position well we could take them within the hour." Creedus whispered the news to Beathan and Corred, who knelt just behind Reed.

Corred strained to see them through the forest before passing the news to Einar and Boyd in the rear.

Einar smiled slightly with the good news and clenched his meaty fists. Each man took heart at having the goal in sight, though the hardest part was yet to come. They did not know how many scouts they were trailing. Scouts were trained for a single purpose: to terrorize and kill without hesitation.

Once they were sure that their quarry had dipped over the hill and out of view, they descended. Swiftly, and with as little noise as possible, they worked at closing the gap without compromising their position.

*   *   *   *   *

Halfway down yet another steep hill, Selcor suddenly stopped.

Tristan, still working on his cords, nearly walked right into him.

They were almost out of the mountains. Only two small hills separated them now from an open field several hundred yards away. In the far distance were more woods, but the land flattened significantly.

Without a word Selcor nodded to the scouts that had been following Tristan and Olwen with spears in hand. One of them returned his spear to his pouch and went about gagging Gwen. Looking back and forth from Olwen to her captors and then to Tristan, she began to cry again.

"Leave her be," Tristan said, turning to Selcor with a scowl on his face.

"You are in no position to enforce such a command," he replied. Selcor's thin frame did not appear very strong but Tristan knew first hand that this was not the case. It was Selcor who had given him his stripes.

Before Tristan could respond in any way, the scout who had been tending him followed suit. Returning his spear to its pouch, he forcefully shoved Tristan's gag back into his mouth and tied it tightly behind his head.

Selcor went about gagging Olwen himself, but she bit him. In a flash he had a spear held to her throat and nodded for the scout beside him to finish the job.

Tristan lunged angrily at Selcor, but he was grabbed from behind and thrown to the ground.

Olwen froze as her gag was placed. She blinked away a few drops of water from the branches above and looked into Selcor's hollow eyes. He slowly lowered the spear, shaking his head.

Turning to the others, Selcor nodded, "Take them." For a

second he paused to look at Olwen closely. With black, beady eyes he admired her beauty. A hint of emotion came to his face, but it was fleeting. Handing the ropes he had been carrying to one of the others, he left the trail, followed by the scout who had been bringing up the rear.

Tristan struggled to his feet as he watched them go. When he looked back to see if they were being followed he received a swift slap to the face. Turning the other cheek with disdain, he glared at his captor.

"Let's move." The scout who had gagged him drew a spear again and held it up to Tristan's nose. "Go."

Continuing the flight with a renewed sense of urgency, the captives once again struggled to keep the set pace.

Every few steps Tristan searched the trees for Selcor and the fourth scout; they were gone. His suspicions were true: they were being followed and an ambush had been set. With a quickened pulse, Tristan resumed cutting at his cords.

Olwen watched her brother's hurried looks and caught a glimpse of his hands fast at work. She immediately looked away not wanting to bring attention to his efforts.

At the bottom of the hill they were forced to begin running again.

Tristan broke through in a matter of seconds, dropping the stone along the path. Holding fast to his cords, he now feigned his captivity, waiting for the right moment.

*   *   *   *   *

No sooner had the rescue party rounded the next hill than Beathan pointed through the trees over Creedus' shoulder. "There they are!" he whispered, trying to contain his excitement. In the same motion he pulled an arrow from his quiver and placed it gently on his bowstring.

From the top of the ridge the rescue party watched as two men dressed in black led three captives between two rocky hills, the last in the Bryn Mountains. They were moving fast.

"Only two scouts," Reed whispered as they crouched low to the ground.

"Don't be so sure," Creedus said. In the same breath he scanned the woods to either side. "They know they are being followed. They wouldn't have taken Lord Wellman's children without expecting it." After a few thoughtful strokes of his beard, he moved on. Glancing back at the whole group he whispered, "Watch the path closely."

Boyd knocked an arrow. With his left hand he held his bow in front of him and with his right he tucked the hood of his coat behind the top of his quiver and out of the way.

Einar and Corred remained in the middle, surveying the forest on either side.

The woods were beginning to thin as they followed the path down the hill. From tree to tree they watched for movement, listened for sound, never losing sight of where they had last seen the captives. Tension hung like the moisture that filled the air.

Halfway down, Creedus and Beathan slowed at a point where the path and the forest floor on either side had been disturbed. Sure enough, there were signs where the leaves had been pressed down, leading into the woods. Creedus stopped and observed the tracks, following their line with his eye.

Beathan and Reed peered through the boughs of the trees, bracing for what might come next.

Corred watched his grandfather's face as he looked

through the forest; his eyes widened.

In a flash of light, Creedus drew the Sword and cut the air as if deflecting an imaginary blow. The shaft of a black spear shattered loudly against the blade.

From the east, two scouts ran toward them. Their soft steps could barely be heard. Each held a spear shoulder high, ready for release. Darting between the trees, they charged the group of armed men with abandon. 60 yards, 55, 50 . . .

Beathan pulled back, leveled his aim, and released the first arrow.

With lightning fast reflexes, the scout coming from higher on the hill ducked between two saplings. The arrow deflected and flew high, missing its mark.

Beathan drew another arrow.

40 yards.

The second scout threw a spear with the force of his whole body behind it.

It sank into the tree beside Beathan's head, causing his second shot to sail wide.

"Corred, Einar, Boyd, save the captives!" Creedus yelled under his breath. "Go!"

Another spear was released. Creedus deflected it again with another equally agile block. It snapped in two on the trunk of the tree beside him.

Without another look at their attackers, Corred and Einar sprinted down the path with the wind on their heels. Boyd released an arrow at the closest oncoming scout and followed them while pulling another arrow from his quiver. His shot hit one of the scouts high in the shoulder, slowing him only a little.

In a rush of sound, the scouts met the three who had

stayed behind. Corred could hear a cry of pain from behind but did not dare to look. He stayed low. Reaching the spot the captives had last been seen, he flew over the final hill, barely touching the ground. Through the rush of wind in his face he could hear Einar's steps close behind him. The ground was wet, and at the speed they were running, it would be easy to lose control going down the last hill. Gliding over the wet leaves, Corred's footing hung on a thread, but he pushed all the harder. When a low branch hit him in the face, he slid down a section of the path with one hand on the ground. Like he had a hundred times before, he picked up a stone in the same movement, his second weapon.

Breaking out of the woods, Einar and Boyd came along side him. Einar's sword was in his hand. Boyd carried an arrow in his right hand, ready to lay it on the string.

The grass was thick, making it difficult to keep up the speed as the light rain mixed with the sweat on their brows, stinging their eyes.

Lord Wellman's children were already halfway across the open field. They too were running, but only as fast as they could be forced to. One of them turned back and spotted his rescuers.

"Tristan," Corred said through his labored breath. He could see Olwen running beside her younger brother. Finding new strength at the sight, he gritted his teeth and pushed harder, drawing his sword.

Einar matched his speed.

Boyd knocked his arrow.

When the scout who followed the group turned to see that they were being pursued, he dropped the rope he had been carrying and turned to face them.

Gwen fell to the ground, exhausted.

Before the lead scout became aware of the situation, Tristan attacked him from behind, taking him to the ground. Olwen struggled desperately to free herself from the wrestling match that ensued.

As Corred and Einar charged with swords in hand, Boyd stopped suddenly and released a shot.

Corred heard it hiss by on its way to the target.

The arrow was true, hitting the scout in the chest just as he released a spear. It soared wide of Einar, disappearing in the grass. Unable to lift his arms for another spear the scout fell to his knees.

Einar rushed in and finished him with one powerful swing, spilling his pouch of spears on the ground.

Without taking his eyes off of Olwen, Corred sprinted to where Tristan fought for his life. Olwen's cords had become entangled in the struggle and pulled her to the ground, threatening to draw her in.

Just as the scout rolled Tristan over and regained control of the situation Corred threw the stone he had been carrying. It struck the scout in the side of the head, knocking him off balance.

Tristan did not respond to the advantage.

Jumping to his feet with a spear already in his hand the stunned scout turned to face his newest attacker.

A second arrow from Boyd's bow struck the scout high in the arm before he could throw; his spear fell to the ground.

Corred met with the injured scout just as he pulled a second spear with his good arm. Their weapons met in the air, shattering the scout's spear. Corred struck him twice before he hit the ground.

In a matter of seconds it was over.

Tristan and Olwen lay exhausted in the grass.

Everyone gasped for breath.

Olwen crawled to her brother's side. He was just now regaining consciousness from a blow he had received to the head. Olwen held back her tears no longer. Turning to Corred she cried out. "Help him, he's been hurt. Help my brother."

Corred responded quickly. Wiping the blood from his sword on the grass he sheathed it. Helping Tristan to his feet, it was clear that he would be unable to run any longer. There was a welt rising on his forehead and his nose was bleeding again.

"I'm okay," he said with slurred speech. "I just need a moment to catch my breath."

Olwen tore a piece of her already ruined dress to wipe the blood from his mouth, but before she could reach him he slumped back to the ground.

Einar joined them. "He's in no condition to walk back to the horses and we haven't much time. These scouts will be expected by their commanders," he exclaimed. He grabbed Tristan's arm and slung him across his broad shoulders. "I've got him. Help her," he said to Corred.

Olwen's quivering hands were clenched as she began to sob, no longer able to control her fear. "There are two more of them. They will come back and kill us."

"They have been dealt with," Einar said confidently, though he did not know for sure. "We have horses not far from here but we must get back to the cover of the woods. Hurry." With that he started running.

Corred extended his hand. "We will not let any more harm come to you or your brother. Come, we must go."

Taking his hand she followed closely, unwilling to let her brother out of sight.

With his bow slung over his shoulder Boyd was already leading the way, carrying Gwen in his arms like a child. She had fainted from fatigue and could walk no farther.

With all the remaining strength that they had, the six of them hurried back to where they had left Creedus and the others in the heat of conflict. Ahead of them Creedus stood at the edge of the woods with his sword still in his hands, watching the field.

By the time they reached the woods, Creedus was down on one knee. Beathan stood just beside him and inside the trees with an arrow on his string. There was a cut on his face and his shirt was torn.

Corred and Olwen arrived first.

"We have killed them both," Einar said under heavy breath as he reached the edge of the woods. He lowered Tristan to the ground softly.

Creedus nodded.

Boyd laid Gwen beside Tristan as she slowly opened her eyes. The color was almost gone from her lips. He pulled a small canteen from his quiver and gave her a drink before pouring some of the water on Tristan's face to refresh him and wash his wounds. Boyd announced the boy's status as he cared for him. "His nose is not broken but he's had a good knock to the head."

"Where is Reed?" Corred asked.

There was a pause. They all looked at Creedus and Beathan.

"He has fallen." Creedus lowered his head.

Corred looked up the path to where two bodies lay next to

each other. One was dressed in black and the other was Reed. Protruding from his torso were three black spears. Driven into the trees around him were two more.

"He took one of them for me once he had been mortally wounded," Creedus said, rising to his feet. "He took the other to save Beathan."

There was a tear in Beathan's eye as he continued watching the woods, nervously feeling the fletchings of the arrow still on his bow.

"I slew the first, hand to hand, and the second ran when Beathan struck him with an arrow. Judging by the speed with which he fled, he was not badly injured." Sheathing his sword, Creedus observed everyone's injuries. "We must go, before he returns with a greater number." Pointing to Gwen and Tristan he said, "Help them to their feet. We have been fortunate not to have all lost our lives, but this trial is not through."

When they came to Reed's fallen form, Creedus removed the spears carefully and picked him up. He trembled not only under the weight of his friend's body but under the gravity that his friend was now dead, another of the Véran lost.

CHAPTER 7

On the bank of a small stream, with the grandeur of the Altus Mountains beyond, Bernd, Gernod and Lanhard stopped to water their horses. Ahead of them stood Mount Elm, surrounded at its base by thick woods comprised primarily of that tree for which the mountain was named. From east to west the open land rolled on, a sea of grass. The blue sky above was spotted with clouds, casting their shadows over the plain as they slowly drifted by.

Dismounting, they filled their canteens with the crystal clear water. Gernod tossed some on Lanhard, starting a short exchange of larger splashes. Normally it would have escalated but they reached an unspoken agreement that it wasn't exactly summer anymore and the water was quite cold.

In the distance a herd of horses was feeding freely.

"There they are boys," Bernd said with a smile. "There must be over fifty good catches."

Lanhard took a deep breath of cool, clean air. "What a beautiful sight."

"It only gets better up close. Let's go," Gernod said placing his water back in his saddle bag.

Promptly finishing their rest, they mounted their horses and waded through the shallows, scattering the minnows into deeper water.

"Should we approach from the east, keeping the lower hills between us and them?" Lanhard asked.

"Sounds good to me. The breezes are coming from the west so they won't spook by scenting," Gernod responded.

Bernd had the final say. "From the east it is, keeping between the hills. Let's hope the breeze holds true."

Taking one last look at their destination, they cut between two bluffs just high enough to hide them from view. They kept their pace to a slow trot, working in and out of the hills. When the occasion allowed it, one of them would ride a little higher to mark their target and track their progress.

The sun had by now reached its height in the sky. With that in mind, they took pains not to rush the process. If they spooked the herd before the time was right, they would be forced to start the hunt over, and that with a far more alert quarry. Even if they caught a desirable specimen, it would take the rest of the day to subdue it to the point where they could control it through the night.

When they were within less than three hundred yards, they slowed to a walk, keeping out of sight until they were within less than a hundred. A couple of buzzards coasted on the winds above, which remained in their favor. Indifferent to the whole scene, they were concerned only with finding some carrion to fill their stomachs for the day. Passing overhead, their shadows flew by as if trying to keep up.

Bernd stopped his horse just before the crest of a large

bluff. Peeking over the top, he caught a glimpse of the back of several spotted horses grazing in a flat section of the plains. Turning to his brothers behind him, he nodded. The wind tossed his hair across his face as he flashed a knowing smile and pointed to his nose. They were in the right position, so close that they could smell their quarry.

At only seventy yards away, Bernd exercised the element of surprise. With a quick kick to his horse's sides he darted over the top with Gernod and Lanhard close behind.

The reaction of the herd was immediate; ears perked, eyes widened and with a host of snorts they were off, a shifting maze of whites, tans and shades of brown. Running into the wind, they headed west, leaving nothing behind but dust and trampled grass. Staying just south of the herd to avoid the cloud, the three brothers each readied their lariats.

Gernod quickly split away and rode into the herd after a young colt as the leaders of the herd began turning north; Lanhard charged ahead and caught up with them. Moving in closer to join him, Bernd singled out a mare on the fringe and pointed her out; she was a rich brown with bright white feet. Working together, Bernd and Lanhard skillfully managed to separate her from the group, allowing Bernd to get his rope around her neck. This scared her even more, and she split completely from the herd as it continued its turn toward Mount Elm. Despite her burst of speed, Lanhard stayed close on the opposite side to hem her in and keep her from pulling too hard on the rope.

Far behind, Gernod was already off his horse and trying to control the young, frightened colt that he had caught. He was having a far easier time than the other two, as the mare Bernd had roped decided to pick a fight with her new masters.

Turning one way then the other, she rose to her hind feet and kicked frantically. Lanhard jumped from his mount with another rope and began the difficult process of convincing their new catch that she had nothing to fear. With the rope wrapped around his shoulders and a bridle in one hand he threw his arms in the air, focused on keeping in front of her as she turned circles. Her desperate movements tested Bernd's skill in keeping her at a safe distance and the rope taut at the same time.

In defiance she rose again to her hind feet, kicking wildly, daring Lanhard to come closer. Armed only with agility, he stayed just out of reach so as to avoid her violent flailing, but close enough to make it clear that he wasn't leaving.

"Whoa, whoa, whoa." Lanhard raised and lowered his voice until she came to rest on all fours. The roar of the herd was fading now and the sound of his voice became her central focus.

Even when she had stopped fighting Bernd's rope she bit it nervously. With a snort she looked at Bernd and back at Lanhard, turning her head to the side to get another look. Her dark ears were low against her head, signaling that she had no intention of submitting.

Bernd loosened the rope just a little as Lanhard took a step closer.

Up on her hind legs she went, tossing her head and kicking, making her displeasure known with a fearful whinny. Stomping hard with her hooves, she turned to run again, but Bernd was right there to pull her rope taut and circle her back toward Lanhard.

"Whoa, whoa, whoa."

Numerous times the process was repeated, each time

enabling Lanhard to get closer. Eventually, he was able to toss a rope over her neck in order to make the transition from Bernd being in control to making himself the center of the mare's attention. Bernd kept his rope around her neck for back up. Slowly, her trust was being earned.

In the distance Gernod was already attempting to place a bridle on the young colt he had caught, a much less formidable project than the one Lanhard had undertaken.

"Hey now, hey. Hey now, hey." Lanhard dropped his volume even farther to soothe the mare's nerves, keeping his hands up and out for her to see. Her ears were now perked, but she continued to back away before Lanhard could touch her.

Bernd kept silent, attentively assessing the situation. Lanhard's mount stayed on the outside of the skirmish, curiously watching the process unfold. Neither he nor Bernd's mount had been captured wild, but rather born and raised in captivity, loyally devoted to their master's will. Quietly waving their tails about, they watched a process they had seen many times before.

"It's okay, it's okay. Whoa now, girl." Lanhard took a step closer.

This time the mare did not back away. She licked the white surrounding her nose and cocked her head nervously.

"It's okay. It's going to be okay, girl," he repeated. He kept eye contact, allowing her to read his intentions.

She continued to twitch nervously but relaxed her stance a little.

"You're okay, you're okay, girl." With one more step Lanhard could have touched her but he didn't. Instead he remained still. Hands extended, he looked her in the eye, speaking softly.

She lowered her head ever so slightly and snorted.

Slowly reaching into the pocket of his shirt, Lanhard drew out half of a carrot and again extended his hand.

Bernd watched from his saddle, the rope that had begun the process now slack, resting in his glove. A big smile was on his face as he admired his younger brother's work.

"I'm not going to hurt you, girl," Lanhard said. He waited patiently, not advancing any farther, always looking her in the eye. His soft facial expressions matched his words of comfort, slowly dispelling the mare's fears. The carrot sat in his hand.

After a minute or so of Lanhard's reassuring whisper, the mare gave in. Taking a step toward him she sniffed the hand that held the carrot. She retreated quickly, widening her big black eyes. With her nose in the air she waited for Lanhard's response.

"You're okay, girl. You're okay," he continued saying.

She was the one changing. Again she stepped forward and this time took the carrot. Backing up again, she enjoyed the gift from a safer distance, still convinced her fears were warranted.

"There you go, girl, you're okay." Lanhard reached for a second carrot and held it out, this time not as extended, drawing her closer to him.

Looking at him thoughtfully the mare responded again. Approaching him gingerly she took the second carrot and let Lanhard's hand brush the side of her face.

"She's beautiful," Bernd exclaimed as Lanhard moved to stroking her neck. Her ears perked and her back shivered at his touch but she stood still, finally trusting.

"She is, she is," Lanhard agreed in the same tone of voice he'd been using. Working his way to where his rope was still hanging from her neck, he lifted it carefully, avoiding her ears. As he finished pulling it over her head, he offered another carrot.

"Here comes the brave horse-tamer himself," Bernd said with a chuckle as Gernod approached on horseback. His rolled up sleeves revealed his thick forearms as he bounced in the saddle. The young colt was in tow, led by his bridle.

"I'll bet ten coins my colt belongs to your mare," Gernod said. "Look at the spot on his nose." The young colt, a much richer brown than the mare, had the same white feet and white spot on his snout. The breeze was blowing through his shaggy mane as he tossed his head uncomfortably, still somewhat insolent.

Bernd looked back and forth from his position in the middle. "Would you look at that," he exclaimed. "I think our timid brother may be reuniting the family here."

Lanhard paid no mind, focusing solely on the placement of the mare's bridle and gently calming her fears.

*   *   *   *   *

Like specks on a vast canvas, Bernd and his brothers were barely visible from the base of Mount Elm, but they had found an audience. Just inside the edge of the forest, three riders silently watched them work.

They each rode a hargus, a horse-like beast from the distant north. Their hooves were broader, their manes and tails were thicker and longer, and their hides were a light shade of gray, covered by dark spots.

The riders themselves dressed in animal skins and drab earthen colors, and their beards and hair were dark, as were their eyes. One of them carried a crossbow, which hung from the side of his saddle, and the other had a long spear that rested in his stirrup. Each of them had a battle-axe slung over his back; one's was double-bladed, nearly spanning the width of his shoulders. They were soldiers.

The middle of the three carried only an axe, but it was twice the size of those carried by his fellow riders. One side was a broad blade but the other was shaped like a hammer, heavy and blunt. His mount was also bigger than the other two, for he was nearly seven feet tall, and twice as wide as a common man. He was a Mallith; Hildan, Mornoc's captain of the North.

Hildan's features matched his size, with a large jaw and deeply furrowed brow. Dark eyes and eyebrows stood out in stark contrast to his short grey hair and thin grey beard. The long green robe flowing from his shoulders and his silver wrist cuffs were not worn by the other two soldiers.

The tightly clustered trees surrounding the three of them all leaned at different angles in a struggle to gain enough light, making travel difficult but providing excellent cover. With no concern of detection the soldier to Hildan's left, with the spear, asked in a low voice, "Do you wish to do anything about these horsemen, my lord?"

He didn't respond immediately, remaining fixed on the horsemen with a cold stare. He hadn't seen any this close to Mount Elm in a long time, and with every passing day he had more to hide.

The soldier asked again, unsure of whether he had been heard.

"Wait for night," Hildan replied. "Do not reveal yourselves." Turning in his saddle, he addressed the soldier who had asked the question. "You go, alone. Kill them in their sleep. We cannot risk them finding us out. The advantage of our silence cannot be lost." His voice was menacing. Returning to observe the scene before them, and added, "The two of you return together."

The soldiers looked at each other in agreement.

After a pause he added in a hushed voice. "The time for open battle is approaching, but we must have it on my terms." With that he slowly turned his hargus around and trotted into the woods toward the mountain.

CHAPTER 8

The return of Creedus and the rescue party to Wellman brought a mix of joy and sorrow. The heavy rain clouds from earlier in the day had since cleared from the sky, rolling back to reveal the setting sun. As it lay now on the western horizon, things were different. Years of comfortable peace with the enemy were over. His boldness to attack was far greater than expected, and had sufficiently shocked Wellman in its complacency.

Details of Lord Wellman's misfortune had spread throughout the town by the time Creedus and his rescue party returned with his children. Three of their horses carried two riders. Gwen rode with Boyd, Tristan with Einar and Olwen with Corred. Creedus had led them out and now he led them back, his shining sword held in front of him to honor his fallen friend. His shoulders hung lower, and his countenance was heavier than it had been earlier that day. His youthful eyes displayed the sorrow of an old man.

Behind him walked the horse of Reed, whose body lay

across the saddle, covered with his own cloak. Upon entering the outskirts of the town, the few men that now carried a sword drew it, holding it in front of them to join in the salute to their fallen friend.

As the party took the southern road toward Lord Wellman's mansion, the whole town began to receive them. Stopping all activity, those in the street and around their houses bowed their heads to show their respect. Initial smiles were mixed with tears at the sight of Reed's body and the sacrifice that had been made to save the captives. It had been a long time since warriors had taken to the field and nearly as long since warriors had been honored. The fading light cast a long shadow in front of them as Creedus acknowledged the homage paid by those on either side of the street.

In the distance, Lord Wellman stood on his steps, dressed in his finest robes, awaiting their arrival. The members of his house and a large number of citizens stood in the courtyard of the town hall straining to see who had returned.

Third in line were Corred and Olwen, exhausted from the day's trials. Corred held his sword in one hand, the reigns in the other and his chin high. For years he had carried his sword as a matter of identity, but until that day he had never used it. A new confidence filled him. He was a warrior, and better yet, he had saved the one he loved. Corred had never felt so alive.

Olwen sat in the saddle behind him. With nothing to secure her, she wrapped her arms tightly around Corred. Only hours ago, bound to a captor against her will, she now freely clung to another. Her long brown hair flowed loosely over her shoulders, partially covering her face.

Unlike his sister, Tristan wore his wounds proudly, looking back at the people around him, unashamed of his appearance;

he too had tangled with the enemy and lived. He was recovering well from his bruises after taking food and water, and though he had wiped his face to remove some of the horror of blood his shirt was stained with it.

It was a quiet procession. There were no cheers or shouts of joy. It was a solemn moment in light of the loss suffered and the awakened reality of the presence of their enemy.

As they drew near, Lord Wellman's wife could restrain herself no longer. Seeing that her children were safe, she abandoned her position of respect and ran to them with her long, graying hair flowing behind her. Tears filled her eyes again, but this time for joy. Her youngest daughter followed behind her. She looked up at Creedus and bowed her chin in respect. "You kept your promise. We thank you, from the depths of our hearts."

Creedus nodded, unable to speak without revealing his emotions.

Corred let Olwen down slowly with one arm. Part of him did not want to let her go.

Olwen paused for a moment, looking at Corred through teary eyes. "Thank you, Corred."

Corred returned her gaze, not knowing how to express the love he held for her in his heart. "You are welcome," was all he could reply.

Tristan too slid from the back of Einar's horse and met his mother and sister with a hug. Lord Wellman remained at his post, playing the leader. His anger could now turn to mourning for the death of his oldest son.

Several of the servants of his house ran to Gwen, along with her parents, humble citizens of Wellman. She slowly let go of Boyd, who had held her since he carried her from the field of battle.

Her eyes were bloodshot from grief and exhaustion, but at last a smile came to her face at the sight of loved ones. She fell exhausted into the arms of her father.

Creedus stopped the caravan at the steps of the Lord Wellman's mansion, sword still in hand. "My lord, your children are safe and the enemy has fled before us."

Lord Wellman clasped his hands in front of him. His uncontrolled temper from that morning had been tamed with contemplation, and now gratefulness. "Creedus, you have honored my house with this deed of bravery and love." Pausing, he observed the horse that followed and its burden. "Is this the horse and body of Reed?"

"It is," Creedus answered heavily.

"May I know how he died?" Lord Wellman asked.

"He was struck by three scout spears before he fell. The wounds that killed him were received fighting for the protection of your children, and . . . his fellow warriors." Creedus struggled to finish.

Those in attendance listened quietly.

"To honor his sacrifice, my best servants will prepare him for burial, with the permission of his family," Lord Wellman announced.

"He was a great man, my lord. Such an honorable burial would be fitting. But permission will not be necessary, for he has no family left living." Creedus bowed his head slightly.

There was by now a great throng of citizens who had followed the party into the center of town to hear the report of what had transpired. Whole families were gathered, having left their dinner meals half prepared and their fires burning bright.

"Very well. At the rising of the sun we will remember

him." Lord Wellman spoke loudly, so that all could hear. He continued to address the rescue party as his family gathered to him on the steps. "You have all shown your bravery and love for your fellow man. I do not know how to repay you for saving my children. I welcome all of you into my house tonight to dine with me, though you must be tired from the day's events." Looking Creedus in the eye he asked, "Will you do me the honor?"

"I will," Creedus responded with a nod.

"And what of your grandson and the rest of you?" he asked. "I feel unfit to thank you. Please accept what hospitality I can give."

One by one they accepted.

He whispered several instructions to his head servant who quickly acted on them. Turning next to the throng that was still watching, enthralled by the sight of warriors returned from battle, Lord Wellman addressed them with hands raised. "Citizens of Wellman, though we have experienced loss, we must not give in to fear, for that is what our enemy would want. Go back to your homes in peace and keep watch over your families. May you find better fortune than my house and I have had today."

With that the crowd dispersed and one of Lord Wellman's servants took the reins of Reed's horse to carry out the preparations for his burial. Only once Reed's body was handed over did Creedus and the others sheath their swords. Again addressing the whole rescue party, Lord Wellman thanked them and asked them to return to his house once they had tended to their horses and families for the evening.

* * * * *

"Bring more ale."

One of the nearby servants scurried away to carry out the order.

Under the light of the great chandelier, Selcor ate at the stone table in the cave of Casimir; it was nearly empty. He grimaced with every bite of meat and drink of ale he took because of the pain in his side. The blood from his wound was still drying on his shirt, as it had not yet been bandaged.

His quarry had proven too much for him. Though successful in killing one of the Véran, even he had nearly refused to fall. Selcor had been unable to withstand the strength of the old man's blows and the archer's arrows, and fled when his comrade was struck down. Finding the other scouts dead in the field he abandoned the fight completely.

On the table next to him was one of his spears. It was not wooden like the others, nor did it have the head of a spear but rather, it was iron and shaped more like a sword. It was chipped up and down the blade and severed near the tip.

He muttered under his breath.

The hall servant returned with a pitcher and placed it in front of him. There the servant waited for either gratitude, which would not come, or another command.

Selcor gave him a murderous look. "Can you not see that I've been wounded? Fetch me some bandages, you fool." Selcor threw a bone after him.

Several scouts eating further down the table stopped talking and turned to see what the commotion was about. Recognizing who it was causing the scene, they went back to eating silently.

Selcor was feared for his ruthless nature and even more so for his unbridled hate. Few had ever stood up to Casimir and lived. Selcor had done it three times since joining his army. He had his Captain's recognition to prove it. Being grazed by an arrow would not slow him, but rather make him all the more vicious.

"Your day is coming, old man," he said through his teeth. He thrust his knife into another piece of meat with added force.

*   *   *   *   *

Under the cover of night, a lone figure approached the shores of Lake Tormalyn. His shadow from the lights of Renken quickly faded, traded for one from the light of the night sky. With a black coat, a heavy hunting knife on his belt, and fur cap on his head, Lowell did not appear anything like he did when accompanying Lord Raven.

His stately air had been discarded for a more stealthful movement. His leisurely walk quickly became a run once he was sure no one had followed him. For a man his size, his speed was impressive, but more astounding was that the dark did not at all seem to slow him or cause him to exercise caution in the placement of each step. He glided along as if the fields around the lake were as familiar as home. The pale moonlight accentuated his thin features, if not causing him to look gaunt.

Making fast work of the distance between Renken and the forests that met the shores of the lake to the north, Lowell slowed only a little as he entered the woods. Again, as if the path he took was well known, he seamlessly leapt over fallen trees, ducked under low lying branches and through brush to arrive at a cabin and stable nestled among the trees. The shining surface of the lake could be seen in the distance. Ignoring the cabin, Lowell immediately entered the stable and set about saddling the horse it sheltered.

The sound of the cabin door opening and closing did not distract him from his careful preparation. Several seconds later, the stable door opened and the light of a lantern outlined Lowell's form against the wood plank wall.

A short, fat man with curly red hair and a thick beard held the lantern up above his head to get as good a look as he could. "Ah, Mr. Abbings. I figured it was you, but I wanted to check. Don't you need a light in here? It's darker than ink."

"The dark has never really bothered me, but thank you," Lowell replied calmly without looking at the man. His run from Renken had not winded him in the least.

"Guess that's how you make it to Port riding through the night all the time," his visitor said. "Very well, I know you're a busy man, Mr. Abbings so I'll let you alone. Just come through on your way out for supplies if you need them."

"I should be fine with what I have, thank you," Lowell replied.

"Very well, have a good ride, Mr. Abbings." Scuttling backward and out of the door, the short, fat fellow left without a second thought and returned to his cabin.

Lowell finished readying his horse without any light at all and led the animal out of the stable. Closing the door behind him, he leapt into the saddle and took off at a trot along a narrow path through the woods. Merging with a main road, Lowell dug his heels into his horse's sides and flew through the night, headed north.

*　　*　　*　　*　　*

The walk back to Lord Wellman's mansion was a long one. From the light of one lantern to the next, Creedus, Corred and Einar walked through the street side by side. The sky had completely cleared, revealing a myriad of stars.

Halfway to the mansion, Beathan and Boyd joined them from a side street. Neither of them carried their bows now, but each had his sword. Their hoods were pulled up on their heads, concealing their features; only the heat of their breath was clearly visible in the cool, moist air. With a nod they fell in line next to Einar.

The soft sound of their steps was uninterrupted by the usual echoing of voices through the alleys. No one was out tonight. The fear of another attack was real, and no one felt immune in light of Lord Wellman's loss. As the group passed one house in particular, a man could be seen pulling a sword from his wall where it had hung decoratively for quite some time. As if suddenly aware of its presence for the first time, he held it, examining its edge and line.

Fortunately for some, the day's events had awakened them from slumber and reminded them of the presence of their enemies. Sadly, it had taken much for their eyes to be opened. It would likely take more to move them to action. The sight of only five men walking to Lord Wellman's house that night was a vivid sign of the complacency of men even in Wellman, home of Creedus, head of the Véran.

As they approached Lord Wellman's mansion, he himself joined his guard in greeting them. Fitted in the attire of a royal and draped with his blue robe, he stood on the top step and waited for them to arrive. Even with the knowledge that scouts could attack as readily as they had the night before, he insisted on opening his doors himself. The spear that had been driven into the front of the house was gone, but its mark could still be seen within reach of the lanterns below.

"Welcome, friends. I am honored that you are here. Please, come in. My table is spread and waiting. My wife will not be joining us as she is mourning, . . . our son." Lord Wellman faltered but forced a smile as he held the door; it was quite a gesture. It was rare that a man of his importance would wait on anyone, let alone common men. Warmth from the fire of the front hall could be felt with the opening of the front door. The aroma of burning wood mixed with cooking filled the house.

"May I take your coats, kind sirs?" A maidservant asked, carrying out her duty for the evening.

"Thank you," Creedus said.

"Thank you, miss," Corred followed.

"Gentlemen, follow me." Lord Wellman led them through the front hall and to the back of the mansion, where an ornate staircase led to the upper levels of the house. Corred took a longing glance at the stairs, wanting only to see Olwen descend them. Little else was on his mind.

Though appearing rough on the outside, with its stone architecture and heavy, crude beams, Lord Wellman's mansion was well adorned on the inside. Where there was wood, there were carvings. Every wall was decorated with some trophy or relic telling the history of the town, from the armor of warriors to the portraits of past lords and their wives. The hard wood floors were covered with fine woven rugs and the hides of bears taken from the Bryn Mountains. There were ornate drapes at every doorway and window, and even the massive crossbeams above were decoratively fashioned.

In the east wing of the mansion was the family dining room, much smaller than the banquet hall, which was found in the west wing, customarily used for entertainment. A large wooden table at the center of the room was filled with every good food available: freshly killed venison, duck, loaves of bread with butter, gravy, carrots, onions, potatoes, tomatoes from earlier that summer, stewed apples, and wine. Each place at the table was set. The smells beckoned them to partake.

Before sitting, Lord Wellman spoke a word of thanks and blessed the food. His voice cracked with emotion in the effort. In the midst of the loss of his eldest son, he voiced his gratefulness for the preservation of his family and the safe return of Tristan and Olwen.

The gentlemen present bowed their heads in respect for his suffering. Creedus alone watched Lord Wellman's face as he spoke, more aware than the rest of having lost a beloved friend.

Just as his words began to grow downcast, Lord Wellman turned to speaking of hope in the Promise, as if for the first time. "And may he who will come to redeem us, come soon. For in this promise we find strength and reason for vigilance. May we not let our swords collect dust or our gaze fix on anything less."

Observing one man, then the next, he appeared stunned by his own words. To bring conclusion to what had become a short and impromptu speech, he awkwardly added, "And may we never grow tired of such things." For a moment, he was one of the Véran. Though he was not an antagonist of the Promise, there were few leaders in those days that spoke of such things publicly. It was like a lost heritage, a dying language.

An "Amen" resounded at the table in response to his words.

The agreement had its effect on Lord Wellman, and he sat with the remains of a slight smile. "Gentlemen, friends, please help yourselves." And with Lord Wellman's blessing they broke bread.

*   *   *   *   *

Hours before dawn, just before the fourth watch, Lowell came upon the city limits of Port. The sole lantern at the western watch was burning brightly and the guard there was on his feet with his spear in hand as Lowell entered his view. The soldier's helm was polished metal, and his coat was a mix of dark purple and gold thread, the colors of Port. He extended his spear and took a step in Lowell's direction.

Recognizing the guard who was on duty, Lowell raised his hand in salute. Without slowing his approach he said, "I've come to see a lord to be."

At this greeting the guard lowered his spear as if the rider he'd seen approach was no longer even there. As Lowell passed by, the guard re-entered a small, three-sided stone hut where a fellow watchman was sitting by the fire.

Lowell heard him say, "Just a local of no consequence," as he passed by. He smiled at the belittling and rode on toward the city limits.

Port was laid out much like Wellman, but with far more glamour and wealth on display in its structure. The town hall, which more closely resembled a castle than a hall, was at the center of the city. Port's officials and all the wealthiest of the region lived in the city square, which was comprised of mansions, storehouses and stables. The markets and trading streets surrounded the city square, and the citizens of Port lived in every direction beyond. The poorest in Port, whom were quite well off by the standards of Renken's western district, lived on the outskirts. It was to one of these cabins that Lowell steered his mount.

The plains surrounding Port were quiet and as far as he could see in the moonlight, not a creature was stirring. The smell of smoke from Port's many fires grew stronger as Lowell approached the side of the cabin and there tied his horse to a small post. Rounding the front of the cabin cautiously, he stood aside as he softly rapped on the door.

At first no sound came from within to suggest that he'd been heard, so Lowell knocked a second time, but no louder than the first. Within seconds the door opened inward a few inches. A low voice asked, "What's your business?"

Responding in a whisper, Lowell said, "To reform the house of Lord Raven."

The door instantly opened wider, but no one stood in the entrance to welcome him.

Lowell slipped inside and shut the door behind him very softly.

The cabin was one room with a fire place along the back wall and several chairs scattered about. Just behind the door stood one of Port's guard, dressed like the one who had been manning the watch point. In front of Lowell and next to the fire, with his back to the wall sat a man dressed in dark robes. Leaning forward so that the light of the fire would illuminate his face, he said, "I've been waiting for an hour." His tone was displeased, but not angry. His whitening hair stood in great contrast to his youthful looking face, which bragged of a young man no more than forty years of age. His skin was not wrinkled or weathered at all.

"I rode hard as soon as I was able to gain dismissal from Lord Raven's presence," Lowell responded blandly.

"Things are going according to plan then?" the white haired man replied.

"Yes," Lowell responded, but offered no additional explanation.

After a moment's silence, the man replied, "You are all so very talkative, you scouts." Leaning back into the shadows, he continued, "Your Captain has once again arranged for us to meet in order to let you know what progress we are making here in Port. It greatly influences your work in Renken. Please, have a seat."

The guard behind Lowell pushed a chair toward him. Cautiously watching him then back up to the door again, Lowell slowly sat before giving the man by the fire his attention.

"The army you have helped to build," he began, commending Lowell, "is complete. Your Captain is set to move in little more than two days' time. The caves will be emptied, and those who have made known their resistance to what must happen will be removed. I have convinced, bargained, and threatened most of Port's wealthiest to follow my lead, and those officials on the council who pose any problems will be dealt with likewise. As soon as we are able, a force will move on Renken." He spoke in a calm voice given the gravity of his announcement. "And so, any more recruits you can send our way by tomorrow night we will take, but after that your mission reaches it end."

Lowell nodded, as if that was all he needed to do to give complete consent.

The white-haired man folded his hands in his lap and

asked, "What of Lord Raven and Renken?"

Lowell crossed his thin arms and gave report. "Renken is just as ready to fall. The city is divided against itself, the poor against the rich. They live together because they have nowhere to go, but it is a city without roots. Even so, some of the Véran live there, and with their help, Lord Raven and his guard could unite the city in a time of need."

"Lord Raven is a supporter of the Véran now?" the man asked, disappointed. "That would be a change for the worse."

"Not a supporter, but a respecter," Lowell said.

After a pause of silence, the man said, "Which is exactly why your greatest task in Renken will be your last, in Renken. Do you have a plan?"

Without even shifting, Lowell responded, "I am a scout of Mornoc, chosen in the service of Ahriman to bring about his will and rightful rule. I will carry out my task without fail and report back to my captain's command."

The white-haired man leaned forward from the wall once again to where his face could be seen in the firelight and smiled. "I believe you. You know, Lowell really isn't a strong enough name for you, I don't think."

Lowell's expression remained fixed and emotionless. "It is not my name."

The white-haired man just smiled. "A new horse has been brought for you, so that you can be back in Renken as quickly as possible. It will be just outside, next to yours."

Standing to go, Lowell nodded. "Long live Mornoc, the rightful king of Amilum." With that, he opened the door slowly and stepped outside into the cold night air.

CHAPTER 9

The sound of the bubbling brook soothed the mare's nerves as she and her colt huddled together.

Lanhard offered them both some apple, which they eagerly took. He was still at work, stroking one then the other. With gentle hands he continued earning their trust.

"Save some apple for me," Gernod said over his shoulder from the campfire.

Lanhard ignored his brother's complaint as if he had been a cricket in the background.

Bernd acted on his brother's request and offered one from his own pack. "Here." He tossed it to him over the flames. "I think I'll have one too. It's been a successful day." Carving off a slice with his knife he smiled. "I love it when things go according to plan."

"Likewise," Gernod agreed, taking the biggest bite he could.

Lanhard paid little attention, but rather checked and re-checked the ropes on their new horses where they were both tied to the remains of a fallen tree.

They had made camp on the outskirts of the foothills, only a few miles from where they had made their catch. The night sky was again clear and bright, casting a glow on the grass around them.

"So, what do you think of her, Lanhard? Will she be good for breeding? She seems agreeable enough for a wild catch," Bernd mused as he carefully carved away at his apple.

"She was quick to trust, especially for having a colt still dependent on her. I'm impressed with her gentle nature." Lanhard patted the mare on her neck and joined his brothers at the fire. "Time will tell."

"It's hard not to trust you, little brother, with your big, pretty, innocent eyes, carrot in hand. I would have fallen for you," Gernod jested, nudging him.

Lanhard was serious when he answered. "She really did trust quickly, quite unlike most catches we've made." He watched the two horses interact at the edge of the fire's light. Running his hands through his hair, he gave a yawn.

"I agree," Bernd said. "It's also been a long day." He whittled a few more pieces off of his apple and tossed the core into the fire where it hissed on the hot coals.

The light winds from the west had shifted and were now coming from the north, a steady, cool breeze.

Gernod placed some more wood on the fire to keep it going into the night, and they all went through their routines of preparation for sleeping under the night sky.

Bernd turned in first, as usual. "Bless the women and children, goodnight."

Gernod followed, pulling his blanket up over his head. "And may it not rain while we sleep. Goodnight."

114

Lanhard did what he always did. Slowly making his bed, he soaked up the night air with his senses. Tonight he was watching for the sake of the horses.

The mare and colt still stood close to each other, quietly observing their new situation. They would eventually sleep as well, once they realized they were not going anywhere.

Lanhard tucked himself under his covers, hiding from the cold. After recounting the day's events and imagining the next, his thoughts began to drift to the stars and his heavy eyes slowly closed. The bubbling of the brook remained constant, lulling them all to sleep.

*   *   *   *   *

From the edge of a bluff a stone's throw away, Hildan's soldier lurked in the grass. Watching the campfire closely, he hugged the ground, keeping to the east so as not to be winded by the horses. Carrying out Hildan's orders, the soldier was alone. He held his long spear flat, taking care not to provide any outline against the night sky. His axe was on his back, slung tightly around his shoulders to hold it in place as he crept along the ground.

It had been over an hour since he had seen the horsemen move in the light of the fire, and now it was no more than a pile of coals with a small flame licking the air.

The soldier slowly worked his way down to the stream. The breeze through the grass and the rolling stream hid any sound that he made. At twenty-five yards, he stopped, eying the horses that were tied to a large fallen tree. For what felt like hours he waited, crouching still in the grass, watching their movements. They had bedded down, but were nervous and not sleeping like the rest. Rubbing his spear with his thumb, he itched for an opportunity to hurl it through the air. Warily, he pulled his axe off of his back and readied himself for an attack. He could not wait for the horses any longer.

Gripping his axe in one hand and his spear in the other, he clenched his teeth.

*   *   *   *   *

Lanhard awoke with a start. Without moving a muscle he looked at the mare and colt. They were bedded down. There was no movement. But a chill ran down his spine, clearing his senses. Something was wrong. Instinctively, he reached for his knife.

The mare perked up. With a snort, she pointed her ears forward. The colt beside her rose to his feet and stared into the dark with wide eyes and a rigid back.

Gernod was startled by the commotion and was on his feet as if he had never been sleeping.

A dark figure now stood against the night sky on the opposite bank of the creek.

"Look out!" Gernod yelled.

Bernd threw his blanket into to the air and rolled to one knee just as a long spear pinned it to the ground, narrowly missing him. He rose to his feet, shifting this way and that to find his attacker. His sword was in his hand.

The attacker lunged from the opposite side of the bank and into the glow of the fire with an axe raised in the air.

The mare and colt went wild, wrenching their necks in an attempt to escape.

Running right past them, the dark specter made Lanhard

his next target.

Lanhard hurled his knife toward him and dove for his bow and arrows, which he had stowed with his pack for the night. He had nothing to ward off the blows of an axe.

Bernd interceded and met the attacker's axe mid swing. Sparks flew as the blades met, dashing the night's peaceful silence.

One blow was met with the other as Bernd warded off the vicious assault.

Lanhard found his bow and knocked an arrow.

Gernod rounded the fire pit with a broken branch from the fallen tree that held the wild horses captive. Wielding his crude club, he too entered the fray.

Seeing that he was now surrounded, their foe fought all the harder, knocking Bernd's sword to the ground with a swift blow.

Bernd lost his balance, tripped backwards, and fell into the fire, showering sparks into the air. With a cry of pain he rolled aside quickly, smacking his burning shirt until he could wrap it in a nearby blanket to smother the flame.

With fell swoops, Gernod stepped into his brother's place.

Unable to defend against the force of his new combatant, the assassin received a blow to the shoulder that rendered one of his arms useless. Striking back in desperation, he broke Gernod's weapon in two, nearly taking his leg with it.

Lanhard released an arrow in the dark.

It found the man's heart and brought him to his knees. Grabbing his mortal wound, he let out a groan and died where he fell.

The wild horses continued to tug at their cords, letting out one whinny after another, filled with fear. It would take more than carrots to calm them now. The other horses had run to the outskirts of the skirmish.

For a moment they all braced themselves for more. But when nothing followed, Bernd looked at the spear that stood driven into the ground where he had been sleeping. With a foot on his blanket, he pulled it out of the ground with his good arm. After a good look at its craft, he tossed it aside. "Thieves don't carry weapons like this."

"Who was this man?" Gernod asked with heavy breath. He observed his fallen assailant with fearful respect. Picking up the axe, he held it close to the light of the fire to observe its design. On either side of the well-sharpened blade, at its base, there were carvings.

"Hildan," Gernod read quietly.

At the name Bernd's eyes grew wide and the color left his face. "A soldier of Mornoc." He whispered just loud enough to be heard.

Lanhard stood in shock. He had never before killed a man, much less a soldier of Mornoc. The horror of it showed in his expression.

Bernd looked at his younger brothers. "We need to leave now."

"What of our catch?" Gernod asked. He tossed the shards of his club on the ground next to the soldier.

"Let them both loose, they will slow us down and wake every fiend within earshot." Bernd tore a piece off of his blanket, gritted his teeth, and wrapped his burnt arm. Picking up his sword, he sheathed it and grabbed all of his things.

With a whistle they called their horses back from the surrounding fields.

Lanhard found his knife on the bank of the stream and

regretfully cut the wild horses loose.

At first they shifted about, unsure of their regained freedom.

"Yah!" Lanhard stepped toward them quickly with raised hands, destroying in an instant the trust he had gained. They bolted into the night.

Bernd kicked dirt on the fire as Gernod stowed the soldier's axe among his things.

They packed in a hurry, unwilling to meet with another soldier so determined to take their lives. Without another moment's hesitation, they mounted up and rode west, back to the Northern Villages.

The night air felt colder now as they rode through the plains. What peace they had found in the stars the night before was gone. The success of earlier that day was gone. There was no prize to return with, save their lives.

* * * * *

On the outskirts of Wellman, in the dead of night, a dark figure lurked, looking down one street then another, searching for something. Elsewhere in the dark, a second shape dodged the light at the edge of town. Casimir's scouts were at work.

All the lanterns were lit, enveloping the town in a faint glow. Without a word, the two of them passed each other on the eastern edge of the town.

A little farther along, one of them overcame his seeming hesitancy and ran into the town with light, quiet steps. Flying by one house, then another, the light from each lantern illuminated gaunt features only for a moment at a time as he approached one, then passed.

Nearly halfway to the middle of town the second scout ran past him from the northern side. As if this were a routine activity they each ignored the movements of the other, focusing only on their respective paths. Like errand specters, they ran through the streets at full speed.

Once satisfied with all that he had seen, the first scout grabbed a lantern from the front step of a house without slowing and headed south. The lantern's flame whipped about, holding desperately to its wick, but at last was snuffed out as the scout cut through an alley. He left the southeastern corner of Wellman, barely touching the ground.

Everyone in the sleeping town remained ignorant of their presence, except for the old warrior, Creedus. From the window of his cabin, he peered through the dark with wide eyes as a single flame flew by, and then vanished. His suspicions were confirmed. The attack of the night before had not been an isolated event. The enemy was moving.

Frozen where he crouched, Creedus gripped the handle of his sword with white knuckles. Creedus silently recited something to himself, keeping watch. Dozing off for a minute at a time, he would awake with a start, only to find he was alone in the dark.

*   *   *   *   *

Three riders from Wellman pushed their horses to greater speeds through the night. One traveled east, one north and the other west. Neither fatigue, nor lack of sleep, or any other obstacle could stop them; all that mattered was the word that they carried. Each rode with a pouch containing several letters. Through hills, plains, and wood they rode as if the wind was always at their backs. They themselves did not fully know how necessary their flight was. Sent the day before by Creedus himself, they had hundreds of miles to cover with one task: to rally the heads of Véran to Wellman.

For several years Creedus had felt the advance of the enemy though he could not see it. After the previous day's events, his fears were being confirmed. If he, Head of the Véran were prey, then this was not simply sport or restless violence. Something more sinister was afoot.

As the glow of a new sun gathered on the horizon, Creedus sat on his front step awaiting its arrival. The thunder of the messenger's hooves lingered in Creedus' mind; urgency weighed on his countenance. Observing his surroundings, he once again noted that one of the houses further down the street had no lantern on its step. Creedus pondered the significance of this odd theft, knowing that regardless of its utility, their enemy was more than present, he was active. He stroked his beard softly, lost in thought. Every now and again he muttered to himself, checking always for the first ray of light to pierce the trees to the east.

As it arrived, the door of the next cabin over opened and Corred quietly joined him to welcome its warmth. He could see his grandfather was deep in thought and did not want to disrupt his meditation.

After a moment of silence, Creedus turned to his grandson with a smile. "Have you rested well?" he asked.

"Yes, I have," Corred responded. "Have you?"

"Not as well as you perhaps, but I am an old man," Creedus responded.

After a quiet pause, Corred asked, "When will the others come, do you think, the heads of Véran, that is?"

"It will be two full days before they arrive, if all is well," Creedus said dryly. After a pause he added, "I only hope that no one will come this morning and bring me news of another tragedy. I saw a scout in the street last night while you slept." He lifted his brow as he said this.

Corred's eyes grew wide at this news. "Three nights in a row," he said. "First I was attacked, then Lord Wellman. Who was it this time?"

Creedus pointed down the street to the only house without a lantern. "It would appear that only a lantern was taken. I walked the town nearly an hour ago."

"I don't understand." Corred responded.

"Nor do I," Creedus answered.

Einar emerged next.

"Come, today we begin by honoring the fallen," Creedus said. He forced a smile across his wrinkled face. Patting his grandson on the back, he beckoned Einar to join them.

Over a breakfast of eggs and buttered bread the three of them spoke very little. As soon as they had finished, Einar and Corred checked their swords to be sure that they shined their brightest.

Creedus spent his time cleaning his shoes and donning his finest cloak. He had no need of sharpening the Sword of Homsoloc as its edge was timeless. As sharp as the day it was forged in Amilum centuries ago, it had not weathered at all. Tightening his belt just a little, Creedus lead the way to Lord Wellman's mansion.

When they arrived at the center of town the funeral procession was assembling. Lord Wellman's finest horses were hitched to a wagon that had been decorated by his servants with wreaths, and blue, white, and green ribbons. In its bed lay the body of Pedrig, dressed in his finest robes and adorned with flowers. He looked as if he were ready to assume his father's chair in the Hall of Wellman. Behind the wagon was gathered the household of Lord Wellman, his wife, his children and servants alike, all dressed in their finest. Next in line was a second team of horses to draw the body of Reed. He too was decorated, but done so in fashion to honor a warrior. His robes were not only blue, green and white but more prominently red. Reed's sheathed sword lay on top of his chest, while his arms rested by his sides.

Lastly, the bodies of the two servants who had been slain along with Pedrig the day before were carried by yet another wagon, decorated much like Pedrig's, but with a simplicity fitting their status in the town. They were not forgotten, but they would not be as celebrated as the heir to the lordship and a victorious warrior.

Collecting himself as best he could, Lord Wellman greeted Creedus with a firm hand, placing his other on the old man's shoulder. "Thank you for coming. You honor not only your friend, but also my son."

Creedus nodded with a painful smile. "It is a warrior's duty and desire to pay his respects."

He then took his place with Corred and Einar in the funeral procession, standing behind the casket of Reed. Joining them were Beathan and Boyd and several other members of the Véran who had not accompanied them on the chase the day before. They all wore their swords and dressed in the best coats they owned.

Corred watched Olwen closely as she held her siblings and cried with them. The depth of his own past loss stabbed at the wound in his heart. He too had lost his brother. It was a void he could not fill, a pain he could not run from, and Corred had no one to hold and share his suffering with, or so he felt. Galena was in Oak Knoll, and she, unlike him, had mourned their brother properly.

Making eye contact with Olwen at one point, Corred nodded slowly, the ache in his chest rising into his throat. Olwen forced a smile and mouthed a few words of thanks. Like healing he could not have found anywhere else, it seemed to give him permission to cry freely and mourn with her. Wiping his eyes, Corred let his hair fall around his face a little. He shuddered at the thought of his own weakness, wiping his wet hands on his coat. He tried to hide it from those around him, but Olwen had seen it.

Several more minutes passed as citizens of Wellman came to honor the fallen. It was a crowd large enough to fill the town square to its edges. Everyone who came also brought dried flowers to throw on the ground before the fallen.

When Lord Wellman gave the signal, a servant on horseback lifted a horn to his lips and blew a single, somber note. In the silence that prevailed, it carried through the town in every direction and to the far reaches of the fields beyond. With the slightest nudge, the servant ushered his horse forward at half-steps. Seemingly aware of his part and the nature of the occasion, the horse did not push the pace administered, but held his head erect, as if proud to be in such a position of honor.

Drawing the Sword of Homsoloc, Creedus held it in front of him with both hands. Its shine was brilliant in the morning light, drawing more admiration from those around him than it had in years. Like an old tool, suddenly and desperately needed, an emblem of the Promise that should have never been ignored was once again being appreciated.

Corred and the rest with him followed suit, holding their swords erect in salute to the fallen.

With a clear blue sky overhead the procession made its way through the northwestern part of Wellman to the burial ground outside of the town. All along the road, a sea of people dressed in blues, greens, and white had gathered to say goodbye. In the midst of it all, Lord Wellman stood tall and hid his grief as best he could, playing the leader. There were no words exchanged by anyone, but rather complete silence was maintained apart from the controlled sobs of the grieving.

The burial ground was hemmed in by several tall oak trees that had by now dropped many of their leaves, sprinkling the barren soil with shades of brown as they cast their own long shadows across the procession.

As the wagons pulled next to the pyres, one for each man being remembered, only immediate family and close friends remained. The remainder of the town that had made the march returned quietly to their homes.

Circling around the wagons, anyone with a sword drawn sheathed it, and each burial plank was lifted out of the wagons and set upon the pyres. Before moving Reed's body, Creedus took his sword and strapped it onto the opposite side of his belt from the Sword of Homsoloc.

Lord Wellman and Tristan along with several of his servants carried Pedrig's body, and several members of the Véran helped Creedus carry Reed's. The families of the fallen servants carried their own.

Once the fallen were laid to rest, everyone who remained sprinkled them with dried flowers, some from jars, some from baskets, while others gave whole bundles. Being so fragile, many of the flower petals fell apart in the act. Life was beautiful, but fragile.

After a continued moment of silence, in which people whispered prayers, a time was given for words of remembrance to be spoken.

"Pedrig, a son of the line of Wellman, my first born . . ." Lord Wellman's voice faltered for a moment as he spoke his son's name but he pushed on. "The pride of our family. At the age of twenty-three, taken in the prime of his life, you left a bright future untouched."

Lord Wellman's wife began to weep more bitterly as she realized at yet a deeper level that her son was gone. Olwen and her younger sister held their faces in their hands. Tristan contorted his face under a wave of grief.

"Though you did not die the great leader you would certainly have become, we remember you for the leader that you were. A man full of life, you conquered everything you put your hand to. Though you never gave your love," Lord Wellman paused to keep his composure, set on honoring his son in full. "Though you never loved or were loved as a husband and father, we know you had the heart to, and the hope." Lord Wellman's lips quivered. "Though so much of your life was not lived, you have touched us all. With your love as a firm believer in the Promise, may you be carried to the halls of the King of Amilum." Lord Wellman lowered his head and at last wept.

Once every last flower petal dropped into Pedrig's grave, everyone turned their attention to Creedus. With his eyes looking into the sky, toward the western horizon, Creedus' expression grew calm. "A son of Homsoloc, a servant of the King of Amilum and a lover of his Promise, our brother Reed has found his rest. As a warrior, he died like a warrior, defending his fellow man." Creedus paused, allowing a slight smile to reach his lips. "Reed, you lived a life of love."

Corred watched his grandfather, struck by such words. He looked around to find that not a single person was looking anywhere else. Some followed Creedus' gaze, but returned to observing the old man's countenance. Many stopped crying for a moment, waiting for what would be said next.

"At the age of sixty years you were strong enough to live another twenty, but you gave your life for what you lived for, and you did so in love. For the hope of others, you fought. Love hopes. You believed, unwavering in what you held to be true. Love acts in faith. You protected others from what you knew to be injustice and wickedness, bringing justice where you were able. Love protects."

In the midst of a funeral, life entered the group once again. Tears continued to flow but the morning light had its effect in the hearts and minds of those who listened.

Creedus lowered his gaze to look at all that remained of his friend. With longing in his voice, he finished. "May you be carried to the halls of the King of Amilum and honored for your life of love." With these last words, Creedus stepped back and let the officiators finish the ceremony.

Oil was poured around the edges of each pyre, and all around each body, but not on them. While everyone present backed away several steps, two men methodically struck a spark to the base of each pyre. Within seconds, a gentle but consuming fire climbed each pile and a curtain of flame was drawn on the lives of the four men.

After a long moment of silence, mixed with inaudible prayers, the group began to disperse. For the first time that day, conversations were started as folks shared memories of either man, beginning the spoken legacy of each that would remain with the living.

Corred wanted to talk to Olwen, but he didn't know what to say. He watched as she and her family stood together, receiving continued condolences for their loss. He wanted to join them, but he could not bring himself to do it. *I don't belong with them, and even if I did, I'm a complete mess. I've got to be stronger than this.*

She noticed that he was watching her and several times returned his stare, forcing a smile. Slowly parting ways, Corred joined Creedus and Einar, and Olwen remained with her family as everyone wandered back into town.

Corred stared at the ground, a mix of emotions swirling within him. *Even in mourning she is beautiful. If only I could hold her now.* He thought of little else on the walk through town, missing most of the conversations around him.

CHAPTER 10

The setting of a Northern Village was unfolding as Bernd, Gernod and Lanhard returned from the plains to the east. At the edge of town, they watered their tired horses. The terror from the night before was far removed from the tranquility of the morning sunrise and those who casually went about their chores.

"Gernod, feed the horses. Lanhard, unpack my things." Bernd gave a few orders while pulling the battle-axe from among Gernod's things. "I am going to speak to Bjorn."

A farmer passed by with his oxen and plow, headed for the field to turn the soil. A few houses down, a man chopped wood with long powerful swings. A stray dog trotted through the street independently, looking for scraps to make a meal. It was just another day in the life of a Northern Villager, but not so for Bernd. With pursed lips he blocked out his surroundings, consumed by the severity of the news he now needed to make known. At one of the cabins, looking much like the rest, Bernd abruptly pulled up and knocked hard.

After a moment's silence, footsteps approached from the inside. The door quickly opened inward, revealing a heavyset man with short dark hair and a kind face. A look of surprise came across his face when he saw who called on him. "Bernd? I wasn't expecting to see you for another few days." He quickly noticed the weapon in his young friend's hand.

"Bjorn, I have something I must talk to you about," Bernd said with a straight face.

"I see," Bjorn responded blandly. "Come in, come in." Backing into his cabin Bjorn pointed at the axe in Bernd's hand. "What's that you have there? It's not for chopping wood."

Bernd extended the handle to him. "No, it is not. This is the weapon that almost took my brother's life last night not far from the foothills of Mount Elm." Bernd closed the door behind him to keep the heat in. "We were attacked by a soldier."

Bjorn started at this news. "Soldier!?"

"Look at the base of the blade," Bernd said, pointing to the head of the handle.

Bjorn walked over to the fire, which lay at the other end of the room and held it to the light to get a better look. "Hildan. One of the four?" Bjorn said in a deep voice. "A soldier of Mornoc wanders the plains of the East?"

"Wandered; Lanhard's arrow found its mark. Not far from the Altus Mountains." Bernd felt his arm, still wrapped from the night before.

"You are fortunate there was only one," Bjorn said. He turned to Bernd with a knit brow at the very thought. "Was there only one?"

"Yes. I am glad for it, but vexed by it. Our enemy has

never been one to spare the use of force, has he?"

"Not in all the history of war." Bjorn rubbed the scruff of his face thoughtfully.

"What do we make of this?" Bernd asked anxiously.

"I don't know," Bjorn answered, becoming lost in thought.

There was a moment of uncomfortable silence, but it did not last long. The sound of a charging horse in the street came to a halt outside of Bjorn's door. Bernd stood aside as Bjorn went to open it.

A messenger on horseback had already dismounted and was extending him a letter. He was haggard looking, and poorly rested, but his arm was steady. "Creedus sends you word. Wellman awaits," he announced with a cracking voice. With that he handed Bjorn the letter, mounted, and hurried on his way. A couple of chickens scattered from his path as he headed west to the next village.

"This is proving to be a very interesting morning," Bjorn remarked as he retreated inside. "It has been some time since Creedus summoned us to Wellman."

The letter was folded, but not sealed, as if prepared in great haste. Returning to the light of the fire to read it, Bjorn held it away from his face to focus on its contents.

Bernd waited silently.

Bjorn mumbled something to himself. Looking at Bernd he noticed his wounded arm. "It appears that you're not the only one who's had a brush with the enemy." Bjorn returned to the letter and read aloud.

"To all who remain faithful to the Promise, now is the time for you to prove your faithfulness. Come to Wellman, giving word to no one of the nature of your travel, save those you can trust with your life. When you

arrive, do not make yourself known, for our enemy has been active and is watching.

Bring full account of your post and the movement of our enemy, thought by some to be silent, known by others to be gathering strength in this very hour. We will meet on the night of the third day. Come quickly."

Bernd's mouth was open, but he was speechless.

"Will you come with me?" Bjorn asked. "You have testimony to give that Creedus and many others need to hear." Bjorn refolded the paper, and after a slight pause tossed it into the flames. "I am leaving as soon as I can pack sufficiently. It is a night and a hard day's ride to Wellman."

Bernd took a deep breath. "I will. I will come and give an account. But afford me some time to leave it off with my family. They have missed me for most of this past month, and I dare not leave again without seeing them."

Bjorn shook his head in agreement. "Go. I will wait for you, but do not linger."

Bernd rushed out and ran back up the street to where he had left his brothers tending the horses.

There was a sober urgency in his voice as he gave them news of his summons.

As Bernd ran inside to tell his wife and children, the echo of the messenger's gallop thundered on. Another letter was dropped off to a member of the Véran, and for another family, the world changed.

*   *   *   *   *

Returning to the base of Mount Elm, a soldier of Hildan rode alone, leading a second hargus with the form of a fallen soldier as its burden, a single arrow protruding from its shoulder. His comrade's failed attempt to kill the three horsemen the night before had become apparent when he did not return by sunrise. The dead soldier's spear had been recovered but his ax was gone. The surviving soldier would now have to report the failure of carrying out his captain's order, a duty that promised wrath.

Riding around the base of Mount Elm, the soldier began to climb. Taking a well worn trail, he fell in with several other soldiers, all coming from the eastern regions of the Altus Mountains. They eyed his load curiously, wondering what had happened, but declined to ask questions when they saw his bitter scowl.

After several miles of thinning forest, the group rounded the northern face and followed the same trail in a steeper switchback ascent. To the north, the fullness of the Altus Mountains slowly came into view. Like an immense forest of jagged cones rising into the sky, they were by far the largest mountains in the Lowlands. Losing their foliage gradually, each individual mountain began as a teeming forest and rose from there to become a lifeless rocky point crested with ice and snow. For as far as the eye could see, they stood like a throng of giants, all equally separated by expansive valleys lined with rivers and forests of immense evergreens. Everything was larger, the trees were taller and the world itself seemed to double in size.

As the soldiers climbed higher, bringing more of this world into view, trees gave way to grass and brush which covered its slopes in green, not yet shriveled from the first winter frosts that had begun to fall at night. A hedgehog the size of a dog scurried out of their way, eating his last few meals before entering his burrow, not to emerge until spring.

Passing several cave entrances along the trail, the soldiers chose a specific entrance higher on the mountain. It afforded room enough for several riders to enter at once and still more to ensure that the hargus were not wary of their surroundings; they were animals to be dealt with cautiously, and feared for their strength.

The rocky passageway immediately branched into several tunnels. Following the first of these to the left, the soldiers kept to the contour of the mountain, until they reached a place where it opened into a vast cavern. It was a space filled with crudely constructed stables for the hargus and plenty of soldiers to tend to them. So as to keep the animals healthy and content while penned up, there were multiple holes cut into the cave walls high above, admitting the light of the sun. The rock floor was coated with straw to aid in cleaning, and there were many troughs for water and feed lining the stables.

Dismounting, the soldier who had returned from the plains handed his own mount to one of the soldiers working the stables. Turning to another he gave orders concerning his fallen comrade. "See to it that this animal is reassigned immediately and get rid of the body before it begins to smell." Reaching up, he pulled the dead man's cloak aside and snapped the end of the arrow off that had ended his life. Without another word the soldier marched out of the cavern and back to the main tunnel where he followed it deeper into the mountain. Grumbling, he braced himself for what wrath his report might bring.

Using the spear as a walking staff, he carefully examined the craftsmanship of the arrow's fletching under the light of the lanterns that lined the cave walls. The further into the mountain the soldier traveled, the less the air moved, becoming heavy and damp. It was not long before he came to a particular tunnel over which was carved the name *"Hildan."* There he paused to lean the spear against the rock wall, take a deep breath, straighten to his full height, and enter.

The tunnel quickly opened up into a larger room, where at the center Hildan and several of his guard were dining at a monstrous wooden table. The soldier entered with arrow in hand and walked around the table to where Hildan sat at the head.

Hildan lowered his meat back to his plate. "Why have you returned alone?" he asked.

"The horsemen were more than we expected, my lord." Holding up the arrow, he avoided the specifics of what had happened. "Apparently one of them was an archer, capable of great precision in the dark." There was a bitter sarcasm in his voice.

Hildan did not reply immediately. He looked around at the members of his guard to read their reactions. Turning again to his visitor, he asked. "What of the horsemen? Do the Northern Villages now know that we are here, in the foothills?" He leaned in on his elbows. His usually cold stare had already begun to flush with a horrible rage.

"It is unlikely, my lord." He chose not to speak of the missing axe. "They fled, and I was sure to gather any evidence that might suggest such a thing. Thieves will be credited for the act. I am sure– "

BOOM! Hildan slammed his fists on the table, shaking its contents violently. "For your sake I hope that is true." Hildan replied quickly. Rising to his feet he looked down at his soldier with a clenched jaw.

The soldier took a step back and braced himself.

Hildan continued. "If I find that our presence is now known on account of your failure, I will not wait for the day of battle to wield my axe." He breathed heavily, each breath, ready to deal a death blow, but he stayed his hand.

The soldier swallowed hard and looked directly ahead, unable to make eye contact with his captain. Each second that passed filled him with greater dread.

"Get out!" Hildan growled.

The soldier took a step back, grimacing at the intensity of his captain's malice.

Having shaken the hall with his voice, Hildan promptly returned to eating, tearing his food as he cursed through his teeth.

Quickly leaving the room and continuing back down the tunnel, the soldier snapped the arrow in half with his fingers and tossed it on the ground. Feeling his neck, just to make sure it was still there, he returned to the stables and to his duties.

*　　*　　*　　*　　*

The cave walls of Casimir were glowing bright, and the movements of his army were beginning to show. As a scout left for one mission, so another returned, saluting his comrade with a raised spear in one hand and a lantern in the other.

Casimir walked the feasting hall daily, inquiring after each mission and the results, in eager expectation of the day he would wield his club openly. Selcor was often the object of his focus. Casimir had been skillfully tending to his young soldier's heart, training him for treachery yet to be carried out. Killing Lord Wellman's eldest son was just the beginning. Casimir had plans for Selcor. Creedus was his high prize and he had already come close.

Selcor remained in the hall, letting his wound heal to a point where he could once again attack the Head of the Véran and take the Sword of Homsoloc. With this deed accomplished, the whole of Mornoc's forces would be unleashed. And so the center of the struggle lay in Wellman: the fading strength of an aged man pitted against the hatred of a traitorous youth, trained solely to strike at the heart of hope.

At the same time, unknown to Casimir, the heads of Véran were gathering. Men were traveling to Wellman as they did every day, but among them were these uncelebrated warriors and warriors to be, representatives of every part of the Low Lands. They arrived unannounced, blending in with the town until the following night when they would gather at the town hall for a council.

*   *   *   *   *

Walking briskly away from Lord Raven's estate, Lowell headed for the busier sections of Renken, closely evaluating the interactions of the people around him. He was not wearing his usual green robe, as he did in Lord Raven's presence, but instead he dressed like a common man, donning a small cap made of fur which he had bought in the market place weeks ago. With beady eyes he looked this way and that, as if in search of something specific, but it was clear that he had no destination.

Merchants held conversation with wealthy customers, a carriage with several young ladies drove by slowly, two gentlemen argued over a sale, and a group of boys ran through the streets in a dangerous game of tag. It all captured his eye, but none of it held his attention; he was in search of something else and before long, he saw it.

Studying the countenance of a young man who was aimlessly weaving through traffic, Lowell picked up his tracks and tailed him for a while to evaluate his person. The young man was dressed in tattered clothing not fit enough to keep him warm, and he appeared not to have bathed in weeks. His shoes had holes in the toes, and he walked with a slight limp on account of it. His hair was disheveled, his eyes hollow and gaunt, and his arms swung heavily at his sides.

Lowell followed him for a while to see where he would go, keeping far enough behind so as not to raise any suspicion. Deep into the western district they wandered, walking through dirty streets packed by wagons loaded down with goods, crowds of people hovering over some table of produce for sale, meats, bread, and every other necessity. Reaching a section where the most desired form of shelter was no more than a shack with one large room and a door on hinges, the young man that Lowell had been following stopped abruptly on the corner of two narrow streets and crawled into a large slat box that leaned up against the outside wall of a neighboring shanty. Once used for housing chickens or some other livestock, it now served as his home. Inside were several thin blankets and other worthless trinkets that served as possessions.

To any other man, this bum would have been difficult to look at, but for Lowell, he was a gem. Walking right up to the box, he stood in front of it and addressed him. "Sir, you look hungry."

The young man had just enough strength left from his

walk to give Lowell an unwelcome look and tell him how he felt. "Whatya know about it? If ya come to mock me, then ya come to waste yer time. No other soul here knows my hunger, and I don't care to tell 'em bout it. They all," waving his finger around the place, he brought it back to Lowell, "and you can fall over dead fer all I care." His voice was raspy, tired, and full of bitterness. He finished his speech with a cough.

Lowell reached into his coat and extended a crust of bread and a piece of cheese. "On the contrary, I've come to satisfy your hunger and tell you about a better life. So for your sake, I hope I don't drop dead, or you won't hear about it."

The young man's eyes grew wide, and the frown left his face at the sight of food. He did not accept it at first out of shock and the suspicion that it was a cruel trick, but when Lowell did not withdraw his hand, he reached out and took it. Holding it carefully he stared at it for a moment before slowly beginning to take bites of one and then the other.

Lowell stood there silently, waiting for his new friend to finish eating. Observing the trust that had been established, he broke the silence. "Sir, there is no reason for you to lie here any longer. What are you doing sitting in a box made for animals among people who do not care about you?"

The young man continued to eat and stared at him blankly, as if the question had never even occurred to him.

Lowell folded his arms behind his back and presented the news as if it made perfect sense. "My master can care for your needs if you are willing to honor his rule, and I do not speak of Lord Raven." Pointing to the food in his hands, he added, "He has far more than that waiting for you if you will only join him in his work."

The young man swallowed and paused before taking

another bite. "Whatya talkin' about? What master?" No sooner had he asked the question, sincerely wanting the answer, than he stuffed the remaining bread into his mouth.

"His name is not important. What is important is that you are fed, made valuable and respected as you clearly are not here. What is even more important is that my master will soon rule these lands, and if you are not with him, you are against him." With that Lowell turned to go.

"Wait, wait!" The young man rolled out of his box, calling over a mouthful of food. "Where can I meet him?"

Lowell stopped and turned to face him again. Looking him in the eye with a smirk, he answered quickly. "Meet me tonight, just after sundown, outside of the town on the northern shore. If you come I will have a new coat for you and a full meal. Don't be late."

CHAPTER 11

Corred was restless. The funeral was fresh in his mind, but he did not want to dwell on it. Strolling through the streets, he greeted those citizens that he knew, and received greeting from those that now recognized him from the evening before. Not surprisingly, he found his path taking him toward Lord Wellman's mansion. Corred's wandering led him straight toward one of the primary sources of his restlessness. As always, there were servants at work around Lord Wellman's property, going to and fro with their errands. Only now, there was a weight of sorrow that covered the mansion. A few of the windows were open, welcoming the fresh morning air in hopes that the life outside would inspire continued life within.

The stable boy, leading a horse around the side of the house, spotted Corred gazing at the windows above. With his horse in tow, he approached Corred tentatively. "Sir, are you one of the men who fought to save my master's children?"

Corred turned to him as if awakened from a dream, startled by the question. "Yes, I am."

With a slight bow, the boy humbly paid his respects. "You are very brave. I hope to be like you some day." He was young, no more than twelve years of age, and only beginning to grow into his hands and feet. Dressed like the other servants, he was not distinct in any way, but he possessed the boldness to approach a man carrying a sword, one whom he knew to be dangerous.

Corred was pleasantly surprised with his forward manner. "What is your name?"

"Andrew, sir. It was my father's name."

"Well, Andrew, I count it an honor to meet you," Corred said, extending his hand.

The young boy beamed with joy at being so kindly received and gave Corred as firm a handshake as he could.

Before Corred could pursue further conversation, he caught a glimpse of someone in the window above. A young woman with long braids stepped back from the window when he noticed her. *Olwen.*

Seeing the conversation had come to an abrupt end, Andrew hurried off to complete his tasks, pulling his horse behind him.

Once again, Corred was alone, staring up into the windows, wanting only to catch another glimpse of Olwen, wanting to know she was safe. Out of respect for the grief of Lord Wellman's family, he resumed his walk through town.

From the back wall of the hall that led to her room, Olwen felt her pulse quicken. A mix of emotions filled her. She watched Corred carefully, keeping just out of sight. As he passed by, she admired his every step. No common man was supposed to catch the eye of a young woman born to royalty. She herself was alarmed at the thought and blushed, bringing back her natural color. But she couldn't shake the feeling of her hand in his.

She closed her eyes and saw him running toward her, sword in hand, covering the length of the field in seconds. As the cords around her wrists pulled at her very strength, he closed in, sword raised.

She opened her eyes. Though it was not the first time she had seen him, it was how she saw him now. The young man she had talked to several times before, when they were both just children, was no longer an acquaintance. After her grip on hope had lost hold, he had come running to defend her. She felt safe just knowing he was near. Looking down the hall to see if anyone had noticed, Olwen chastised herself for feeling joy in the wake of her brother's death. But she did. In a mix of painful loss and hopeful love, her tears threatened to spill over.

At that moment Gwen turned the corner at the end of the hall and walked Olwen's direction. Her head hung low as it usually did, but mostly for mourning the death of Pedrig. She wiped a tear from her weary eye and approached Olwen shyly. The scratches on her face from the day before had been cared for but were still quite fresh.

Extending her hand, Olwen met Gwen and embraced her, blinking back her own tears. There was no social separation between them now, as there once had been. Tucking Gwen's hair behind her ear, Olwen lifted her chin. "Not even when they had taken us from our home could they claim us. You are far more loved than you believe, my sweet Gwen. Let the light of day brighten your face."

Gwen straightened up and allowed a smile to cross her lips. Hope returned and she breathed deeply, releasing her anxiety. "Thank you, my lady. We do have much to be thankful for. Please, forgive my sulking." She wiped her face with the back of her hand and continued on her way.

Once Gwen had rounded the corner, Olwen let her tears roll down her cheeks freely, baring her weakness in secret. But her weakness was real, and she longed for the strength that she did not possess, strength that could not be shaken.

Outside, Wellman too carried on as it did every day, but changed; its eyes were open. A sober air filled the streets; chores once taken for granted were now welcomed. The lives that they had simply been drifting through only a week before were more precious with every breath, because untimely death had again become reality. The funeral of Reed earlier that morning had been a vivid reminder. There was a sense of urgency to live a normal life while it was available. The man carrying a pail of milk and the woman gathering eggs from the chicken coop, like Corred, knew that life in Wellman had changed.

While crossing the main road that led to the center of town from the west, Corred looked into the distance. As the sun reached its highest point in the sky, he spotted something gliding along the horizon, just above the tops of the trees. *What is that!?* He stopped in his tracks, straining to see more.

It was clearly some sort of bird in flight, but for what Corred could make of the creature, it was not only larger than he'd ever seen, but different. Soaring effortlessly over the highest parts of the forest, it dove between two mighty oaks and out of sight.

The sound of hooves right behind him broke Corred's concentration. Jumping aside, he made way for a wagon full of firewood. The rider looked at him oddly and half yelled, "What are you doing in the middle of the road?"

Rising to his toes, Corred ignored him, searching the distant fields. The wagon blocked his view, so he crossed to the other side of the street; nothing. He had the boyish urge to mount his horse and ride straight for the place he'd last spotted the creature, but he pushed it aside. *This isn't exactly the time to explore the woods in search of a bird, no matter how unique it is.* With a wry smile, he thought, *besides, who would go with me and not think that I've lost my mind?*

Gradually becoming aware of how warm it had grown and how thirsty he was, Corred turned north so that his wandering would at last bring him to one of the wells there. From there he would be able to see the Altus Mountains, though their majestic peaks were but a hazy outline. It was a favorite view of Corred's whenever he had the chance to enjoy it. *Perhaps there will be some folks arriving from the Northern Villages.* Whatever he found, it was something to keep his mind occupied, and that was what he needed.

The northern end of Wellman was spread much thinner than the southern side, occupied by many poorer citizens, some of whom found means by working as servants of Lord Wellman. The huts were smaller in most cases, with small gardens along the side or in the back. Only a few owned a horse for any sort of labor or travel, and most had little livestock beside. There was rarely enough work to keep these folks from wanting for something, though they were all better off than most in the western district of Renken.

Corred passed a garden where a mother and her children were working the soil slowly. For the younger ones, it was nothing but fun, and this alleviated some of the burden for their mother, even bringing a smile to her face.

Corred bid them good morning, receiving the strongest

response from the youngest. With hands held high, he gripped the soil tightly, displaying his mess quite merrily. His mother bowed her chin respectfully, trying not to laugh at her young son as he tossed the dirt into the air. Her daughter was much more conscious of her manners and curtsied with a "Good Morning," offering some harsh correction to her younger brother in the same breath. He grinned foolishly and took the abuse as some sort of compliment.

Continuing on, Corred observed several more households gathering the fruits of their labor and turning over those crops which had finished their giving. Quite in contrast to the young children who had been helping their mother, several houses along, an elderly couple worked side by side. They both had well weathered skin, wrinkled and leathery from so much time spent in the elements, and their heads were arraigned in silver, a testament to their many years. The old woman took notice of Corred first and initially gave him a suspicious look.

"Good day," Corred said, nodding her direction. With a small wave, he smiled.

Allowing a weak smile to wrinkle her face further, she held up a dirty hand with her other still clinging to a clump of the weeds that seemed to thrive in all weather.

Not wanting his work to be distracted for more than a second, her husband looked up for the briefest of moments to a give a tight dip of his chin. The vine he was attempting to reinforce was well filled with ripe peppers, red and green, some of which he had already placed in his grass basket. His old fingers moved slowly but with no less dexterity.

Corred's walk took him through pictures of life as it had been in Wellman for generations. Only once or twice did anyone recognize him from his past visits to see his grandfather.

"Kind, sir?" A soft voice spoke from behind him.

Looking over his shoulder, Corred stopped and turned to face a young girl and boy who had stepped out from behind a cabin.

"Yes?" Corred asked as softly. He felt awkward that they were so shy.

"You're Corred, aren't you?" the girl asked. Eyes wide with wonder, her little brother stood just behind, stepping out only to get a better look at Corred's sword.

"Yes, I am. And who might you be, miss?" Corred asked, squatting to meet them both at their level.

"Delian, sir," she answered with a bit of a gasp. "And this is my little brother."

Corred smiled, amused by the fact that she referred to him not by name, but as her little brother. The small boy, no older than three years, blinked curiously. Before Corred could respond they both ran back around the corner of the cabin.

How do they know my name? Thinking no more of it, he turned to go, but before he could get another step, a man rounded the corner with Delian and her little brother in tow.

"Excuse me, Corred," the man said, approaching Corred with a sense of urgency. He pushed aside his long hair with the back of a dirty hand, revealing how young he really was. Extending his right hand in greeting, he hesitated, as it too was quite dirty with the work he had been doing.

Corred quickly responded and shook the man's hand firmly.

"My name is Grady," he said, standing to his full height which was several inches shorter than Corred. "I believe I owe you a great debt in the rescue of my daughter, Gwen."

Corred blushed with honor and discomfort. Nodding a little, he replied, "I was only one of six men who made the ride, and it was my honor to fight for you and your family. Your daughter, Gwen is a brave girl."

Grady backed away somewhat and with the most humble strength replied, "She gets her great courage from her mother, you know." His strong hands, arms and shoulders seemed contrary to his meek and self effacing manner. His whole appearance was that of a man who could wrestle an ox if he set his mind to it. Though not bulky or intimidating, his strength was the deceptive kind.

Corred nodded again, and sought to build that man up. "Our enemies were wise to take their captives under cover of darkness, for I am sure they would have been unable to contend with you."

"You pay me kind words," Grady replied. "I'm not an aggressive man, but I do love my family."

You may not be aggressive, but I wouldn't cross you. "I'm pleased to meet you Grady, and pleased more that you and your family are safe."

"As am I," Grady replied, taking Corred's hand again in his tight grip. "And may it stay that way."

Watching the man return to his work, Corred felt another wave of confidence, that a father, a man many years older than himself had stopped him in the street to pay him honor. Having longed to show himself the man he aspired to be, the reality of it caught him off guard.

With his head held that much higher, Corred cut between properties toward where he best remembered the well to be. He heard horses watering before he could see them. Rounding a newly built cabin, he came upon the sight of several armed men silently watering their horses.

Men from the Northern Villages? Corred thought. *The heavier coats and long bows in their packs seem to say so.* The men of the Northern Villages were known for the bows that they made from a type of fir tree unknown in the southern parts of the Lowlands. They were well constructed for the typically longer shots that were necessary for hunting in more open lands.

Taking notice of Corred right away, one of them with a head of thick messy hair immediately looked at Corred's sword and then lifted his chin in salutation. He couldn't have been much older than Corred. Neither he nor his companions carried a sword on their belts, but without too much effort Corred caught sight of a hilt protruding from the saddle pack for two of the three.

Corred approached cautiously, with his left hand rested on the hilt of his own sword. "Welcome to Wellman," he said.

Looking up from where he'd been filling the trough for their horses, the oldest and heaviest of the three stared at Corred for a moment before answering. "Good day to you." He latched the rope back onto the handle of the bucket and tossed it into the well. Stepping forward he extended his hand in greeting. "Bjorn." His thick jaw was nearly wider than his ears and his short dark hair stood on end like coarse wire.

Corred took his hand with as firm a grip as he could but found Bjorn's hand far too large to actually squeeze. "My name is Corred," he replied, looking his acquaintance in the eye.

Glancing over his shoulder, Bjorn pointed to the young man who had taken notice of Corred first. "This is Bernd, and that's Rickert. We've had a good long ride and we're wondering where there might be some lodging for men who could use a good meal and some rest."

Northern Villages it is, Corred concluded. Turning back toward the center of town, Corred motioned to where the highest point of Lord Wellman's estate could be seen rising above the rooftops. "That tower you see is very near the center of Wellman. In the town square there are several lodgings, and the best would have to be Targen's Tavern."

Before Bjorn could continue the conversation, another rider came from between two cabins and into the main road, headed for the well at a slow walk. His hood was pulled up over his head, but not so much as to shadow his face. Dark stubble covered his jaw, but it was not quite enough to call a beard. His features were sharp and his clothes looked well worn and ordinary. His horse was nothing like him, a rather remarkable creature. The bright white patches that covered its stomach, part of its back, and even one of its ears drew a sharp contrast with the dark brown of his hide. Corred had only seen a few horses like it, rumored to be one in five thousand.

Judging by Bjorn's reaction, he could tell that the man was not part of their small party. When Bjorn had evaluated the man in silence, certainly more impressed with his horse than with him, he nodded but did not lift a hand in greeting.

The stranger nodded back in like fashion, allowing a bit of a smile to curve his lip. Leaned over in his saddle, he did not change his pace, but merely walked up to join the group and water his horse like the three that had arrived before him.

He must not be a horseman, though perhaps he is also arriving for the gathering, Corred thought. *He looks enough like it.*

"Well, Corred," Bjorn continued, as if the conversations had never paused, "thank you for your kind greeting and for the recommendation of Targen's Tavern. That is where we'll stay." Returning to his horse, he stroked its face and neck as it

150

had its fill of water, appearing to ignore everything else around him.

Bernd smiled slightly and approached Corred with an extended hand. Under his breath he said, "Don't mind Bjorn, he gets a little tart when he's tired."

Corred nodded, imagining Einar after a long day's work. He smiled at the thought. "Understandable."

"So, are you from Wellman?" Bernd asked.

"I am not, but my grandfather lives here and has for many years," Corred replied.

"What is the name?" Bernd asked very directly.

"Creedus," Corred answered.

Bernd raised his eyebrows a little. "The one who carries the Sword," he said.

Quite used to the response, Corred nodded, directing his attention over Bernd's shoulder to the fourth rider. He had now dismounted and was already drawing the bucket from the well to replenish the trough. "Bernd, it was nice to meet you. I will look you up tomorrow, perhaps."

"You know where I'll be, and if not, I will see you tomorrow night?" Bernd asked.

"I will be there with my grandfather," Corred responded, proudly. "Enjoy your stay here at Wellman. It's an honor to meet a brother from the Northern Villages."

"It is an honor to meet you, Corred, grandson of Creedus," Bernd replied.

Watching them all silently as he pulled the bucket up and dumped it into a second trough, the stranger who had arrived last smiled as Bernd and Corred finished their exchange. He pulled off his hood, revealing long hair pulled back from his face. His skin was not weathered so much as it was dirty; he looked as if he had not bathed for some time. Not waiting for Corred to initiate, the man attached the rope to the bucket once more and threw it in. "Good day, friend," he said.

"Good day," Corred quickly replied.

"I'll have a drink here for you in a moment," he said, as if he were a local just stopping by the well after a daily ride.

"Do you live in Wellman?" Corred asked. *I don't recognize him, and I've never seen such a horse.*

"No," he replied lightly. With long smooth strokes he pulled the bucket up from the bottom of the well.

"Have you traveled far?" Corred asked.

"I have," he replied, again not giving any more information than was needed. After a few more quick pulls, he hoisted the bucket up onto the edge of the stone that surrounded the well, and looked at Corred. "You are thirsty?"

"Yes, I am," Corred replied. *Seems like a very agreeable fellow.* Taking the bucket Corred lifted it to his lips and took a long cold drink. The surge of pain in the back of his head reminded him just how cold well water could get in the fall. Shaking his head to clear his vision, he handed the bucket back.

"Guess I'll sip a little slower," the stranger said with amusement.

"Yeah, it's pretty icy," Corred said, taking a step back as the pain cleared.

After a mouthful, which he was sure to let warm a little in his mouth first, the stranger asked Corred, "What do people call you?"

"My name is Corred," he responded.

Drying his hand on his shirt, the stranger stuck it out. "I'm pleased to meet you, Corred. That's a good name."

"Thank you," Corred replied, not used to such a

compliment.

"Named after your father?" the stranger asked.

"No, my grandfather," Corred replied.

The fellow nodded and held the bucket out for Corred to have some more.

Accepting the offer Corred was sure not to take too much too fast this time, as refreshing as it was. As he handed it back to the man he asked, "And what is your name?"

"My name is Remiel," he replied. With another big mouthful, he set the bucket on the edge of the well and retrieved a canteen from his pack.

Never heard of you. Corred wanted to ask him outright if he was a member of the Véran, but he maintained his sense of caution. "So are you here to trade?"

"No," Remiel responded dumping the remaining water from his canteen on the ground.

"Do you have family in Wellman?" Corred asked.

"No, do you?" Remiel asked intently filling his canteen without spilling a drop.

"I do," Corred responded. "My grandfather lives here in Wellman, and I often visit him." Corred cringed a little, realizing he knew nothing about Remiel, but that he was already revealing a lot about himself. Ever since being attacked near Hill Top, he'd felt vulnerable, or at least uncomfortable telling folks about himself, unless he knew them to be trustworthy.

Replacing his canteen among his belongings, Remiel rubbed his horse's side as it drank from the trough. With his eyes fixed on Corred's, Remiel simply smiled before looking past him and at the town all around him. As if giving voice to his thoughts, Remiel said, "Wellman is much like I imagined it would be."

Remiel's piercing gaze unnerved Corred. "Have you never been here before?" he asked, hoping to learn more about his new acquaintance than Remiel already knew about him.

"No, I haven't. I have wanted to see Wellman for some time, so it is good to finally be here," Remiel responded. Whispering to his horse, Remiel moved to now stroking its neck. "Do you know it well? I would very much like to see some of it before I find a place to rest," he said.

"I do. I could show you the town," Corred quickly responded. He was beginning to grow uncomfortable with Remiel, as something about him made Corred uneasy.

"I would like that," Remiel responded with a smile. Stroking his horse's side, he spoke under his breath and the animal stopped drinking. Not bothering to take the reins in his hands, Remiel followed Corred back toward the center of Wellman with his horse right behind him.

Astonished at the horses' calm nature, Corred couldn't keep from smiling. "Where did you find him?"

"Naveed?" Remiel asked. "Well . . . we sort of found each other. I needed a horse, and he needed a rider."

"That seems to have worked out well," Corred replied, not sure what else to say. "He is a magnificent animal."

"He is, and he has been an excellent companion," Remiel responded. "He does not tire like other horses."

Passing back between many of the cabins Corred had seen earlier, he received even more curious looks than his first pass. Most of the looks were for Naveed's unusual and beautiful appearance, but also because Remiel was truly a stranger.

In some ways the lack of recognition and therefore surprise from some of the citizens of Wellman put Corred at ease because it confirmed that Remiel had at least not lied about it being his first time to Wellman. *I'm just being suspicious. I can't always distrust everyone I meet because I haven't met them before.*

While pointing out certain aspects of the town, Corred slowly let down his guard. Remiel's unassuming, yet confident nature seemed nothing to be wary of, and by the time they reached the town square, Corred felt as if they would fast become friends. With the sun beginning to set, they parted ways. As Remiel walked toward the southern end of Wellman, Corred admired Naveed for a moment longer before returning to his cabin.

CHAPTER 12

A large, horse-drawn wagon carrying a few remaining hay bales slowly strolled into Oak Knoll. With a piece of straw in the corner of his mouth, Garrin occasionally snapped the reigns, staring straight ahead, lost in thought. He couldn't shake the conflict that resided in his own mind. Corred's words from several days before still rang in his ears. Though he tried to explain them away, they remained. The tone of his cousin's voice and the news of the scout attack haunted him.

The shouts of young boys engaged in a pretend battle broke his trance. Sticks made swords, and the heat of conflict filled the air. Measuring the force of their blows, two of them carried on, allowing the advantage in the fight to swing one way, then the other. The other boys stood back after a while and watched, fixed on the drama unfolding before them. At last, with a quick thrust, the one lunged and pretended to run his enemy through. Playing along, the other held the stick to his side with his arm and fell to the ground as if dead. But, the fight wasn't over, the victor ran for his life when he saw his enemy reviving. The boy who had feigned death jumped to his feet in pursuit.

Garrin admired their zeal with a knowing smile as he passed by. Gone were the days when he had felt such liberty, running freely through the town, pretending to be like his grandfather, Creedus. "The days of the warrior have passed," he said softly to himself.

As the sun was finishing its descent once again, he grew restless as an argument renewed in his mind. His final stop for the day was with his parents, a continued source of the argument itself. Garrin's big brow was knit tightly at the thought of discussing the very topic he had been trying to shake for days.

Pulling his wagon along the side of the house, he took no notice that the lantern was missing from the front stoop. With a sigh he jumped down, tossed his chewed piece of straw on the ground, and approached the door. Before he could knock, his cousin, Galena opened the door and smiled brightly.

"Garrin, I saw you coming up the road," she said joyfully, giving him a hug. "It is so good to see you."

The simple gesture relieved the tension in his mind as the heat from inside warmed his face. He couldn't resist such kindness. No matter how much he disagreed with his parents, he could never dislike his cousin, Galena.

"Come in, son," Logen said, joining Galena. "Have you had a long day?" He extended his hand.

"I have, but it was good. There were a lot of folks who needed hay today." With a big arm still around his cousin's shoulder, he greeted his father with a firm grip.

"Your mother is preparing dinner as we speak." Logen sat back down in his chair to enjoy the fire for a while longer.

Before he could answer, Shae came in from the kitchen, spoon in hand. "Son, I am pleased to see you." She too hugged her boy, unconcerned with getting dirt on her apron. "Clean yourself up. The stew is almost ready," she said as a sort of command. She made her request known with less subtlety than her husband and returned to tending the pot.

"Yes, ma'am." Garrin knew no other way to respond. He was hungry, tired, and it was growing cold outside. A bowl of stew sounded inviting enough to endure whatever conversation might arise.

"I'll get some water for the pail," Galena said, following her aunt into the kitchen and to the back of the house.

"You will be staying the night?" Logen half asked, half suggested. He pulled up a second chair for his son. "Corred was here two days ago." He offered the news off-hand, unaware that his son knew of the event.

"I thought I might as well be getting back to Renken after dinner; the horses need to be fed and watered," Garrin said, taking a seat.. Ending his work for the night and resting his horses was an appealing idea, but staying with his parents meant discussing their interests.

"I don't think that would be wise," Logen said. "As for the horses, you can feed and water them here." Turning to his son he continued. "Corred was attacked coming home from Hill Top but three nights ago. He barely escaped with his life. Not only that, but I received word this morning that Lord Wellman's son, Pedrig was killed the night before last." He paused to let this shocking news sink in for a moment. "You would be tempting fate to travel tonight."

Garrin was silent. He had been ready to dismiss the first warning, having heard it already, but the second caught him off guard. "Pedrig?" he was stunned.

"Lord Wellman's son and daughter, Tristan and Olwen were taken captive but they were rescued yesterday with efforts lead by your grandfather, Corred, and Einar." Logen returned to watching the progress of the fire with folded arms. "We all hope that this is not the beginning of something more sinister."

Garrin again had nothing to say. The argument he had assumed would transpire had been replaced with evidence, and he was now in the wrong. He knit his brow again, but this time out of anger toward the injustice.

"Are you ready son?" Logen turned and looked him in the eye. "You know there is an enemy, but are you ready to believe in the Promise?" His words were soft but spoken plainly.

Garrin cracked his knuckles loudly. The question that had vexed him his whole life was once again raised. "I know there is an enemy, but what am I to do with a promise, made hundreds of years ago, by a king I do not know?"

Logen remained silent for a moment, thinking it through. Before he could continue, Galena announced the completion of the evening meal and that the washing pail was full of warm water.

"Let's talk around the table, son." Logen stood up and waited for Garrin to enter first.

The smell of stewing venison and potatoes beckoned them in. As there was for every evening meal, a loaf of bread sat in the center of the table with butter beside. The house Garrin had grown up in knew him as well as he knew it. Every shelf and item on them, the planks in the floor, even the very plaster on the walls was as familiar to him as the air itself. Leaning in to get a better smell of the stew, his mother chastised him for invading her space. He was right at home.

After washing up in the back of the kitchen, Garrin took his seat with his back to the shelves. It was his chair, the one he had sat in since he was a young boy. As Shae served them all a bowl of stew, Galena sliced some bread.

Taking their places they looked to Logen to bless the food, as was his role.

Bowing his head Logen spoke the words Garrin had heard a thousand times. "May this food bring nourishment to our bodies and may we be truly grateful for its provision, and the provision of the Great Promise and its fulfillment to come. Amen."

"Amen." All present agreed in word, whether in their hearts or not, because that was what they did. Garrin's heart was divided.

They all ate in silence for a short while until Shae couldn't take it any longer and opened the discussion. "Garrin, do you have much hay left after your rounds today?"

"Not much, but I would rather like to run out. It would be better for business." Garrin dipped his bread in the stew and took big bites, wiping his mouth with his sleeve. He stayed focused on his food, but the question he had asked his father was repeating in his head.

It didn't take long for his mother's intuition to take hold. "Garrin, is there anything you want to talk about?" Shae posed the open-ended question as a hint that he better start talking.

Aware that if he didn't, more questions would follow, he asked the burning question again. "I know there is an enemy, but what am I supposed to do with a promise made hundreds of years ago by some king I've never seen?" He sat up straight and looked back at his father. As if surrendering to the difficulty of the question, he dipped his bread into his stew and continued eating. He didn't expect an answer, or to understand it.

Logen put down his spoon and leaned back with his arms crossed. "If our hope is in this place, then there is nothing more. But, even without the stories that have been passed down for centuries, men know that they are not at home here in the Lowlands. Something more calls us."

Garrin listened but gave little satisfaction to his father. He had heard it before. He wanted to hear something new, something different. He blurted his usual response. "But we've never been without the stories, how do we know that?"

"Where is your hope if not in something greater than yourself?" Logen asked. "Do we look to men around us who weaken with age and die? The question is still of hope. Did some man one day contrive these stories to comfort himself?"

"Sometimes I wonder," Garrin returned, taking another bite of stew.

Galena ate quietly, watching the struggle unfold. It made her visibly uncomfortable to see her cousin so resistant to what she held as true. Looking from one to the next, she waited to see who would respond. When silence continued, she overcame her fear and spoke up. "Why would those who believe be resisted if it weren't true?" It was a question Logen had put to his son before. But now it was coming from his young cousin.

The other three at the table looked at Galena, surprised that she had opened her mouth at all. Logen tried hard not to smile, leaning forward a little.

Galena's face was animated. "Why would someone attack those who believe in the Promise, killing the son of a good man? Why would they try to kill my brother, and my grandfather?" Her eyes welled up with fear at the thought, and love for the only family she had left. She looked straight at Garrin and continued. "Why do I only have one brother left? Did my father simply disappear, or has he deserted us because he lost hope? And my mother, do you think she died from grief and despair only because he left, or because of what he became?" Wiping away a tear, she looked at Garrin with pain of loss that weakened her very features. "Why have you been unharmed?"

Garrin stopped chewing and swallowed hard. Unable to look into his cousin's eyes, he turned away. The realization struck him like a blow. The enemy existed only to crush hope. Why would evil men attack the Promise unless it threatened them, unless . . . it was true?

Shae put her arm around Galena as she let loose her anguish. Her tears were very real to Garrin and he felt his heart break for her.

Logen leaned back toward his food and picked up his spoon again; he locked eyes with Garrin. "Son, the enemy attacks those he fears, and he fears those that oppose him. One thing is certain; Corred is on the right side."

*　　*　　*　　*　　*

On the shores of Lake Tormalyn, a large row boat with a sail waited patiently for a passenger to come. In it sat the man who was clearly responsible for the craft. He was a large fellow with a full beard and a pipe hanging from the corner of his mouth. His long coat was worn and weathered like his face. In the other end of the boat was his hired hand, a thinner man wearing the same worn coat; he was stretched out across the bottom of the boat with his arms behind his head, gazing at the stars.

The vessel was suited for carrying upwards of eight passengers comfortably and there were just as many overcoats lying in the boat, each accompanied by a closed basket. A light wind was steadily blowing, and the night sky was crystal clear. It would be a good night for traveling on the lake.

Standing stoically on the sandy beach was a short man with a small fur cap atop his head. It was Lowell, once again without his green robe. His arms were, as usual, folded behind his back as he watched the outskirts of Renken. Against the light of the town, several men could be seen approaching, each coming alone and from different directions. Their features were indistinguishable in the dark. One of them started to run when he noticed that he was not the only one making his way to the same place.

"Make the sail ready," Lowell said over his shoulder. "It looks like these fellows are pretty eager to be going." He said it with a crooked smile.

Arriving completely out of breath, the same young man that Lowell had spoken with that morning fell to his knees. "Please sir, I arrived first!" He coughed heavily before continuing "Let me meet your master, don't cast me away."

"Young man, there is room enough for you. Get on your feet." Lowell stepped back, showing his disgust for the man's groveling.

The young man jumped to his feet and stood shaking with fatigue and emotion. He attempted his best to stand up straight, but he kept shifting in his shoes out of discomfort. Several of the others who had been walking through the fields behind him arrived and appeared just as surprised as the first to see that they were not the only ones. They were all clearly from the western district and younger in age, but none of them as hapless looking as the first.

One of them walked right up to Lowell and asked blatantly, "Where's the coat you promised me?"

"If you wish to receive a coat at all, you will stand in line beside your new friends here," Lowell responded. When the beggar did not immediately obey, Lowell snapped his fingers. The larger of the two men who had been preparing the sail got out of the boat and came to join them with a club in his hand.

At the sight of such an imposing figure, the beggar tripped over his own feet and fell awkwardly into the sand. When the sailor continued his approach with the clear intention of beating him, the beggar found his senses and took off running with all his strength back toward Renken.

Lowell watched him go with a smirk and turned to address the rag-tag group of six that still stood there shivering in the wind. "Gentlemen, it will serve you well to remember from where you have come. In bringing you here I am offering you another life, but this is not because you deserve it. The whole of Renken despised you and left you in its streets to rot without a home or a meal fit for a pig. I am offering you food, shelter, clothing, and respect in return for service to my master in whatever he desires. But it's not just food and shelter that your service will bring you. It is citizenship in the real kingdom that you will gain. The king spoken of in our history, the history of Homsoloc is not real. It is the contrivance of men who want to keep control. It is a tactic, not a truth. If it were true, would you really be as pitiable as you are now? If the people around you really believed in this King, or that he was coming to save them some day, they would be concerned with how they lived, with preserving the good of those around them. Do the wealthy on the east side of Renken really look like they expect to leave this supposed land of exile? They seem pretty well established, pretty well fed for people who claim to be in exile."

Lowell paused to look them over and observe the effect of his words. "I am calling you to join my master, for he will not suffer these hypocrites. My master will soon be the only master of these lands, and those who aide him in establishing justice will rule with him. Those who have become rich at your expense, and wealthy at your cost . . . they will be your servants if you join us."

Standing with eyes wide open, the beggars and drunks waited on his next word.

"When you enter the boat, you will find a coat to keep you warm and a basket full of food. If you choose to take what food is not yours, you will be thrown into the lake and drown like the rats that you are. If you take your place and show gratitude for what you have been given, and these men choose to take you across, then know that this is the first true kindness you have ever known, and you owe your lives to my master."

The group of beggars nodded in understanding, several of them now convulsing with cold.

"We're ready when you are, Lowell." The thinner of the two sailors announced their readiness for departure.

Lowell stepped aside and held out his hand. "I wish you luck in your new life. Remember what I have said. You owe your lives to my master." Lowell watched until all six of them were on the boat and in their coats before giving a hand in pushing them off.

*   *   *   *   *

After the sun had set and lamps were placed on the front stoop of every home in Wellman, a host of men slowly made their way to the town hall. In groups, or one by one, they emerged from their cabins, cut through alleys, and crossed streets, each with his hood pulled over his head and a sword at his side. Creedus, Corred and Einar walked together.

The town was asleep, but it was quietly stirring with those who had remained vigilant to the present day. They were the faithful, watching when all others had decided there was nothing to see. The Heads of Véran were gathering.

Filing into the town hall where the fires on either end were burning brightly, they filled the benches that lined each side. To add light to the dark hall, several lanterns were lit and hung along the walls. Corred and Einar took their places on either side of Creedus.

Looking around at those who had already arrived and were seated, awaiting Creedus to begin, Corred looked for the men he had met the day before. Without much trouble he spotted Bjorn, Bernd and Rickert, but he did not see Remiel. Giving it no more thought, Corred gave his attention to his grandfather as he took the floor.

Upwards of one hundred men, young and old, faced the main floor giving their attention now to one man who stood at the center. With his left hand propped on the hilt of his sword Creedus looked around him, nodding with satisfaction. A smile came across his face, showing through his long beard. For a moment the silence continued as recognition was given simply for the fact that hope in the Promise lived on. Each man looked at the other, and whether he knew him or not, he beheld a brother.

"Welcome to Wellman, brothers of the Promise." Creedus held out his hands and took yet another good look at them all, allowing a longer look at Corred. "Though you did not know the nature of my call, you came all the same, leaving what you held dear to answer. Much has taken place in the last few days, all of which we must address here, tonight. Events as of late have been troubling."

Creedus paused before sharing the worst of it. "Pedrig, Lord Wellman's eldest son, has been slain by an enemy scout." There was a slight stir among the few who had not yet heard, having only just arrived in Wellman. "With the heroics of some of the brothers here in Wellman, greater loss was averted. Lord Wellman's young son, Tristan, and oldest daughter, Olwen, were taken captive in the same hour. After a day's chase and the sacrifice of a man's life, they were saved."

There settled over the hall a deafening silence. The beat of a heart could be heard. Every eye and ear gave full attention to Creedus as a tear fell freely down his cheek.

"Reed, a son of the family of Bryn, has gone to be with his fathers." With these words, he nodded to Einar who came out from the crowd, carrying a sword in front of him. Holding the sheath, he extended the hilt to Creedus who drew it slowly and held it up for all to see.

Corred swallowed the lump in his throat. Across the room men were solemn, not for fear or cowardice but for respect and admiration. Some of them beheld the sword of a man who had been a great warrior before they were even born. Others who had known him well, remembered him with tears, unashamed.

"Though his body returns to the dust, his sword shall not rust." With a renewed gleam in his eye, he looked them over. "Which of you will carry this man's sword?"

There was a moment of hesitation as most were slow to assume so great an honor. It was not common for such a question to be posed; a great warrior's sword could not simply be claimed as if it were the spoils of war.

Creedus looked around, disappointed at the lack of response. "His sword must go on to fight for another's hope as sure as his legacy will live. Who will take it?"

Before he could finish speaking, a man from the darkest corner of the room stepped forward. His hood was thrown back revealing his face in the dim glow of the lanterns. He had a gentle expression but the hair on his chin and a heavy brow gave him the rough look of a man not to be trifled with. Coming before Creedus he bowed a knee in respect. "I did not know this man, but I will honor him by carrying his sword." His voice was gruff but soft.

"Please, rise. You have made known your desire to be a warrior of the Promise. May you be honored and become as great a warrior."

Looking up at Creedus, the man took every word to heart.

Creedus returned Reed's sword into its sheath carefully. He nodded to Einar, who then gave it to the man.

"What is your name?" Creedus asked him.

"Fenton," he replied with a slight bow.

"Fenton," Creedus said, returning a bow of respect, "add this to the sword you already carry. In the days ahead, you will need both."

The man smiled, feeling the weapon's weight as he returned to his seat.

Creedus' words hung in the air as he resumed his pose in the midst of the floor and took a few paces before continuing. "Mornoc's scouts have been busy. A week ago I saw what I thought to be a specter fly by my window in the night. Its pale face shone in the moonlight for only a moment, and then it vanished. I thought it to be a dream. I now know that it was not. They have been among us, in our streets, on our very doorsteps. I do not know for how long or why, but lanterns have gone missing here in Wellman. I fear that it is not the mischievous activity of a few, but the planned effort of many, and a forewarning of war."

The room stirred. Not even rumors of war had been heard for so long that the reality of it seemed unreasonable, if not hasty.

Creedus quickly continued, "I have always feared our enemy for many reasons, but above them all, I fear him because he will stop at nothing to subject us to his will. He is so determined to do so that he would even remain silent to accomplish his purpose, for he knows that his very presence reminds us of the truth from our past. He was not the only one banished from Amilum. Our great father, Homsoloc was also banished, but . . ." Creedus shook his finger in the air, "he was banished with the hope of redemption. The writings of our fathers, kept safe by faithful men in Shole tell the Story, and many of us know it by heart. Mornoc wants this to be forgotten and taken for granted. If his silence can accomplish this, he would stay even his bloodthirsty hand to see it happen." Creedus began pacing as he continued, "Brothers, a serpent that waits for its prey to draw near may be silent, but he is not idle. He watches. He harbors his malice. He prepares to strike." He lowered his voice. "Mornoc is that serpent."

There were some words among the men, both in agreement and disagreement. But before any arguments could take course, someone stood up from among the crowd and advanced to the middle to join Creedus. It was Bjorn.

"Brothers, if I may have a word," he said, looking to his superior for permission.

"Go ahead, Bjorn," Creedus said. Giving the floor to another, he sat down between Corred and Einar.

Bjorn felt the light growth on his face thoughtfully before addressing the group. "I was approached by a good friend of mine the same hour that I received the summons to this gathering. He came to me distressed, and for good reason." Turning toward the bench he had just left, he extended his hand. "Bernd, would you show them what you showed me?"

Without hesitation Bernd joined Bjorn on the floor with an axe in his hand. Holding it up he said, "This is an axe from a soldier of Mornoc. My two brothers and I were attacked by this soldier in the plains by the foothills of Mount Elm, before the Altus Mountains. It is a new weapon, unworn and recently sharpened."

Again a stir of responses among the Véran filled the hall.

Bernd continued, raising his voice. "We were ambushed as we slept. All three of us escaped with our lives. We left his dead body lying in the field as we fled." Bernd lowered the weapon as he did his voice. "I have never before seen sign of a soldier in the foothills, and now I have been attacked. I share the fears of our leader."

"As do I," Bjorn added. He patted Bernd on the shoulder as he returned to his seat. Bjorn continued. "Brother Bernd failed to mention one thing. At the base of that battle axe is engraved the name of one of the four: Hildan."

The very name brought an end to continuing conversations and arguments alike.

"If one of the four has a soldier who would attack so readily on the northern plains, we have just concern and must take action." Bjorn spoke confidently about these things.

Another of the group stood. "There was only one soldier?" he asked with slight contempt. "Mornoc's men do not spare the use of force when they mean to kill."

Bjorn responded quickly. "That is a point that must be considered. If Mornoc musters his strength for war, then he would not put it on display before its time. This soldier was no doubt expected to be successful in his attack to ensure the secrecy of his regiment."

There were some murmurs and a request to see the axe. Bernd freely passed the weapon around at the behest of those skeptics who argued the legitimacy of the account.

"Brothers, I have given account of my post in the Northern Villages." Bjorn returned to his seat, giving the floor back to Creedus.

"Who else has a report to give of his post?" Creedus asked, opening the floor. "Stand and give account where you are."

Immediately a man stood from the back of the room. It was Fenton, now with Reed's sword also hanging from his belt. His countenance was now one of deep concern. "I would like to give account of my post in the eastern city of Port." As the room quieted he began, "Those who remain true to the Promise in Port are treated as the local fools. Though our land is fertile and we have grown into a city of commerce and great wealth, our people have regressed. The hearts of our leaders have clearly been led astray by their own success. There is evidence of council from within the Court of Lords that openly opposes all committed to the Promise. We are more than derided. If ever there were a time when Mornoc would strike our city, it is now. We are like a harvest ripe for picking." His voice grew louder with these last words. "As I traveled here, I was followed by a rider until I passed Renken. I do not know who it was and I thought it best not to confront him. He never revealed himself and I do not think he knew of my destination. But I am known as a member of the Véran in Port, and I have been watched. I beseech you all to give great consideration to what must be done to determine our enemy's intentions before it is too late." With that he sat down.

A few of the men to his right and left spoke words of encouragement, openly showing their respect for his steadfast devotion in the face of contempt. They were a brotherhood, regardless of whether they agreed on anything other than the Promise itself.

Einar stood next. "Brothers, our times are becoming increasingly ruled by the pursuit of wealth and power, not conviction. As a member of the Véran in Renken, I too have seen the drift of our leaders from the foundation on which we built our towns and cities. Lord Raven as well has shown that he is satisfied to merely live out his life in these Lowlands and forget the past and the Promise. I have reason to believe that there is darker councel behind it. There is a man that attends his guard who clearly does not belong. If we, who do not believe in coincidence, think that this is not some work of our enemy, we deceive ourselves. I do not know of the depth of his workings, for I admit I too have grown comfortable in peace. But as Fenton has just stated, we have not been vigilant enough. If we are to send men to seek our enemy out, I will go.

My sword is sharp and my hope is fixed. I respect his strength, but I do not fear him. I would rather face him on my terms."

Some agreed whole heartedly with Einar's impassioned speech, but most remained unmoved. They nodded, acknowledging the accounts, but they dismissed the severity of the implications.

Corred rose to his feet. His spine shivered with pride as he began. "Brothers, I have an account of my post at Oak Knoll."

A gentleman to his right said aloud, "Speak up, son," and a wave of encouragement followed. Beads of sweat formed on Corred's forehead under the light of the chandelier above.

"Four nights prior to this, in the woods between Oak Knoll and Hill Top, I was hunted and attacked by a scout as I returned home. Along the path that I have run since I was a boy, he waited to take my life. At the last moment, he gave himself away, providing me with the chance to make an escape. I was hard pressed to stay ahead of him as he ran me down and narrowly missed me with his spear, cutting my shoulder. The next morning the same spear was driven into my front step, my blood still on its blade, and my lantern was gone."

He had their attention in full. Realizing this fact stunned him, but far more than that, it energized him.

"Our enemy has grown bold. We have posed no threat to him. Is it not our destruction that he has planned since the day he was condemned? He has no purpose apart from it. My grandfather and I have been marked. Either we live to see the day of a champion from the West or we hold our enemy to an account for his wicked ways. Neither has taken place." Corred shifted his weight nervously. "My whole life I have dreamed of using my sword; I have dreamed of living up to my name. If we wait for Mornoc to strike first, we have played into his grip.

If we are to take action, I also will go." He quickly sat down.

Corred received even more approval than Einar had. Boyd and Beathan patted him on the back from behind. "Thank you, friends," Corred replied quietly. His heart was racing. If the last two days had given him confidence that he too could be as great a man as his grandfather, worthy of carrying the Sword, this did even more. He had spoken, and men he admired had cheered.

Creedus once again took the floor. "Brothers, we have heard these accounts and need to hear no more. Whether our enemy is gathering in strength or cowering in caves, we must seek him out. If we do not, he will, as in these events, come to us. Will we wait for him to strike? Will we wait for him to snuff out our lights and harm our families?"

The group's response as a whole was not what Creedus had hoped for. Even after the accounts that they heard, most were timid in their response, revealing their lack of will for action. Well-spoken words had been more easily accepted. Indeed it seemed that only those who had already encountered the enemy also clenched their fists.

Creedus led them anyway. "Who will work with me to organize our own scouting expeditions, to find our enemy's whereabouts and determine his strength? If he intends to strike again, we must be ready for him, or more innocent people will die."

Another elderly gentleman on the opposite side of the room stood to give response. He was not much younger than Creedus, but he did not appear as fit for battle. His belt hung below his protruding belly, and his shoulders were rounded from years of resting on past accomplishment.

"Brothers, and especially those who have shared their

concerns of the movements of the enemy, I would like to give an account that has not yet been heard."

The room quieted down to give the floor to yet another. Creedus likewise returned to his seat with a look of knowing what was coming.

"It has been many years since the horror of war has raked our lands. Living within sight of the Black Mountain, and the waste that surrounds, I am one who is reminded everyday of the presence of evil. And so, I do not seek to minimize the occurrence of it. But . . ." Pausing, the gentleman shifted his weight, not in a manner of being nervous, but as if to set his feet. "If one man is stung by a hornet, should he expect his neighbor to go looking for the nest, risking the same sting for himself?"

"More than one man has been stung, brother Loyde," Creedus audibly replied.

As if expecting the answer, and to hear it from Creedus, Loyde continued, addressing the rest of the gathering. "And how many stings does it take to require that the nest be disturbed?"

As agreement and disagreement arose among them, Loyde raised his voice. "Won't prodding the bushes with a stick to find the nest only provoke fury; indeed, fury that may *not* have been in store?"

The jubilation that Corred had felt only moments ago at inspiring the room into fervent response dissipated among the voices of dissent. Feeling cheated, he looked from one man to another, searching for the conviction he thought they all shared. Lastly he looked to Einar, and then Creedus. His own feelings were reflected very clearly on their faces. Corred was not alone in his dismay.

Standing with Loyde, a younger fellow sitting among those from Shole and its surrounding region, joined the conversation. "I understand the stings, and the fear of the nest. But what I believe is more important than winning one side of this gathering to the other, is the realization that the strength of the Véran is one of unity in purpose." He spoke loudly, holding out his hands to ask for silence at the responses that were given in anticipation of his conclusion. "*If* we do anything divided, one side or the other will fail in their part."

"Which is why," Loyde bellowed, building his argument off of the younger man's wisdom, "an organized offensive of any kind is to beat the bushes with a stick, at the expense of our neighbors."

Like a tide, the room began to turn in Loyde's direction.

Creedus shifted in his seat angrily, but held his tongue. He knew that consensus could not be shouted into existence, and an offensive could not be a split decision. It was true, that a force divided would never succeed.

"Brothers, brothers," Loyde continued, feeling that his persuasion was quickly winning the evening, "my children and grandchildren have not known war. Before tonight, none of us had cause to believe that they might. In the western Lowlands, that is still the case. And having seen war . . ." Loyde slowed down, letting his years and wisdom weigh heavily on the men around him, "I *will* refuse to do anything to jeopardize our present peace."

"What of Lord Wellman's son?" a voice called out. "His death is not peace."

"I will mourn him, as will you," Loyde very quickly replied. "But while I do so, I will not do anything to bring similar loss to my family." He said it with deep emotion. "War in the

Lowlands means certain desolation of the villages near the Black Mountain. Without fail, we never escape Mornoc's fury and fire. If Wellman is in danger," Loyde said carefully, "Wellman is right to exercise extra caution to protect itself. But in so doing, I beg you not to stir the hornets' nest throughout the land." With that he held up his hands and sat down.

Once the room had been taken by debate for a while, Creedus stood and took the middle of the floor to bring the meeting back to attention. After a few turns, waiting for everyone to acknowledge his presence again, Creedus nodded in Loyde's direction. "Thank you, Loyde for your sincere words."

Knowing his stand was not unanimously supported, Creedus quickly declared the compromise. "Thank you all for your thoughts, your reports, and your concerns. Thank you, most of all, for being men of conviction and caring. As stated earlier, and it is true, we cannot take offensive action unless we are undivided in it."

Corred waited for his grandfather to put Loyde back in his place, and call for a renewed, organized vigilance. Moving to the edge of his seat, he waited anxiously for the one who carried the Sword to grab their attention again, and command them.

"Instead," Creedus said, "we will take action as we always do, each man at his post. It is true that we are not at war, but I believe we must better prepare ourselves and our people for it. For if it comes," Creedus said, looking over the room, "our enemy will be the architect of it. We will be the prey in his snare."

A sober air filled the hall, as this point was not in the least arguable.

"Go now," Creedus concluded, "return, each of you to his home and live differently in light of the attacks and signs of the times that warn us of ever-present evil. Live aware of all that has been shared tonight. Keep your eyes on the Promise, and keep your swords sharp." Bowing in respect of all who were in attendance, Creedus left the floor and proceeded to greet old friends, and make new ones of the next generation. Despite his evident disappointment, he did not lose the opportunity to encourage increased vigilance on a personal basis. Some stayed to further discuss the events of the night amongst themselves, but many wandered too quickly back out into the dark town.

Corred looked around, feeling that the meeting had ended too easily. *That's it? No plan of action to find out our enemy? Nothing?* He felt the same disappointment he could see in his grandfather's face. *What good was that?* He blushed, ashamed that the Véran had become a group of men who had lost sight of the imperative of their calling: to be vigilant not just in title, but in action. Einar's words about the comfort of men echoed over and over in his head.

Across the room from Corred, standing just outside of the chandelier's light, Remiel stood with his arms crossed in front of him. The smile he had been wearing when Corred had met him was gone. Replacing it was a look of serious contemplation as some of the men around him stood and left as silently as they had come. With one last look at Corred, Remiel pulled his hood down over his forehead and filtered out with the rest of the men around him.

*   *   *   *   *

Thin clouds drifted in front of the moon. The Véran had

long since returned to their beds for the night and all was quiet.

From the edge of the woods, across the fields, Wellman was being watched as it had been for weeks. Unknown and undetected, Casimir's scouts shifted in the shadows, watching and waiting for the opportune moment to strike; a serpent was indeed harboring its malice.

Selcor, leading the band of scouts, still had a mission to fulfill. The wound he had sustained from his first attempt was well wrapped and healing. His countenance was one unchanged, of hatred and determination. Letting out a light whistle, Selcor kept his eyes fixed on the edges of the town and the points of light scattered throughout it. When the other four scouts joined him from behind, he gave some last instructions.

"The old man is all that matters. We have lamps enough to light Casimir's halls. Creedus has an appointment with our lord, Mornoc."

Boldly leading them into the fields, Selcor's fast steps built into a jog and then became a run. Following a row of grass between the plowed fields, they approached a barn on the outskirts of town, keeping it between them and their target.

They ran in a tapered row with Selcor at the point like an arrow sent to its target. When he drew a spear from his pouch the others followed his example. When he picked up the speed even more, they kept pace.

As they reached the first houses, the light of the lanterns cast their shadows against the grass. Without a sound they swiftly flew through the streets.

Quickly coming to a halt, Selcor approached one of the cabin doors. Stepping aside he waved two of them to the door itself. Carefully, he lifted the guard from the lantern on the front step and set it aside. The lantern's flame grew taller and brighter in the slight breeze. Selcor licked his fingers and smothered the wick.

CHAPTER 13

Many miles west of Wellman, through the northern regions of the Bryn Mountains, beyond the Plains of Shole, lay the city of Shole itself. The largest of all the cities in the Lowlands, it was also the oldest, built by Homsoloc and his sons. Placed on an immense plateau, it overlooked the region around it for miles in all directions. It was a fortified city, originally built for the sole purpose of defense. Made of stone at its center, it had withstood sieges, fires, and the fiercest weather the Lowlands had ever seen. The rock wall that surrounded the city limits, standing four feet high, had witnessed it all. The architecture of Shole was like that of a large puzzle, as if its builders had more than once considered it incomplete. But with each passing decade it had grown larger, its citizens adding yet another section, slowly filling the plateau. Settlers now also inhabited the region surrounding its soft slopes to the north and the east.

Still further west, on the opposite side of an expansive

valley of wooded terrain stood the Black Mountain. It rose into the sky like a scar on the landscape. Once a flourishing wilderness, the woods immediately surrounding the mountain were now dead and colorless, like a pile of ashes in the midst of a healthy green field. The very mountain itself had died and hardened. On its peak and along its slopes lay the twisted forms of trees, like men left dead on a battlefield.

At the foot of the Black Mountain there stood a large gate, a lattice of long, sharp spears. For hundreds of years it had remained unchanged, maintaining the dark color of the ore from which it had been forged. Joining together an arching stone wall that ran to the north and south, the gate faced the city of Shole like bared teeth. The wall, standing ten feet tall and five feet thick, curved back toward the Black Mountain in the shape of a crescent, forming a large courtyard of dust, gravel and rock.

On the other end of the courtyard was a pair of guards, each armed with a large battle-axe, standing watch at the entrance of an enormous cave. They were soldiers of Mornoc set apart for their size and strength to be the guardians of the Black Mountain. They wore no helmet but had full heads of thick black hair pulled back from their eyes and tied behind their heads. A fierce, but stolid expression was written on their faces. The chain mail shirts they wore were impenetrable, heavier and thicker than any known to man. Even so, they seemed more ceremonial than anything, as these soldiers were not likely to lose a fight hand to hand.

The cave itself had a roughly hewn entrance, but the floor of it cut deep into the heart of the mountain like a well-worn road. Once the mouth of the cave and the light of day were lost from sight, pairs of torches were set in either side of the cave wall at intervals. Despite these lights to lead the way, it was an unearthly, suffocated place.

Like the main road to a hidden city, smaller tunnels branched off of it, leading to the far recesses of the mountain. Some of these passages were watched by an armed guard while others were merely marked by a lantern.

As the tunnel continued, in time, it gave way to several sets of stairs carved into the floor, leading to higher ground. At the top of these stairs the cave walls opened up into a great hall and the ceiling doubled its height. In this hall, an elaborate array of torches lined the inside of ten massive columns carved from the walls, five to the right and five to the left. On the opposite side of each column hung another lamp lighting the face of the walls and the entrances to yet more tunnels, running to more rooms within the mountain. In the center of the hall, three monstrous chandeliers hung from the ceiling, lighting the way to the far end.

There, with a king's court all to himself, Mornoc, the father of rebellion and pride, sat on his throne. Positioned against the far wall, facing east, it was cut from the stone floor. Its arms yielded to the shape of his grip and its seat and back to the posture of his body. The right arm of this throne was carved in the shape of a large hand, clenched in a fist. Resting in its grip was Mornoc's spear, over ten feet long and razor sharp.

The fine garments that would normally have adorned such a magnificent throne were instead carved into it; no ornament of cloth, gold, or jewel was present. Without a single crack or fissure, it displayed such decorations in its surface and structure. But it was colorless. Mornoc himself wore robes in shades of gray and black. Even his skin color was a dingy gray, and his bald head did not shine in the glow of the lamps. His face was worn, lined by centuries past, wrinkled by bitterness and a desire for revenge. His eyes were gray, cold, and piercing.

Staring at the other end of the hall and drumming his fingers on the arm of his throne, Mornoc wore a smug smile. His dirty nails clicked loudly in a slow and ominous rhythm. It was not joy or happiness that moved the corners of his mouth, but expectant malice. Content to remain silent in his hall, he was waiting, patiently waiting.

"One day soon. One day soon . . ." Mornoc whispered to himself. "I will have mine."

With these words he jumped down from his throne and began to pace back and forth. With both arms held behind him, his robes flowed loosely, barely touching the floor. Turning sharply at the base of one column, he headed back toward the other with a measured pace, following a clear path he had worn into the stone floor. And every time he turned he would look toward the entrance. The guards stationed there remained at attention, not daring to observe the movements of their lord.

Pausing, he brought a hand to his chin. Staring into the thin air in front of him, he muttered under his breath, "I will have mine."

He did not look upon the splendor of his hall or the size of the chandeliers above. His eyes were peeled on the one thing he had failed to attain so long ago. "I will have my own name, my own kingdom, my own . . ." His thoughts trailed off once again to a place he could not go. Scowling, he released his chin and clenched his fist. "I will have mine!" he said in a deep, suppressed yell. His words pulsed off of the rock walls. With a huff he returned to sitting on his throne and staring at the entrance to his hall.

No sooner had he resumed his place than someone ascended the last stair to enter the hall. He was head and shoulders above the guards that stood on either side of the entrance. They both remained at attention, not daring to block his path. With long strides this giant of a man slowed to a stop and dropped to one knee in the middle of the hall. There, carved carefully into the floor was a large signet with the sign of Mornoc at the center; a clenched fist, raised in defiance. With his hands extended outward, revealing the length and strength of his arms, the giant bowed with his face to the ground. After a short, reverent pause, he arose and continued across the hall. In front of the throne he stopped, adjusting his stance, and folded his arms behind his back. As he waited to be addressed he looked at the feet of his lord.

Apart from the gray cloak clasped around his neck, the giant was clothed from head to foot in the hides of animals. Under the light of the chandelier above, his short white hair shone brightly and his once youthful face was revealed. Though his appearance was more pleasing to the eye than that of his lord, his cheeks were scarred, as if burned by tears, and his countenance was just as cold. Standing at nearly eight feet, his size added weight to his already intimidating air.

"Sobieslaw, what news of war do you bring?" Mornoc asked. His voice filled the hall.

Sobieslaw smiled. "My lord, I have received word concerning Creedus. It is done."

Mornoc smiled and gazed into the distance once again. For a moment he paused, savoring the message. Standing up on the step of his throne, he took a deep breath. "So, the hour has come, and our silence has paid us well. The strongest of men has been subdued and with him the sword that has denied me my rightful rule."

"Yes, my lord. Scouts from the halls of Casimir visited his cabin last night as he slept," Sobieslaw continued. "I have also unexpectedly received word that many of the Véran are in Wellman. What would my lord have?"

Mornoc cocked his head at his captain's last comment. "Hmmm. The Véran, though leaderless for now, will find another to replace Creedus. But, it will not be enough. To begin, Wellman must fall, and it must fall hard." Mornoc paused and sat down in thought. With a furrowed brow he raised his voice. "Too long have these zealots refused me. They will die for their obstinacy." Mornoc slammed his fist on the arm of his throne in angry resolve. "Casimir shall be the first to move. He has shown himself worthy of such an honor. Crush Wellman and we will conquer east. We must strike every city before the first snow falls in the north."

"I will send word, my lord." Sobieslaw bowed low and turned to go.

"Sobieslaw, send word also to the spies," Mornoc added coolly. "Every leader that may oppose me must fall."

"It will be done," Sobieslaw answered over his shoulder with a deep voice. Spurred on by the call to arms, he quickened his stride when he reached the stair, and marched down the main hall to one of its many tunnels. There, under the engraving of his own name, Sobieslaw addressed his guard with authority. Taking one of the torches from above its door he disappeared down the tunnel.

The guard quickly carried out his orders. Marching as fast as he could without breaking into a run, he headed for the courtyard. He did not stop to inform anyone of his task. Only the sound of his steps could be heard through the cave, a hurried messenger's approach.

At the entrance to the cave, the guard slowed to share a few words with the guardians of the mountain concerning his mission. One of them immediately accompanied him through the courtyard to the gate. Using the head of his battle-axe as a tool, the guardian unlatched all ten of the gate's locks. He then rapped on the door three times as a signal to the guard on the opposite side. Leaning against one side of the gate with his full weight and strength, he was able with the help of the guard on the other side to open it enough to let Sobieslaw's messenger through. As soon as he let up his effort, the gate drifted back into place. With three more raps on the gate, the guardian methodically replaced all of the locks and returned to his post.

Along the path that led through the center of the courtyard were multiple large rocks laying to one side or the other. The guardian of the Black Mountain passed them by without a thought, for his daily view consisted of that same sullen ground that did not change for the wind. But hidden behind one of these rocks, a miracle was taking place. Just breaking the soil's gravel surface, a small green shoot labored to emerge, unfazed by its parched surroundings. For as long as the courtyard's walls and gate had been standing, no living thing had dwelt there. But the evil that had killed the mountain itself had not stopped this tiny plant from taking root; and it was growing.

*   *   *   *   *

"Einar!?" Corred burst through the cabin door. "My grandfather is gone!" Corred was out of breath and shaking with emotion.

Einar paused over the wash pail, hands full of water halfway to his face. "What do you mean?"

"My grandfather's door is open, and he's gone." Corred was pale with fright. "There is a spear driven into the center of his floor . . . with blood on it. The Sword is gone!"

Einar dropped the water from his hands back into the pail and rushed past Corred. Flying off the front step, he ran through the open door of Creedus' cabin. Sure enough, in the middle of the floor was a scout's spear, blood covering the blade, driven into the boards. Einar scanned the room. Creedus' cloak was still hanging on its peg, coals glowed faintly in the fireplace, and there were no signs of struggle beside. "No!" Einar compulsively yelled. "No!"

Walking slowly out of the cabin and into the street, Einar held his hands on his head, trying to contain his shock. The town around them had no idea the depth of tragedy that had struck them this time, again, in the dark of night. Scanning the town around him, trying to process what was happening, Einar looked back at Corred.

"My grandfather . . ." Corred said, staring above the houses around him to the horizons beyond. Tears welled up in his eyes. Drearily looking to Einar, he said very softly, in disbelief. "And the Sword . . . it's gone."

Einar let out a groan of disappointment that could not be expressed in words. Pulling his hands down over his face slowly, he began to pace about the street. Before he could gather any words of comfort for Corred, wrath for their enemy, or thoughts of response, the sound of horse's hooves broke his trance.

Remiel, coming from further in town, slowed to a stop when he saw Einar and Corred standing listless in the street.

"Is everything alright?" Naveed looked at them both sideways, as if he shared his rider's sense of concern. Steam billowed from his flared nostrils as he nervously began to back up, casting additional glances at Creedus' cabin.

Corred was slow to acknowledge him, looking up from his feet with tears streaming down his face. At first he could only mouth the words, but on his second attempt, he replied, quite simply, "My grandfather has been killed, taken . . . and the Sword with him."

Without hearing another word of explanation, Remiel jumped from Naveed's back and ran past Einar to see for himself.

"No!" Einar yelled again. Running his hands through his hair, he began pacing even faster in front of Creedus' cabin. "This can't be happening," he said. Casting repetitive glances at his young friend, Einar still had nothing to say.

Corred sat on the steps of his own cabin, his head spinning. The sun began to cut through the morning mist as his heart sank within him. The confidence he had gained the night before, over the last three days, was gone. He was empty, broken in a moment. *When will this end? Am I going to lose my whole family? Will everyone I've ever loved be killed right in front of me? This is too much for me.* Dark questions filled his mind, drowning out the light.

Remiel reappeared on the porch as Einar continued pacing the street. He quietly observed the loss that these two warriors were experiencing, and his heart broke with compassion. Removed enough from the shock, he acted first.

"I will try to call the others together before they all leave Wellman. This would not have been done unless Mornoc means war." There was no fear or panic in Remiel's voice, but rather, well-known urgency. Looking at Einar and Corred, who had only half acknowledged his offer, he raised his voice a bit more, "The time is coming," he said. "Einar, Corred!" He called their names to gain their attention.

Einar looked at him with confusion, blinking tears away from his eyes. "Who are you?" He shook his head, even more confused that a complete stranger was addressing him. "How do you know my name?"

"I am your friend," he said. With familiarity he offered words they had heard hundreds of times before, words they knew without thinking. "Do not mourn for what is passing or long for what you cannot keep . . ." He trailed off, looking back and forth from one to the other, searching them for a response.

Corred regained his composure and looked into the sky. With a cracked voice he recited what he had heard his grandfather say a thousand times. "But long for the day of your redemption, which is your hope and the Promise fulfilled." He knew it, but his heart was not in it.

Remiel nodded, clenching his jaw. "It's still true." Remounting Naveed in a hurry, he made for the center of town at full flight. He didn't speak a word along the way, but the sound of Naveed's pounding hooves was enough to finally stir those living on Creedus' street. Families filed out of their houses, some with a mouthful of breakfast, others from their beds. A few dared to grumble at the rude awakening, but most were rightly alarmed by it.

Corred watched him go, unable to move at first. Rising to his feet, not knowing what else to do, he felt weak. *I'm not fit for this fight. I can't do this. I'm not strong enough.* Corred wiped his eyes and loosened his grip on hope.

Einar walked past him and into the cabin with a deep scowl. His grief quickly turned to wrath. "This evil will not triumph while I have breath in my lungs!" he said as he forcefully belted on his sword. "Corred, your grandfather will be rescued, or he will be avenged. The Sword must be recovered. It can not fall into Mornoc's hands!" Shaking his head in disbelief he added, "We have been fools to let this happen, to think that the attack on Pedrig would be the only one! Mornoc has always wanted the Sword."

"What will we do?" Corred asked, following him back into the cabin to grab his own sword. "He could have been taken anywhere, if he is even alive."

"We will fight back!" Einar growled. "We will look for a blood trail, any trail!"

"But, we are leaderless, none of us have been to war, and I am not ready to become the next Creedus. I wouldn't be ready even with the Sword, and now it is gone!"

"With such thoughts filling your head, you certainly won't be," Einar replied. He stared Corred down with an intensity he could not help.

"I have no other thoughts to think!" Corred gasped. "I am not ready to lead! I am no Creedus."

Einar finished strapping on his dagger forcefully. "You are Corred, born into the line of Creedus. It is your destiny, and it has been your desire. Throw your fears aside; you do not have the luxury of them." Einar pointed out the door at the town that was beginning to stir with anxious inquiry. "They may fear. They have not kept their swords sharp, nor do they all care about the past and the future promise. Fear is a fetter, and we must take swift action. Throw your fears aside!" With that, Einar walked out the door, jumped off the cabin steps and ran

191

toward the town hall.

Corred still felt frozen. He wanted to follow, he wanted to run, but his feet were stuck to the ground. He felt sick. The very thing he had longed for his whole life, to be like his grandfather, lay before him, and he was entertaining cowardice.

Closing his eyes he took a deep breath and started out the door.

When he opened his eyes, he could see Lord Wellman's mansion in the distance and the window he had come to watch vigilantly the last several days. He remembered the feel of Olwen's arms around him as he returned her safely home. He remembered the look of fear in her eyes and the powerful desperation that he had felt as he ran across the field to where she struggled with the enemy. He remembered the weight of his sword in his hand. He remembered . . .

With each recounting he took another, stronger step.

The town bell sounded, ringing through the streets, filling the air.

Corred began to run.

*   *   *   *   *

Below Lake Tormalyn, at the southern end, was a watershed full of wildlife, known for its fishing and hunting. Further south, the overflow from Lake Tormalyn gathered into one source, the Southern River. The region surrounding it was especially good for hunting wild boar, a hunt traditionally relished by the royalty of the area, especially by Lord Raven. He was an avid boar hunter. With his finest mount and sharpest spear, he rode with three of his guard and Lowell.

The morning was young when they jumped their first boar.

A large male, it had been feeding heartily on the fallen acorns along the western bank. Much to his dismay, he was not the only one looking for food. The hounds flushed him from a thicket where he had hoped to be passed by, and the chase was on. With a squeal he headed for thicker brush but was continually cut off by the dogs, forced to run in the open woods.

In the dress of his own guard, Lord Raven took the lead. With a dignified air he pushed his horse to catch up with the dogs. When the boar came into view, he readied for a throw.

Lowell was close at his back, the only one in the group not dressed in the colors of Renken's guard. He was distracted from the hunt itself, but rather more concerned with the movements of his lord. His face was cold, expressionless.

Lord Raven stood high in his saddle and threw the javelin straight and true, but he over-threw his prey and narrowly missed one of the dogs.

"Lowell, your spear!" he said loudly.

Lowell quickly came along-side his lord and handed him his spear for another throw. This time Lord Raven drew closer for a better chance and pinned the boar to the ground.

"Excellent shot, my lord," the captain of his guard congratulated him on the kill. "Though not the largest I've seen in these woods, he will make quite a feast."

"Thank you, Emer. He certainly will." Lord Raven remained in his saddle as the other two guards in his party proceeded to dress the boar.

Where Lowell normally would have been complimenting Lord Raven's every move, he remained just behind him, observing the process in silence. There was evident tension in the air, and Lord Raven sensed it.

Backing his horse up a few steps, he addressed his counselor, "Lowell, you are very quiet today. Are you unaccustomed to the sight of blood?"

"On the contrary, I am quite used to it, sir," Lowell replied. "But, I have never seen a boar hunt, and I seek to learn as much as I can by watching."

Content with this answer, Lord Raven nodded and walked his horse in to get a better look. "How much does he weigh?"

"No less than 250 pounds, my lord," one of his guard replied.

"Even smaller than I thought," Lord Raven muttered to himself.

Emer was far less comfortable with Lowell's silence. He had been suspicious of him ever since he entered Lord Raven's hall months ago, and had made a point of watching him closely. He kept a firm grip on his spear and watched Lowell out of the corner of his eye. There was something different about him. He seemed more calm than usual, and it unnerved Emer. Though keeping his contempt hidden, he was distracted, not watching the other guards.

Lowell's eyes were fixed on Lord Raven's back as his right hand slowly made its way to the side of his saddle and his hunting knife.

Emer now made it clear that he was staring at Lowell, in hopes that it would intimidate his odd behavior. To his great alarm, Lowell pulled the knife while returning Emer's gaze with an air of defiance.

Before Emer could open his mouth Lowell threw it into the ground next to one of the other guard. "There; use my knife. It is made for such work," he said.

"Thank you, sir," the soldier replied with a smile. "This

should do the job," the guard said to his comrade. They had begun struggling with the boar's thick hide using the tools they had.

Emer looked back at Lowell, who was smiling at him haughtily. The captain of the guard had half a mind to challenge him to fisticuffs he was so angry. But, he held his tongue, unimpressed with Lowell's stature in the first place, thinking him a short, conniving man.

"Alright, let's be on our way, gentlemen," Lord Raven said.

At this Lowell reached to the other side of his saddle and this time drew a sword.

"My lord!" Emer cried lifting his javelin to intervene.

He was too late. Lowell lunged at Lord Raven as he turned to lead the group home. With little time to react, the blade pierced him in the side and he fell to the ground with a cry.

Emer threw his javelin, missing wide as Lowell had anticipated it.

Lowell next attacked the two guards on the ground, cutting down the guard he had given his hunting knife only a moment before. The other dashed for the base of the nearest tree.

Lord Raven lay helpless on the ground, disabled by his injury.

Emer drew his own sword and charged, cutting Lowell off before he could finish the job. With crushing blows he attacked the assassin, but Lowell was much stronger than he looked. Testing his skill, Emer found him a formidable match.

The third guard, who had run for shelter, retrieved Lowell's spear, which had been used to kill the boar. He charged from behind the tree to aid his captain.

Unable to defend against both, Lowell turned about to use Emer as a shield from his new attacker.

With deadly accuracy the guard on foot did not let him succeed. He timed his throw perfectly.

Pierced through, Lowell fell from his mount and died where he landed.

Emer jumped from his horse and ran to Lord Raven's side. "My lord, can you hear me!?"

"Yes, Emer. I hear you," Lord Raven responded, short of breath. He looked down at his wound and placed his hand over it. "How could I have been betrayed like this!?" Lord Raven's face had already turned quite pale.

"Calm yourself, my lord," Emer said. Turning to his remaining guard, he cried for his assistance. "Get him on my horse!"

Mounting his horse he pulled Lord Raven into the saddle in front of him with the help of his comrade. "Yah!" Without a second thought Emer charged through the woods on an errand of life and death. The sweat on his face felt cold in the wind as he navigated through the boughs of the trees. Bounding over brush and thistle, his steed pushed hard, feeling his master's urgency.

Lord Raven became heavier as his own hold on the horse's mane loosened. Through his groans of pain he tried to communicate his regret at being fooled by a traitor. "I should have listened to you Emer. You always said . . . he was trouble. I should have listened . . ."

Just as the city came into view, Lord Raven slumped over, unconscious.

"Yah!" Emer held him fast, pushing his horse as hard as he could run.

*   *   *   *   *

The halls of Casimir were well lit and filled with the coming of war. Several hundred scouts swarmed the tunnels, all headed for the surface and the light of the sun.

Each scout's pouch was full of spears and his pack of supplies filled to capacity. The day had arrived. Casimir himself led them out into the woods and north toward Wellman. He carried his club in one hand and pumped the other as he set the pace, his black hair flowing behind him. Eagerly answering the call to battle, his hate-filled, hardened heart drove him.

In a steady flow, they poured out the mouths of the cave, filling the woods, scattering wildlife in every direction. United for the first time, an army of scouts that had covered the whole region on foot for months set its course to make good on its work. They knew every strength and weakness of every town and village within thirty miles, and now the residents of those towns would pay dearly for their lack of vigilance, starting with Wellman.

Flying high above them were three black birds, each clutching a small parchment in its feet. Though their feet were large and their talons sharp, they were but crows. On the wind they flew together, side by side. When they had passed the head of the army below, they gave a harsh cry and separated, one flying east, one north, and one west. With speed unbecoming of their size, they carried word of the activities below to the other Malliths and their armies, still waiting for the moment that they too would be unleashed upon the Lowlands. By the end of the day they would receive word of the impending demise of Wellman and the beginning of war.

Mornoc would have his kingdom, whether by the free submission of its subjects or by the subjection of their wills and the annihilation of resistance. The later was preferred.

CHAPTER 14

As the sun began its descent, Wellman crawled with activity. At the center of it all were Einar, Corred, and now Remiel. No sign of Creedus' capture other than the bloody spear driven into his cabin floor were found. His attackers had not left tracks as they had when kidnapping Lord Wellman's children. So, with much grief and concern, it was agreed that Wellman's defenses should be the primary focus. Once the town was secure and ready to face an attack, scouting parties could begin hunting for Creedus and the Sword. Even so, they all knew it would be no better than hunting a mouse in a cornfield. There was no way to know where or how to begin.

Most of the Véran had left that morning before Creedus was found missing. Among those remaining were Bernd, Bjorn and Rickert from the Northern Villages, as well as the few that had come from the area surrounding Renken and Oak Knoll. Those that had come from Shole and Port had already begun their journeys home. With leadership from the thirty heads of

Véran still in Wellman, war-time preparations were under way. Another attack was believed to be imminent.

Watchmen were sent to the outskirts of the field and into the forests that surrounded Wellman in all directions. Each guard carried a horn and rode the fastest horse he could find. Beathan and Boyd were sent south of Wellman in the direction that they had pursued the enemy only days ago.

Corred helped to arm men and boys alike in the town square before Lord Wellman's mansion. Tristan assisted him in distributing the weapon store from his own house. With cuts on his face from his first encounter with the enemy, he boldly fitted his fellow man to fight with him if there was to be another.

The town of Wellman was indeed poorly equipped. Those that had kept their swords had reduced them to decorations, as if they were great relics of a past age. Many had melted and forged them into plows or other farming tools. Now there was no time to change what had been done. The best they could do was to sharpen their tools and wield them as weapons.

Armor was harder to find, having been repurposed more often than swords during decades of peace. A few breastplates were pulled down from the walls where they too had been decoration, and helmets were fewer than a couple dozen. Shields were scarcest of all, and were now being made with what materials were available. Every carpenter and blacksmith was put to work.

Einar organized a group of archers from those who were hunters and gave them posts around the edge of the town. Anyone who had skill with a sword was easily distinguished as they were few and far between. Young men who had insisted on playing with their father's old swords were now set apart on account of such childish dreaming and taught others what should never have been forgotten.

The air was heavy with tension and fear, but for the time being, purposeful urgency had won every mind in Wellman. There was much to do if they were to last a single battle. Tasks were assigned to every able body, and those of the Véran that had stayed the morning provided the leadership needed.

Remiel saw to it that every lamp was filled with oil, livestock were brought in from the surrounding fields, supplies were counted out and secured, windows were boarded up, and above all, hope was not lost. Always he carried himself with a confidence that was mysterious to Corred and the others, for he was a stranger to them all. He was suspected to be a spy by some because he had not come with any of the others from Shole, yet he was supposedly from that region. Einar was one of them. With a careful eye, he watched as Remiel took charge of his tasks.

Shortly after the town had received news of Creedus and begun organizing, Einar had pulled Corred aside and expressed his concern that Remiel's sudden arrival at Creedus' cabin was no coincidence. His misgivings only grew stronger when Corred told him of their meeting on the northern edge of town.

"We cannot be too careful," Einar said. "I know he has shown deep concern for the needs of Wellman and its people, but he may only be trying to gain our confidence. Anyone can speak as if they believe in the Promise, even make it sound good."

"I must admit, I know very little about him and have not met anyone that seems to be in his company," Corred said. "He may just be a loner from the edges of the Northern

Villages to the east."

"All the more reason to watch him carefully," Einar said. "It seems much of Port's ill influence comes from that region." Spotting Remiel's approach, Einar ceased his conversation. Patting Corred on his still healing shoulder, he winked at him, and returned to where several men were sharpening arrow heads.

Smiling as he approached, Remiel took notice of Einar's departure. "I hope I have been of some help today. If what we fear is true, and I am inclined to believe it is, we are doing the right thing to prepare for attack immediately."

If he is a spy of some kind, he is a well-disguised one, Corred thought. Corred offered a weak smile while Remiel rejoined him at the mansion with Naveed in tow. "I am glad you have remained with us, Remiel," Corred said sincerely. "You seem to have experience with these things."

Einar's suspicions were growing on Corred. *How is it that he arrived just as we found the spear?* Corred tried hard to hide his emotion. Part of him did thank Remiel for his sudden and selfless assistance, but the other wanted to question him.

"No more than you, my friend. Of this I am sure. What I do know is our enemy and his cruelty. He is capable of the greatest atrocities thinkable." Softening his voice as he watched the town's preparation, he added, "Mornoc seldom attacks half heartedly. In the past he has struck from all sides at once, many villages at a time."

Corred remained silent. A chill ran the full length of his spine. He thought of his sister Galena, his uncle Logen, aunt Shae, his cousin Garrin. He feared for them. With a long swallow he pushed back the anxiety that threatened to undermine his composure. *At least they should be well warned.* "I have sent word to Oak Knoll and Renken of the events of this morning. The riders should be returning shortly," Corred told Remiel. Though, it was more a matter of reminding himself, as he grasped for confidence in the role he was now trying to fill. He was a grandson of Creedus and the only one of his line both living and believing in the Promise. He was not only part of a remnant of those who believed in the Promise, but a remnant of his family.

"Good. They will be well able to prepare for what is coming," Remiel replied.

Corred observed his friend's countenance. Remiel looked to him exactly the same as he had when he first arrived at the well to water his horse two days prior: reserved, strong, and kind. Corred marveled that he was seemingly unshaken. *Only a stranger, unaware of the danger facing him could act this way. Or, he knows exactly what is happening. But why, if he were a villain would he tell me all this? He can't be.* Remiel seemed the very opposite.

A soft tap on his right arm startled him from his contemplation. Turning sharply he beheld Olwen, dressed in a white gown with her long brown braids tied high on her head. With a timid smile she curtsied.

"Olwen, I hope you are well." He bowed instinctively, though he wished to hold her more than respect her status.

"I am comforted to know that you are here to protect us." She looked him in the eye, searching his thoughts. In her hands she held a bundle wrapped in purple cloth.

"I regard it the highest of honors," Corred replied, staring into her green eyes. "If there is anything that you need, I will gladly see that you receive it." He broke his gaze as Olwen met it. He feared that his own boldness would betray his feelings completely.

"I wish only to give you a gift," she said. Un-wrapping the bundle, she presented him with a blade. It was a large knife, nearly unused, with a braided leather scabbard. "It belonged to my brother Pedrig, given to him by my father. He gave it to me only a year ago." She paused uncomfortably, looking at the blade and then at Corred. "I want you to have it."

Corred's eyes widened in surprise, "I cannot. It is sacred to you." Corred took a half step backward. "What would your father say?"

Remiel watched Olwen carefully without becoming an audience.

"My father has ordered our house to mourn for my brother no longer. We will celebrate his life for years to come, but we cannot dwell on his loss when our town is in danger of attack." Her lip quivered with emotion. Taking a step toward him, she held out the dagger. "I owe my life to you, and gladly give that which is dear to me, and mine to give." She looked into his eyes again, searching for approval. "It would honor my family if you would receive this gift." A tear rolled down her cheek. "It would honor me."

How can I refuse you? Taking the blade, Corred carefully strapped it onto his belt. Focusing again on Olwen, he held her hands. "I will honor your family by accepting this gift." Lowering his voice, he added, "I will honor you, beautiful, Olwen."

She blushed brightly, but left her hands in his, staring into his eyes. "And I want you to know," she said, her face turning more serious, "that my prayers are for you in your loss, and for your grandfather, as we must not lose hope for him."

Corred felt as if he would break apart. He had lost his greatest hero, and he was gaining the girl he loved at the same time. Corred wanted to believe her too, that there was hope for his grandfather. But he didn't. It was the Sword that they had come for, plain and simple. Without Creedus, the Véran would find another leader, but without the Sword, they no longer had the one weapon that had never failed them in battle against Mornoc's forces, the only weapon that could slay a Mallith.

Corred could barely mouth, "Thank you." The lump in his throat was unbearable. There was no sense in vocalizing his doubts. He had to appear strong, even if he wasn't. After a moment had passed, Corred let go.

Olwen realized they were being watched by some of those around them and withdrew a step. Nodding toward the knife on his belt, she said, "May it serve you well, and may you find strength for what lies ahead." With that she turned and retreated to her father's mansion.

With a last glance, Remiel smiled and went again to water Naveed at the well on the northern side of town.

Corred watched her go until she was out of sight, unaware that his interest was easily seen. Only once Olwen had slipped behind closed doors did he again concern himself with the tasks at hand. Though heavy inside, Corred felt as though there was a new spring in his step. Resting his right hand on the hilt of his new blade, he rejoined Tristan who was now busy outfitting an older gentleman and his young sons with swords and shields.

"How does the weight of it feel?" Corred asked the father, who was gripping the handle of one of the swords.

"A little heavy, I think," the man answered. His two younger sons were already testing their abilities with some short blades meant for boys such as themselves.

Corred pulled another sword from the few that remained

and compared it with the one the man held. Their blades were both rather dull but they held a sharp point.

The man timidly took the second blade and compared it with the first. He held one then the other, entirely unsure of what to think.

Tristan kept quiet and looked to Corred for a better opinion.

Corred watched the man's awkward assessment and spoke up, "If you were to be suddenly attacked at this moment by a man who wished to take the life of your boys, what would you do?"

The man was taken aback by the question and furrowed his brow as if offended at the notion. "I don't suppose I know exactly, but I do know it wouldn't be pretty for him." He raised his voice slightly and the color rose to his face at the mere thought. With little more consideration he handed the second sword back. "This one will do just fine" he said, raising the first in an awkward salute. It suddenly appeared much lighter in his grip.

"I would agree," Corred said with a nod and smile. "When it comes to it, it's the man holding the sword, not the weapon itself."

The man called his sons and led them home with their new found, dangerous toys.

Together they joined the rest of the town in finishing preparations for nightfall. Every home needed to be ready and every man braced for what he could only imagine was coming.

Corred turned his attention again to the town square to observe the preparations. From amongst all of the activity something caught his attention. Cautiously stepping from between two cabins and into the open of the square, a hefty fellow looked around curiously. His expression was one of confusion, or disbelief, as if he were lost.

I know that face. I don't believe it . . . "Garrin!? Over here!" Corred ran to meet his cousin.

At the sound of his name Garrin awoke as from a stupor. Turning to see his younger cousin running toward him, his face turned bright red. He looked at the ground and then at a woman nearby who noticed the commotion.

"Garrin, did you meet a messenger on the road?" Corred stopped suddenly before him, seeing that he was upset, and for good reason. Softening his voice, Corred extended his hand. "Thank you for coming. How are your parents? How is Galena?" he asked.

"They are preparing for war. It was a blow to the whole town to learn the news of our grandfather." Garrin's voice was weak. "Corred, am I such a fool that it would take this for me to give up my doubts?" He looked in Corred's eyes, pleading with him. His eyes were bloodshot from crying.

Corred drew a step closer and put a hand on Garrin's shoulder. Fighting his own grief, he forced a smile. "Do not be so hard on yourself. Be thankful that our grandfather stood for something so great that he was willing to die for it." He was now crying as well, blinking away the tears to focus on his cousin. "He would be proud beyond words that you are here." With that he could speak no more and embraced his cousin freely.

In their younger years they had been like brothers. As they grew older, it was not a difference of opinion, but rather, a difference of conviction that had divided them. In a family where failed expectations were more common than unity, they finally saw eye to eye in an hour of crisis. They had both always loved their grandfather, and now Garrin was beginning to understand how much.

*   *   *   *   *

As the sun slowly set in the west, Boyd and Beathan kept watch. The woods were cast with rays of sunlight, cutting through their view from the side as they watched the southern borders surrounding Wellman. Any shift in the breeze sent the beams dancing across the forest floor, playing with the shadows. The birds were singing as they usually did in the evening, and a pair of squirrels chased each other over fallen branches through the maze of underbrush.

This was unlike any hunt they had been on before. Their senses were not directed toward detecting the arrival of life, but the coming of death. As first defense, Wellman now depended on their keen eyesight as never before.

Beathan could see Boyd several hundred yards away on the first of many ridges that grew to be the Bryn Mountains. His horn hung at his side, waiting to be used. Both of them were on foot, having left their mounts tied a few trees away. They too waited patiently for action.

With little to do but wait and watch, they scanned the forest in every direction. Every movement was analyzed and the source of it identified. Beathan did not have an arrow on his string as he had earlier. After a full day of vigilance, he was feeling the fatigue of readiness. His bow lay on the ground within reach. His will to act had relaxed and he was becoming increasingly aware of his need for sleep.

A check to his attentiveness arrived in a flash. Moving toward him from the opposite ridge, a large brown shape passed between two trees. There was no sound that accompanied its movement. In the fading light Beathan could not make it out through the trees. In one quick motion he picked up his bow, drew an arrow, and sought to relocate the movement. A large winged creature was flying through the woods at an alarming speed, headed right for him. Beathan froze with fear and awe as the magnificent creature, with one powerful flap of its wings, passed over him no more than twenty feet away. A flash of red and brown caught his eye as the creature vanished on the other side of the ridge. "Wow," Beathan said under his breath.

His mount gave a snort, shifting about where he was loosely tied to the lowest branch of a tall ash tree. Beathan escaped his state of wonderment just enough to whisper a few words of reassurance to his horse, eyes riveted back toward Wellman to catch one more glimpse. Having been stirred from his rigid watch by the creature's sudden appearance, Beathan realized his hunger. From his pack on the ground next to him, he made a meager meal of some crusted bread. With his water half raised to wash it down, he paused. The birds had stopped singing; it was silent. Crouching down to get a better look at the opposite hill through the trees, Beathan held his breath.

Breaching the crest, running straight for him was a tide of scouts numbering in the hundreds; they moved through the woods with frightening agility and speed. Beathan cast a quick glance at Boyd who was already mounting his horse.

Tossing his water skin over his shoulder Beathan stashed his arrow, tucked his bow behind his quiver and lifted the horn to his lips. Letting loose a long hard blow he ran to his horse which was now pulling on his reins, eyes wide, ears pressed against his head. It let out a disturbed whinny, shivering with anticipation of the coming danger.

Without looking back, Beathan jumped into his saddle and flew down the hill toward Wellman, blowing his horn the whole way. Dodging low branches and jumping underbrush, he tore up one of the thin roads that led out of the Bryn Mountains. Several hundred yards away, Boyd's horn bellowed loudly, echoing through the trees.

Urging his horse on, Beathan strained to see the end of the woods. Hugging his horse's mane, he blinked away a tear as the wind whipped him in the face; every hundred yards or so he lifted his horn to his lips.

At last the fields came into view. With one last sound of his horn Beathan broke from the shade of the forest into the last rays of daylight. Racing across the southern fields, he joined Boyd. Riders from all directions retreated from their posts with the wind on their heels.

Waiting to meet them at the edge of town were Corred and Remiel, standing in front of a barricade constructed of two wagons laid on their sides. Before they could ask, Beathan called out the report.

"Hundreds of scouts, maybe thousands, are headed this way. They are on foot, but moving fast. I have never seen anything like it in all my life." Beathan's horse turned about anxiously as he yelled the news.

Boyd likewise tried to calm his horse, which refused to believe he was yet safe.

"And night is falling," Corred said with a deep breath. "There will be no rest tonight. Are they coming directly from the south?" he asked them both.

Beathan answered first. "Directly from the south, though I doubt they will attack from one point. They may even outnumber us."

Remiel spoke up. "Go through the town and warn the women and children to take cover. Be sure that they have plenty of water. Tell the men to take their positions."

Corred looked at Remiel with widened eyes. "Do you think they aim to burn the town?" he asked.

"How would you besiege a town at night?" Remiel asked plainly. "Fire will send us into panic, distracting us from the fight."

Einar looked on from behind, his face reflecting his agreement.

Corred nodded. "You're right." Noticing Remiel had only his sword, he asked, "Do you have a shield to use?"

"No. My sword will be enough," Remiel replied.

Corred returned to his cabin to retrieve his own shield. *How can he still be so calm? No shield? I just hope he's not a fool.*

All around him the town was in a flurry. Some of the young children were crying, afraid of what they did not understand as their mothers hurried them inside. Older children helped in final preparations of securing their homes, wide-eyed and unsure of what to think. The men were gathering in the streets with their older sons as the heads of Véran had instructed them.

Remiel remained at the edge of town, watching the southern border, patiently.

CHAPTER 15

Just inside the woods to the south of town, Casimir stood tall with club in hand as Wellman fell under the dark of night. A malicious grin wrinkled his scarred face, revealing several of his bent teeth. With an army spread behind him and on either side, he waited for the glow on the western horizon to fully fade.

His scouts rested from the day's run while orders were given. With a leader for each task, the plan of attack was laid out in detail. Among those taking the lead were scouts who carried not only pouches of spears, but also large earthen vessels over their shoulders. Several fires were burning, with more being lit every minute.

Returning from where he had been addressing a group of scouts, Selcor approached Casimir and stood at his right hand. With his eyes fixed also on the growing lights of the town, he reported to his captain, "Your army awaits your command, my lord."

Casimir smiled even wider. "Very well; you will lead the attack on the northern side." Turning to Selcor, he added, "Bring me honor, soldier of Mornoc." With that he turned to face the army that filled the woods behind him.

Selcor called his fellow scouts to attention, "Hail your Mallith!"

In a quick shift of feet on the forest floor, all came to attention and lifted a spear in salute.

After a moment of deafening silence, Casimir quickly raised one of his own spears, longer and larger than any other present. "Our time has come!" he yelled. "Those who once despised you will now fear you. Light your torches, soldiers of Mornoc, and let them hear you!"

*   *   *   *   *

The whole of Wellman turned in unison and looked to the south. Every person with ears to hear heard the roar of voices from across the southern fields. Conversations died, men stopped in their tracks, dogs barked, and young children held tightly to their mothers' legs.

Remiel remained where he was, leaning on one of the wheels of the overturned wagons. Clenching his jaw, he squinted to see the source.

Corred rejoined him where he stood with a thick wooden shield in his left hand.

Garrin was right behind him. With a huge broad sword and a crude metal shield, he looked around nervously, trying to make sense of the moment. A man who had only hours ago acknowledged that he had an enemy, he now found himself immersed in the reality which he had so long denied. The battle cries in the distance sent adrenaline pulsing through his core, awakening in him a fearful and desperate resolve.

For as long as a minute the cries kept up, rising and falling in volume. At first its source could not be seen, but in time, the woods began to glow, growing brighter, until it appeared as if the trees themselves were on fire.

"Here they come," Remiel said quietly.

The bright glow slowly began to disperse along the edges of the woods and fan out into the field. In the areas of highest intensity, dark shapes could be seen walking to and fro, all the while advancing on the town. Their intentions soon became clear as they advanced to surround Wellman in a sea of torches.

Garrin could do little but stare at the scene in wonder. He had never imagined such an army existed. His huge arms felt weak for the first time in his life.

"They are going to burn us!" Corred exclaimed.

"The town will be ready." Remiel turned to his new friend and looked him in the eye. "Remember, Corred, your fear is their strength."

Corred met his gaze and nodded, his confidence strengthened. "I am going to the northern side. Will you remain here?" Corred asked.

"I will. This is the post that Einar marked for me. Go and show our enemies that true hope cannot be crushed." Remiel placed his hand on Corred's shoulder. "I will see you when the sun rises."

Before going, Corred shook Garrin's arm. "Stay close to Remiel. He will fight with you."

Garrin nodded, looking back at Remiel, yet another stranger he was going to depend on in a life and death struggle.

Corred ran through the town calling to the first people he saw, "Draw water and wet your roof tops! Fill every bucket you own, they are coming."

Snapping from a state of shock, Wellman began to take action. Every able hand lent itself to gathering water from the wells that were scattered throughout the town.

Confirming for the citizens of Wellman what they had feared all day, Corred ran through the town toward the northern side, shouting orders.

He stopped to help a young boy carry a large bucket of water across the street. Too young to face the battle, he would still not be spared; the defense of Wellman had come to rest on him as with everyone else. Starting at Corred's presence, he quickly trusted and spoke his mind as only young children will, "Sir, is it true that bad men are coming to burn our town, the same men who killed Lord Wellman's son?" His voice trembled as he fought back tears.

Corred stopped him in his tracks and knelt to the boy's level to gain his full attention. "No enemy will ever harm this town while I am alive, and no one will harm you if these men can stop it." Corred pointed to a group of men with swords at their sides, several of them members of the Véran. "Stand fast, little friend, for we will all be tested, but we must prove true." With that he patted him on the back and picked the bucket back up. "Come; let's show bad men what good men can do."

More important than his orders, Corred carried himself with an air of confidence that he did not possess. Surprised at his own words, he saw the effect of his determination. People nodded when they saw him, as if to say, "We will follow you."

Pushing on toward the center of town, Corred avoided the flurry of people at the well in the middle of the square. He met

Tristan on the mansion steps where he stood frozen, overwhelmed. Even from the center of Wellman, the lights in the distance, now surrounding the town in every direction, shone brightly. The enemy was advancing quickly.

"Tristan, come with me. I am going to the northern side; we will need your help!" Corred beckoned him forth.

Lord Wellman opened the doors of the mansion just as Corred was calling Tristan out. He was fit for battle from head to toe. "Corred, it is I who will join you on the northern side. Tristan, stay and lead the house in doing what is necessary." With his spear and sword he descended the stairs. "Show me where I may best avenge the death of my son and show our enemy who he has offended."

"Yes, my lord." *I can't believe I am leading him!* Corred led the way, running around the mansion. With a quick glance at the windows above, he sped on through the cabins that spotted the northern part of Wellman.

The homes were all dark and the windows boarded as women and children had retreated further toward the center of town with the first sounding of the horn.

Corred and Lord Wellman joined a line of defense on the northern side of the town just as the torches were meeting together from east and west. The road was still being barricaded with an assortment of carts and wagons, and on the roofs of the houses along the edge of town several archers stood post, arrows knocked.

With every opportunity Corred spoke words of encouragement and support to those who would receive it, but it was the sight of Lord Wellman with his sword on his belt that lifted their spirits the most; they would follow their leader. Lord Wellman was among the few who had ever seen a battle of any kind, and that when he was a young boy.

If there had been anyone with something of value to say they would have spoken up, but in the presence of a leader who had lost his eldest son and now led them in defending their town against a superior foe, silent respect prevailed. Lord Wellman faced them all and nodded. "Men of Wellman, it is my privilege to stand with you in this dark hour."

* * * * *

Standing three hundred yards out, the scouts stopped their advance on Wellman. Each with a lit torch, they stood side by side, waiting for the command to charge. Some itched in their shoes, others stared at the town in awe that such a moment had actually come.

In an awkward moment of silence, each side of the battle beheld the other.

The occasional voice from Wellman could be heard, urging the haste of some preparation. The lamps burned brightly as they always did, and the chimneys smoked just the same, but this was an evening the likes of which Wellman had not seen in a hundred years.

Selcor stepped out from the line toward Wellman and drew a spear from his pouch. Once every scout in the line had followed suit, Selcor began a slow march toward the town. On all four sides of Wellman, a distinguished scout from among Casimir's men led the horde, inching closer.

As if allowing Wellman the chance to feel the tightening of the noose around its neck, they quietly approached. Each with a torch and the point of his spear directed at its target, they descended upon their prey. The smell of burning oil filled the air.

At two hundred yards out, Selcor fell to a run. The flame of his torch licked the air fiercely but did not lose any of its strength. Falling in behind him, Casimir's army charged Wellman.

At 100 yards, Selcor and the other three leaders dipped the heads of their spears into the flame of their torches. Having been soaked in oil, the blades caught fire instantly. Each scout did the same in step.

Within range of the archers on Wellman's roof tops, the four leaders of Casimir's army released their spears into the air. Each fell sharply from the sky and struck the ground at the entrances to Wellman along each of its four main roads. The flame quickly climbed the shaft, burning brightly.

Everyone who had seen it stared for a moment at the burning spear before them. It was only a taste of what would come next.

"Take cover!" Lord Wellman yelled.

Everyone who had a shield held it aloft.

A barrage of flaming darts hung for a moment before descending on the edges of Wellman like a thousand shooting stars. With a hiss they struck everything in sight, peppering the rooftops. Homes began to catch fire before any defense could be raised. An archer to Corred's left was hit directly and fell to the ground dead.

As a second flock of burning darts filled the air from closer range, the archers opened fire. Cries of wounded men could be heard approaching the edge of town. The ring of torches was almost on top of them.

"Stand your ground!" Lord Wellman cried. He was on his feet with his broad shield held high and his spear ready for its first victim.

One man lost his nerve and fled into Wellman, only to be brought to the ground by a falling spear. In a matter of seconds, Wellman's outer ring was littered with fire. Some of the homes whose roofs had not been soaked in time were already becoming enveloped in flames.

"Do not let them take this town, men of Wellman!" Lord Wellman ran forward and drove his spear through the first scout that reached the mouth of the northern road. With a cry of rage, he left it and drew his sword, running to meet the invading army head on.

Corred was right behind him. With full knowledge of the odds they faced, several others followed them to meet the enemy at the poorly constructed barricade. Just as Lord Wellman reached the wagons, more than twenty scouts descended upon them. Arrows from the left and right caught several of them in stride, bringing them down, but the numbers were hardly evened.

With shields guarding their torsos, they met and deflected most of the spears that flew their direction. Some were too slow to react and fell to the ground with black shafts protruding from some part of their bodies.

"Ahhhh!" Lord Wellman knocked away one scout's spear with a swing of his sword and ran him through. Absorbing another close range assault with his thick shield, he struck down another.

Corred had as many to fight without having to take another step. Unable to see his enemies well, he swung at everything that carried a torch. Hacking, slicing, and jabbing his way through the tangle, the rush of adrenaline drove his movements. His attacks were almost as unexpected to himself as they were to the enemy.

In an instant, five scouts lay dead around him. Two spears that he had defended against were now so deeply lodged in his shield that they were but inches from his chest. Forced to hold his shield further from his body, so as to avoid the razor sharp points, he felt his senses sharpen all the more as yet another spear zipped past his head. With all the speed he could produce, he spun around, lowered to one knee, and jabbed where he fully expected his next attacker to be. Finding the scout out of reach, he had just enough time to react before a second spear was thrown. Leaning to the side and slicing the air he deflected the blow, sending the weapon end over end into the dark field behind him.

Staring at each other for the briefest moment, neither Corred nor the scout continued the fight. The scout moved first, rolling to his right, determined to make an end of his opponent from a safe distance.

Matching the movements of his attacker, Corred, shifted to his right so as to remain on the other side of the invisible ring in which they now competed. Reaching for yet another spear from his large quiver, the limber scout did not hurry to take another shot at Corred, but rather waited, as if determined not to make the first move.

Anxious now to close the distance between them, which would very soon be a disadvantage, Corred feigned a charge. To his surprise the scout backed up and nearly tripped over a broken shield. It was the chance he needed. With a few quick steps, Corred moved in. To his dismay the scout was not only ready for him, but took hold of one of the spears protruding from his shield. With a violent thrust, the scout attempted to drive the spear further through the shield and into Corred's ribs.

Turning away from his shield as quickly as he could, Corred narrowly escaped the tactic. Instinctively he broke the shaft of the spear with the base of his blade. The defensive move pulled his enemy off balance. Seeing this, Corred twisted the shield upward with all his strength and attacked from underneath, stabbing at the scout's midsection with the full length of his arm. A feeling of subtle resistance met his blade as he pierced him through.

The scout went rigid where he stood, his own spear halfway to Corred's neck.

Corred pulled his sword out and backed away, unsure if the fight would really be over.

A tremor ran the full length of the scout's body, but he did not make a sound. Even in the dark, Corred could see his face contort with pain as he crumpled to the ground, breathing his last.

Corred shuddered. The sounds of struggle all around him returned, as did his own urgency to survive. Breaking the shaft of the other spear that still protruded from his wooden shield, Corred sought to regain his bearings, unsure of what to do next.

With the ferocity of cornered animals, the men of Wellman's outer ring fought for their lives. Cries filled the air, warning the next line of defense to make ready, lest they too be swallowed.

Seeing an elderly gentleman singled out and under attack by two scouts, Corred found his next fight. One was jabbing and slicing at the villager with a spear while the other stepped away and sought to attack the man from the other side. His black dart was raised, ready to bring the old man down.

Corred loosening his grip on the straps of his shield, took a step toward the fight and swung his arm around from the side. Halting his movement short, he straightened his arm as best he could. The shield left his arm and became a weapon. To his dismay, the shield sailed just wide of the second scout's head, but it startled him enough that he turned to defend himself. Seeing that Corred was actually still fifteen feet away, the scout smiled slightly as he pulled back his spear to throw.

Regretting his decision to throw away his best defense, Corred felt the panic in his mind begin to take over.

With a quick snap of his arm, the scout sent his spear straight at Corred's heart.

"Ahhhhh!" Half closing his eyes Corred sliced the air and spun sideways in an attempt to make himself as thin as possible.

The spear missed Corred's left shoulder by less than an inch, the fletching of the weapon brushing his shirt. He opened his eyes again just in time to see Lord Wellman knock the scout on the back of the head with his shield, before finishing him off with his sword. With a rage that stunned Corred, Lord Wellman then assailed the second scout, cutting the spear from his hand. With a savage yell, he dispatched the scout with a single cut from his shoulder to his hip. Turning toward the next scout, Lord Wellman drove him through the street.

Seeing their leader gain the upper hand, those still standing rallied to him. Corred chased after them, not wanting to be caught alone again in a fight he could not win. Retrieving his shield from among the fallen, he slipped his arm back through the straps. Something warm and moist had soiled them both, and now covered his sleeve, wetting the back of his hand. He instinctively paused, straining to see what it was, but he knew.

Nausea stirred his stomach. All at once he realized the wet slick feeling of blood further up his arm, and on his neck. *I'm covered in their blood.* Gripping the straps even harder, he shut out the horror of death around him. *I've got to get back to the center of town! Olwen.* Just her name made him quicken his pace.

Most of the scouts had already run straight through the defenses, avoiding the fight altogether to carry out their raid deeper into the town. Emptying their pouches of all but a few precious spears, they threw their torches against a cabin or store of feed and resumed the attack. Many penetrated far enough into Wellman that they found themselves surrounded. Some were killed, but most escaped to fight on, knowing the layout of the town almost as well as its inhabitants.

The most serious damage was done in a matter of minutes as the people of Wellman frantically scrambled to save their homes in the middle of a battle. Water lines were formed by those not caught in the midst of the bitter fighting, dousing the fiercest flames first; some homes burned so violently that they were beyond saving.

In the midst of the ensuing chaos, Casimir's scouts did not quickly withdraw. Just when it appeared that the enemy had gone and efforts to fight Wellman's fires became organized, another scout would attack and raise the alarm.

While standing guard at a large cabin that was on the verge of being saved, Corred saw a scout run out from behind the flames. Before he could open his mouth, the scout pierced a man through, even as he threw water at the base of the flames.

"Catch him," Corred yelled. Burning with anger, he gave chase before he knew whether anyone had joined him.

"Stop and fight me you coward," Corred yelled uncontrollably. Though out of breathe he forced the insults out at a high pitched scream. "Fight me, you spineless weakling!"

The insults worked. Much to Corred's surprise, even as the scout was beginning to pull away, he skidded to a stop before rounding a cabin. Turning where he stood, the scout hurled a dart with the full force of his body behind it.

Corred had no time to dodge as its speed was fatal, but by fortune it sailed wide. He felt its wind as it passed his face, flinching only after it had gone.

The scout slowly pulled a second spear and waited as Corred continued to charge him. Stepping just around the corner of the cabin and out of the moonlight, he waited for his pursuer to come into his line of sight again.

Corred rolled to his left and hugged his shoulder to the front of the cabin, suspecting the scout's intentions. He reached for the hunting knife Olwen had given him the day before. Switching his sword to his left hand and the hunting knife to his right, he spun around the cabin only a moment after he would have arrived if he'd kept running the same line as the scout had anticipated. Lowering his attack only a little, he chopped where he expected the scout's head would be and stabbed a foot below that with his hunting knife. Both weapons struck wood.

The scout, who had backed away just far enough to avoid Corred's blades, jumped at Corred's fierce strike. The scout released his next dart prematurely and it struck the side of the cabin, remaining there. In a flash he turned to run again.

Having the hunting knife in his right hand, Corred felt the weight of it. Without a second's hesitation, he threw it after the scout. It rotated evenly and the blade sunk between the scout's shoulder blades.

With a shriek he fell forward and slid along the ground, limp from head to foot.

Corred approached the scout cautiously, afraid it was a trick. Not a sound came from his enemy as he lay on the ground. Running him through to be sure brought no response. With a quick pull, his hunting knife came out of the wound with a sickening crunch. *I hit his spine.* Corred gagged. Wiping the blade off on the ground as best he could, he quickly made his way back to where the chase had begun. The cabin had been saved, but it was terribly damaged and it was only one of nearly a hundred that had caught fire.

Many homes, stables, and storehouses were lost. Fires burned through the night, with very few targets saved. Not a soul rested. Families were scattered from one end of the town to the other, as fathers and mothers tried desperately to protect their children from attack, even as they lost their homes.

It was approaching morning before the last scout fled Wellman.

As light began to gather on the horizon, Lord Wellman was helped back to his mansion bleeding and faint from his efforts. Corred too had received his share of cuts and bruises. Not a single man on the outer ring was left unharmed. When the last scout was struck down by an archer and killed, Corred sheathed his sword with heavy hands and fell to his knees, exhausted.

The southern side of the town had sustained the greatest damage and the largest loss. Remiel, Beathan, Boyd and Garrin were among the few still standing. Most around them had been killed, wounded, or had fled to the center of town. With a few helping hands, they quickly went about covering the dead before the sun came up; wives and children would again be entering the streets.

Casualties had not been confined to the men. During the night women and children became victims to those scouts who had frequented the town most over the past months. So familiar with Wellman from their nightly visits, they knew the fastest way in and out and exactly where to place their torches. The results were devastating. Livestock too were not spared, rendering many families homeless and without the animals that they depended on daily.

Wellman had not been crushed, but it had been badly crippled and would not sustain another night of such fury. Unfortunately for the town, it was only the beginning. Cries of despair could be heard as much of what had happened was being discovered in the light.

Corred slowly made his way back to the center of town to meet the other heads of Véran. Reaching the mansion steps before any of the others, he sat heavily and observed the billows of smoke that filled the air around him. To the south there were still fires burning, consuming the remains of what was no longer worth saving. The town was much like his clothes: torn and covered with sweat, blood and smoke. His mind was numb from the horror around him.

When he heard the door of the mansion opening, he quickly rose to his feet.

Olwen looked out, unsure of whether it was safe; her brunette braids hung over her shoulders as her wide eyes searched the landscape. When she saw Corred, her face changed from apprehension to one of relief. The hesitancy she had shown only a day before in expressing her affection was now tossed to the wind. She ran to him and embraced him.

Corred held her tightly. Shutting out the pain and agony

around him, he simply listened to the rise and fall of her breath as she cried softly. No words were spoken, for there were none that could do justice. Worlds had collided, destroying the peace they had known all their lives.

Looking beyond Corred's shoulder to where the sun was only beginning to glow on the horizon, Olwen broke the silence. "Is there really a place with no darkness and death?" she asked softly.

Corred held her at arm's length and looked into her green eyes. "There is such a place, Olwen. There are nights, but they are not dark like here. Even the nights are full of light." He wiped a tear from her cheek. "Now more than ever, you must believe it."

As members of the Véran began to arrive, Corred slowly let Olwen go and descended the stairs to meet them. She remained on the steps, watching as a tattered crowd came from all directions, assembling before the mansion.

They were in the lowest of spirits. One man still held a broken sword in his hand. Looking at it helplessly, he sheathed what was left and folded his arms, not caring to wipe the blood from his face. Garrin too emerged from the smoke in one piece. His shield was cracked through the middle but still strapped to his arm. In shock from all that he had seen and done, he stuck his sword in the dirt at his feet and let his shield hang loosely at his side.

"What is the report of the western side?" Corred asked heavily.

Einar stepped forward, cradling his left arm. "We have lost almost all of our defenses on the outer ring and even those that are left are injured. Most homes are destroyed beyond use, if not burnt to the ground." Einar's shoulders hung low and he stared at the ground, forlorn.

Corred looked at him, but he would not make eye contact.

"What of the eastern side?" Corred asked.

Bjorn spoke up first. "We have fared only a little better. With half our men either killed or injured too badly to fight on, we will be in a desperate place if we are attacked again." He was uninjured but deep discouragement showed on his face.

Corred again paused to look the group over, reading for any sign of hope at all. Speaking up he gave a report of his own. "On the northern side, we saw and felt the same as all of you. We lost a lot of good men. Lord Wellman is in his house being cared for after fainting on the field of battle. We fought hard. Though most of the houses around us were destroyed, we did not give up until every last scout had fled or was killed." Corred paused to shift his weight, wincing slightly at his bruises. "If my grandfather were with us, I know that he would be proud. I also know that he would not despair, even after a night such as this, because we fight with faith." Corred raised his voice and pointed to the south. "They have no hope! They cling to nothing but hate. They are the ones who have despaired, not willing to hope for redemption and a better life." Corred looked from one man to the other, seeking to gain an audience.

Tristan joined his sister on the steps of the mansion.

"Will you let such men deny you that which you have hoped for, longed for, waited for your entire lives? The very thing your fathers and their fathers longed for? And your children, will they have the chance to return to Amilum?" Corred became increasingly animated as he continued, raising his voice even louder. "Let them come and do their worst, for I will either fight until I am saved, or die defending what cannot be taken from me." Corred paused and let his message sink in with his comrades.

Corred's passion brought a smile to Remiel's face. As he listened he watched those around him, assessing their spirits. At the same time, he watched the sky as it grew steadily brighter.

"Now . . ." Corred said with a commanding tone, "who will ride to warn Oak Knoll, Renken, and the Northern Villages? There will be scouts placed along our borders to oppose you, but our friends and family must know what is happening, lest the same fate overcome them."

From among them three young men quickly stepped forward, weapons in hand.

*   *   *   *   *

Casimir stood in the southern fields, watching the smoke rise into the sky. He had not joined the attack the night before but waited in the southern fields proudly, watching the progress of his army. In a little while he would have his way with the town; he personally would deal the crushing blow.

Selcor and several other scouts gave report to their captain, gaining a smile and a nod of approval with every word. Casualties among his scouts had been few, and the damage dealt had been even greater than he had hoped for. Victory was certain; Wellman was a prize for the picking.

While the army recovered in the woods to the south of Wellman, Casimir remained in the open, studying his prey. He had scarcely moved since the night before. Occasionally he leaned on his club, but more often he held it by his side, feeling its weight in his hand.

After Selcor had waited some time for his next order, Casimir addressed him. "When you have regained your strength, prepare my army to attack again. This time, I will lead the way."

Selcor bowed humbly. "Yes, my lord. As you wish." His humility was a façade; no scout respected his leader. They could not kill him, and any resistance to his authority was dealt with harshly, thus a status quo was maintained. It was fear and hatred that held them together and in submission.

Selcor thought only of his victory over Creedus. Having claimed the leader of the Véran, he had been filled only with a greater thirst to take or destroy what he did not have. He was now completely given over to his hatred; the bitterness of his heart was turning him colder by the day, but he did not feel his own life leaving him.

Joining a group of scouts, he ate some of the dried meat that they had brought for the campaign. Grinding it harder than necessary, he washed it down with some of the crude ale that certain men were devoted to supplying to the army.

With the sun breaking the horizon in full, more than a thousand strong rested in the shade of the trees, gathering their strength.

*   *   *   *   *

From a thicket near the banks of the Northern River, Fenton crouched low to the ground, watching something in the distance. He instinctively felt for his sword, but it was strapped to his saddle along with Reed's, which he had received at the gathering of the Véran the night before.

His horse was behind him, waiting patiently for his

master's lead; smelling the air carefully, he was growing steadily more nervous with every passing minute. With no less ease than his horse, Fenton watched the outskirts of his home, the City of Port. The area surrounding crawled with the activity of a vast army, numbering more than he could count. It was clearly not a peaceful occasion, but there appeared to have been no resistance. Congregated around the western watch of the city, a large number of them were marching toward the Beryl River. They were all dressed in dark colors, such that from where Fenton viewed their movements, they looked like thousands of black ants swarming the countryside.

A deep, sinking feeling settled over him. Port had no such army, or even much of a guard for that matter. There was only one conclusion: this was an army loyal to Mornoc. A tear rolled down Fenton's cheek as he considered Port's fate. With an army of this size from their own region, someone had to have known of it and carefully kept it hidden. Treason was at work.

"Has it come to this at last? A city of men belongs to Mornoc." His hardened countenance was full of sorrow. Fenton wiped away tears where they had formed in the corners of his eyes. Years of faithfulness in a city of opposition had accomplished nothing. Few had responded. None had followed his lead. If he returned to his home now, he would certainly be killed.

Fenton cautiously backed away from the brush, letting the branches rejoin to close on a scene that for years he had seen only in nightmares. But there was no time to mourn. Without hesitation he mounted his horse and returned the way he had come, keeping to the trees so as to avoid being seen. If he acted quickly he would be able to give Renken fair warning.

Sensing his master's urgency, Fenton's horse needed little

encouragement to make fast his flight.

CHAPTER 16

Wellman began picking up its pieces. In a dazed stupor, many went about uselessly assessing a home they would never again live in. The full range of reactions was present. Wailing grief was mixed with orderly discussion by people who knew nothing else than to move forward. Everyone knew someone that had been killed during the night. Every eye accompanied by a beating heart shed its share of tears; what action accompanied these tears began separating the strong from the weak.

The leaders of the Véran that had survived the night again provided what leadership they could to a broken people. At the forefront of every mind was the realization that the attack on Wellman the night before was only the beginning. They had not been prepared, or strong enough to withstand the first blow, and there was more to come. From the sky, Wellman was a vast ring of smoke, its outer edges a smoldering ruin.

And it was to the sky that Remiel was giving his attention.

As he went about lending aid and comfort to families that had been torn by the loss of loved ones, left homeless, or simply shaken, he kept looking to the horizons expectantly. His valiant fighting the night before had not only left him untouched but had proven his skill with the sword.

Einar and Corred puzzled over him, and they weren't the only ones.

"Any more news of the southern side?" Einar asked, still watching Remiel out of the corner of his eye.

"No more than what has been given," Corred said wearily. "He slew more than Beathan could track with or count."

With a sense of dissatisfaction, Einar nodded, "Not that it's easily counted when you are yourself embroiled in the attack."

Corred paused for a moment, feeling stretched thin. Looking over his shoulder at Remiel, his new friend was unmarked from the skirmish. He didn't even have blood on him. "I don't understand it either," he said, "but I can't believe he could be a spy, or a traitor."

"I don't know if I believe it," Einar said. "There must be another reason the southern side held." But even as Einar openly stared at Remiel, his expression quickly changed. His mouth fell open as his eyes grew wide with amazement.

What ever could . . . ? Corred turned to see what had so suddenly stunned his friend.

Breaking from the trees to the north a large bird became visible through the rising smoke. The bright white of the underneath of its wings caught every eye turned its direction. With the occasional flap of its large powerful wings it glided toward Wellman, following the northern road. Dodging effortlessly between the rising clouds of soot and ash, it silently approached. In its claws hung another animal, whose form could not yet be seen. Standing still, Remiel awaited the arrival of this magnificent creature with a wide smile on his face.

"It can't . . . it can't be," Einar said, with quiet voice. "Such a thing is . . . I have never seen such a creature."

"I have," Corred replied, addressing no one in particular. The glimpse of a soaring bird on the outskirts of town only several days ago came vividly back to him. The white of the bird's wings, its strength, speed and elegance.

Not taking his eyes from the animal for a second, Einar found it hard to form his words. "You've seen an eagle before?"

Corred nodded slowly. "I think . . . I have."

The eagle circled low over their heads, dropped its catch at Remiel's feet, and with measured beating of its wings, landed carefully on Remiel's outstretched arm. With a few quiet words, Remiel greeted the bird and stroked his back. They looked each other in the eye for a moment before Remiel lifted his arm quickly as if to throw the creature back into the air. Beating its wings smoothly, it rose again to perch on the roof of a house nearby, one of the only ones in the area that had not been harmed by fire.

Corred marveled at the fact that the same powerful talons with which the bird had crushed its prey had not even left a mark on Remiel's arm. Absent mindedly he said, "I thought you only saw an eagle when you died."

Einar closed his eyes and shook his head, trying to clear his thoughts. Looking again to where the eagle had landed, he beheld it still. With a quick turn of its head, the eagle looked right back at him. Einar ran his hand through his short hair. "Never in all my loftiest dreams did I think that this was possible." Half laughing, he turned to Remiel and once again became serious, but not in the way he had been only minutes ago.

Remiel gently knelt to examine the prey that the eagle had dropped at his feet.

Corred and Einar slowly made their way over to see what the eagle had brought, struggling to pull their gaze away from the creature.

"Brothers, come see this," Remiel said with a wide smile. He leaned over a jet black crow, still clutching a rolled parchment in its grotesquely large feet. Remiel pulled the parchment from its dead grip and looked at it curiously. He then handed it to Corred.

Carefully unrolling it, Corred held it closely to read its small print. The first thing he noticed was the signature. Chills ran down his spine as his mouth fell slightly open.

"What is it?" Einar asked, watching his young friend's reaction.

Corred did not respond, but instead handed him the note.

Einar maintained greater composure, but stammered in beginning. "It . . . it's a note of some kind, signed by . . . Casimir."

Remiel's expression hardened at the name, but it did not affect him the way it did those now listening on. His eyes narrowed and he pursed his lips. "One of the Four has sent a message. Please, read it. What does the fiend say, who is it to?"

By this time a small crowd was assembled, most of them to stare at the bird now perched over them. But as it had grown very quiet, most could hear what was spoken next.

Einar straightened up and read the contents, not aware of the number of ears now listening.

To Hildan and the Army of the North.

By the time you read this, Wellman will have fallen into my hands. Upon receiving word from our Lord, I have carried out his commands as my pleasure. With many of the Véran destroyed and its leader, Creedus, along with the Sword of Homsoloc taken captive, these lands are ripe for conquest.

As a servant of our Lord, I hereby signal your attack. Once Wellman is crushed and Port is taken by Ahriman's forces, the Northern Villages must fall. With the horsemen of the Northern Villages scattered, we will together surround Shole from the east as Sobieslaw's forces advance from the west.

Death to all who stand in our way. Amilum belongs to us.

Captain Casimir

Einar lowered the note slowly.

Bjorn and Bernd shifted in their shoes, fearing for their families, wanting to believe that this really was the message that would have doomed them if not intercepted. Would Hildan receive word of his orders another way?

For the members of the Véran, news that their leader, assumed dead, was now a captive of the very ones besieging them brought mixed emotions.

"He is alive!" Corred said. His physical pains left him at the thought.

The crowd around them looked at each other, speechless. Those who had doubted the surety of any plan on their behalf or any hope of redemption were again stirred to believe. Some providence was on their side. The word immediately began to spread around the town as people ran to tell their loved ones.

Remiel smiled widely as he watched their faces brighten, their backs straighten, and this in the midst of a town trapped in the chaos of survival. Looking to the eagle that had interceded for them all, Remiel nodded and whistled lightly.

Rising into the sky once again, the bird gave a call that

pierced the skies as it flew into the distance, returning the way it had come. Those who hadn't seen it certainly heard its shrill cry. A cry full of life and freedom, it carried to the woods in every direction and echoed in the hearts of those who heard it.

Remiel fondly watched the creature depart.

When the bird had faded from view, the crowd awoke as if from a trance and turned to look at Remiel in wonder. Though many of them had seen him over the last few days, they began to ask each other who he was for the first time.

"That was . . . an eagle?" Einar asked gently, feeling awkward to even suggest such a thing.

"Yes." Remiel smiled proudly. "That is Oswin. He has been my friend since I can remember." Remiel paused before pulling his attention away from what had just happened. He looked at Corred directly. "It appears we have another battle to prepare for. Casimir is going to overrun us." He said it with righteous contempt.

Corred caught the fire in his eye.

*   *   *   *   *

Oswin's arrival and departure had not gone unnoticed by Casimir. Feeling the growth on his face, he immediately dismissed that it could be anything other than a large bird. But even that baffled him. Most wildlife had fled the surrounding area with the coming of his army. It was indeed strange to see such a magnificent bird flying over a place of desolation and death. But the conflict of logic did not hold his attention, for he was not given to logic. It was hate that drove him.

Casimir turned to see Selcor approaching with his pouch once again full of spears. His steps were much lighter after a morning of rest.

With a slight bow he gave the impending report. "My lord, your soldiers are ready to follow you into battle."

Casimir judged the height of the sun in the sky and smiled at the thought. "Assemble them. We will advance at my command, together, from the south. I want to address Wellman before I crush it under my club."

"Yes, my lord." Selcor turned and ran back to the woods to carry out the command.

*　　*　　*　　*　　*

Remiel waited at the southern edge of Wellman, standing next to the smoldering remains of what had served as a blockade the night before. It was as if he had not changed position since the day before. With an unassuming air, he faced the woods to the south, waiting patiently.

To his left and right were Boyd and Beathan, stationed among the ruins of the outer rim. Reinforcements had been pulled from everywhere to once again strengthen the southern defense. Corred now stood with him while other members of the Véran helped Einar call every available hand to make ready for battle.

It was, once again, a waiting game. This time, no horn would sound for a second attack, for another was inevitable. But, with a sense that providence had smiled upon them, Wellman and the leaders of the Véran were filled with hope. The communications of their enemy had been thwarted. By the admission of one of the most evil beings that breathed, Creedus was alive, and the one who had interceded for them had been an eagle. Not only so, but a man who had remained untouched and unstopped the night before stood with them . . . the friend of an eagle.

Word of these mysterious revelations had spread throughout the town and even Lord Wellman was again on his feet with his sword and spear ready. Though pale from fatigue, the fire of vengeance was still burning in his eyes.

In the distance, without a word, Casimir began the march on Wellman. The whole of his army assembled behind him like a black wave, slowly covering the fields. No torches were lit this time. They were coming to kill, hand to hand.

Casimir waived his club about gently, ever measuring its weight against the strength of his arm. He loosened and tightened his grip, itching for the first blow. With the other hand he adjusted the pouch on his back full of spears made only for him.

Pacing himself, Casimir advanced on Wellman, enjoying the sight of destruction that became clearer with every step. For nearly fifty years he had been waiting to wage war once again on those who had been promised what he could never again have. The raging torrent of fury that had been building up inside of him was ready to be unleashed with abandon.

"Here they come!" Alarm began to arise in Wellman. Any women and children tending to what remained of their homes ran for the center of town. When it was clear that the attack would be from the south, men left their posts around the rest of the perimeter to meet the advance head on.

Wellman's defense found its stance, sizing up its enemy, this time in the sunlight. Tattered, weary, worn, and poorly equipped, they now faced an army of scouts that may well have been twice their numbers, trained for one purpose: their destruction. Unlike the night before, their number could now be plainly seen. It brought little comfort.

Corred and Lord Wellman joined Remiel where he stood awaiting the attack.

"Confidence is a shaky thing when its basis is unknown," Remiel said, turning to Lord Wellman. "What do the men you lead place their hope in?" he asked. Remiel posed his serious question with marked calm.

Lord Wellman looked at him blankly. "I can only speak for myself that my hope is in the continuation of my line, of Wellman, and of good men." He began to frown at their conversation and even flush with anger. "This is hardly the time for such conversation. I suggest we watch these fiends and choose a number to kill before they are upon our children. We can speak of confidence when it is regained from a battle won."

Remiel listened and heard not only his words but also the desperation and doubt in them. "A battle won," Remiel repeated quietly.

One hundred yards from the southern road into Wellman, Casimir stopped. Holding up his hand, his army halted behind him. Reaching into his clothes, he pulled out a piece of white cloth. Against the backdrop of black around it, the cloth stood out like a star against a dark night sky.

Placing it on the end of one of his spears, Casimir turned and called one of the scouts from behind him. Without hesitation he joined his captain at the front.

Casimir handed him his spear with the white cloth and addressed him sternly. "Advance to the opening of the southern road to see if they will hear your message. If they do not attack, but allow you to approach, this is the message you are to give them."

Head and shoulders above any scout in his army, Casimir appeared to the men of Wellman like a man among children. Most were rendered speechless with fear.

"Does such a man exist in the Lowlands?" Lord Wellman exclaimed. "He is taller than my spear."

"He is hardly a man," Remiel replied. "He is a Mallith. Nothing with a heart of stone is truly alive." Remiel's voice grew deeper. "That is Casimir."

Lord Wellman looked at Remiel wide-eyed. His astonishment gave him away; he had hardly believed that such a being really existed. Not until now. His mouth hung open as one who beheld a ghost. "A Mallith?" he asked silently.

"One of the Four, and arguably the cruelest," Remiel replied as he squinted under the sun. He did not seem disturbed to say it, but rather his voice seemed even stronger with the admittance.

Fully expecting a barrage of spears followed by a charge, the men lining the edge of town relaxed a little when a lone messenger began walking toward them with a flag of truce.

"It appears that Casimir would like to have a word with us before he attacks," Corred said to his companions. "Hold your arrows. Let him approach," he yelled to his right and left.

As the scout traversed the gap between his fellow scouts and the edge of town, Casimir began pacing back and forth. In a moment of silence, all eyes were on the messenger, eager to hear what this giant had to say.

Standing erect with the throwing spear in his hand, serving as a flag of truce, the messenger addressed Wellman's defense with the loudest voice he had.

"Lord Casimir, Captain of Mornoc, defies you all." He spoke more with contempt than authority. "He calls your best man to bring his weapons and fight him in this field, if there is such a man willing among you." His delivery very quickly turned to mocking. "Let him who has half a heart come forward and fight. If no such man can be found, Casimir will surely leave your town in ruins, and every life will be taken." After a short pause, he added with a sneer, "Let the hero of your forefather's stories fight for you, if he will." With that the scout stuck the spear into the ground and ran back to his army.

The men of Wellman cowered behind the smoldering remains of their houses. Deafening silence was all that followed Casimir's challenge. Whether at the hand of Casimir or his army, none would be spared, that much was clear.

The heads of Véran, Einar included, stood frozen to the ground. Corred observed those around him, watching their courage leave them like dust in the wind. His throat was dry. He couldn't speak through the fear that had gripped him also. Only his grandfather in his youth, with the Sword, would even stand a chance.

Even Lord Wellman, who had fought valiantly the night before, remained where he was. He swallowed hard, searching for something to say as his men began to shift their weight and draw back a step.

Remiel promptly drew his sword.

Lord Wellman started at the sound, looking at him with wild eyes. "He will destroy you! You yourself said that he is a Mallith!" Lord Wellman looked again at their enemy. "No man has ever defeated a Mallith!"

"One man has," Remiel replied.

"But he lived in Amilum," Lord Wellman replied. "He had the Sword! See reason, man," he pleaded.

Pointing his sword at the giant, Remiel spoke with an

authority unbecoming his appearance. "Heart of stone or of flesh, he has breathed his last murderous threat." With that, he set out upon the southern road into the fields. With his every step the sun seemed to shine more brightly, and Remiel himself began to look larger and stronger than the men of Wellman remembered him.

Casimir smiled in satisfaction at the sight. Walking forward with long strides to meet his challenger, he mocked the man's very arrival. "Have you come to end your life sooner, little man?"

When his challenger did not respond, Casimir drew one of his spears and held it high. With his club in his other hand he ran forward to make a quick end of him. But that is when he saw his opponent's face. Running to meet him, sword held high, Casimir's challenger had not the least bit of fear in his eyes. With a piercing gaze, his face was firm. The double edge of his sword shone in the sun like a flame.

When Casimir recognized who it was, he was overcome by shame and rage. "It can't be!" he whispered harshly to himself. With his nostrils flared and teeth bared, he gave a horrible cry. Releasing his spear with all his might he raised his club for a powerful blow.

Remiel rolled to the side, avoiding the first attack as Casimir's spear sailed wide and buried itself in the worn path that lead into town.

Meeting where the southern fields and the southern road joined, Casimir released his hatred in an opening blow that could have felled a tree.

Staying light on his feet, Remiel narrowly dodged Casimir's second attack. Avoiding a flurry of blows, Remiel weaved about his enemy, deflecting one strike after another with his sword.

Sparks flew into the grass every time their weapons met as the sound of metal upon metal mixed with Casimir's angry screams, echoing through the fields. Remiel's sword sliced through the air like a flash of light with every artful swing.

Each side of the battle stood in awe, watching Remiel closely. It appeared to them all that Remiel knew exactly where to step and when to deflect each blow such that Casimir was really no challenge at all. Casimir's scouts grew increasingly nervous as the men of Wellman found confidence with Casimir's every failed attack. For several minutes Remiel remained on the defensive, as if tolerating his enemy's attack.

It was not long before Casimir's rage began to take a toll on him, and his blows weakened from their initial strength. With less accuracy he sent large pieces of earth flying into the air with each wild swing. Still barring his teeth like a wild beast, his breathing became heavy and his curses fewer.

Even the sweat of Remiel's brow seemed to shine as he moved to avoid each blow, any of which could have ended his life. With confidence unwavering, he did not back down. Addressing Casimir for the first time, Remiel spoke as a master to a servant. "You know why I am here, Child of Death."

Casimir straightened to his full height and looked Remiel in the eyes. Shame deeper than words could express contorted his face. Pain and anguish gripped him, leaving nothing but rebellion, his only remaining strength.

"Today I will take your remaining life, and administer your final judgment, nameless one!" Remiel lunged toward him.

With lightning fast reflexes, Casimir tossed his club aside and pulled two spears from his pouch, one in each hand. Deflecting Remiel's strike with a downward thrust of his crossed spears, he stepped back.

Remiel continued advancing so as to stay close enough that the fight would be determined by his skill with the sword, but Casimir would not have it. Dropping back quickly he released one spear, then another, pulling and throwing with both hands.

Back on the defensive, Remiel deflected the spears with his sword, leaving each one splintered on the ground. Moving from side to side, he followed Casimir, anticipating his every attack.

When there was only one spear left in his pouch, Casimir paused for breath.

Remiel paced back and forth, knowing the end was near. With eyes fixed on Casimir's heavy arms, he steadied his breath and gripped his sword tighter.

Though it was becoming clear that he could not win, Casimir remained as defiant as he had the day he'd become a rebel. Casimir slowly pulled the last spear from his pouch. This was unlike his others, for in fact, it was not a throwing spear at all; with a long thick shaft and large double-edged blade, he gripped it in both hands, mimicking Remiel's stance. Spitting at him, Casimir spoke through set teeth. "I am Casimir, and I have no King!" With renewed vigor, he assailed Remiel, and the field was once again filled with the sound of metal upon metal.

Casimir's army began to stir, having never seen their Captain challenged before. Some scouts shifted nervously, others cursed under their breath; there were none left who believed Casimir could win. This stranger struck a fear in their hearts that they had never felt before.

Selcor watched the exchange with an icy stare, hiding his

growing dread. One thing was becoming clear: with Casimir slain and this great warrior opposing him, Wellman would not be easily taken. A plan for safe retreat was already in the forefront of his mind. Selcor had a prisoner to present to Mornoc whether Wellman fell now or later.

Wellman watched with the same eager attention. In awe of this stranger's stand, many began advancing, gripping their swords in growing expectation of victory. Each blow and block became their own as Remiel fought for them, doing what none of them could ever have done. The stir among the men of Wellman was also one of inquiry. Some even dared to ask the question: "Is this the one we have waited for? Could this be a champion from the West?" As their minds weighed the possibility, Remiel's sword made quick work of Casimir's last defense. In a series of quick slashes to the center of Casimir's spear, he broke it in two, sending half of it flying into the field.

With what he had left, Casimir made one last desperate thrust. Stepping aside, Remiel pierced him though, cracking Casimir's heart of stone.

Casimir took his last venomous breath and fell to the ground. With a weak hiss, his soul was sent to its second and everlasting exile.

The cheers that arose from Wellman were deafening. Not a single man was cowering now. With swords lifted high, they charged Casimir's army. Arrows filled the air, peppering the scouts as they turned to flee for the woods in every direction.

Lord Wellman was again leading the charge, pursuing the enemy with abandon.

Remiel joined in the routing, striking down every scout that crossed him. Some turned to fight, but in vain, for they could not stand against him.

Corred, Einar, and Bjorn were all there, fighting side by side.

The southern fields were littered with the bodies of the enemy as the sun began its descent. Casimir's scouts fled south, back to where they had come from. Food, drink, spears, torches, and every other thing they had carried was abandoned.

The tables had fully turned; chaos and fear filled the enemy when only a night before they themselves had been cause for trembling. All this had been accomplished by one man.

He is more than a man. Corred marveled at Remiel. Never before had he seen such confident bravery and a willingness to fight for others in the face of death. *And to think that he had arrived so unnoticed. He even gave me a drink of water before he took his own.*

Talk was on the lips of every man, woman, and child. Talk of redemption. As surely as Casimir's body was left lying in the southern fields, so some began to believe that the long-awaited warrior, promised to their fathers, had at last arrived, a deliverer from the West who would bring renewal and an end to exile, for the hope of every heart and the life of every soul.

But even for those who knew the whole Promise, word for word, they did not know in full how it would be fulfilled. War had only just begun and it would not suddenly end with the death of one of the Four. Those that had remained in Wellman from the Northern Villages knew that from the words of the late Casimir had come orders for a far greater force to attack their homes. Not taking for granted that that news had been providentially intercepted, Bjorn, Bernd, and the others they had traveled with did not wait for morning before they began their ride home. They beseeched Remiel to accompany and lead them, but he sent them on with a blessing as he had already decided to join the effort to rescue Creedus and the Sword.

*　　*　　*　　*　　*

Sobieslaw's robe flowed behind him as he made his way through the halls of the Black Mountain with long strides; a small parchment was in his hand. Ignoring the commotion around him, the news in his hand carried him forward.

Bounding up the steps to Mornoc's hall, his usual display of reverence was slightly more rushed than usual. Approaching Mornoc, who ever drummed his fingers on the arm of his throne, Sobieslaw held out the parchment with the full length of his arm, not daring to touch his lord's throne.

Mornoc rose and received it. For a short moment he read silently.

> Lord Mornoc, the true King of Amilum.
>
> As surely as you read this, Wellman has fallen into my hands. Upon receiving your wishes, I have carried out your command: to strike at the heart of hope and render your enemies leaderless. Many of the Véran have been destroyed and its leader, Creedus and the Sword of Homsoloc will soon be a trophy of your power. These lands are ripe for conquest.
>
> Captain Casimir

Seeing that his plans were in motion, Mornoc returned the parchment to Sobieslaw and addressed him. "Send Captain Casimir my congratulations. Inform him that Creedus is to be brought to my hall immediately, lest the Sword fall into the hands of another man as courageous as he."

Sobieslaw bowed slightly. "And what of his next task, my lord?"

Mornoc continued as if the question had not been asked. "Port will have fallen by this hour, as it is a city worthy of paying allegiance to me. It will not have resisted save for a few weak-minded individuals who have misplaced their hope." Mornoc sat down slowly, thinking. The war he had so patiently planned was finally under way, and it brought a contented smile to his face. His terror would once again reign. Turning again to Sobieslaw, he finished, "I thoroughly expect that Ahriman is carrying out his plans for an attack on Renken. Casimir is to join him there after killing or converting every man, woman, and child in between."

Sobieslaw again bowed, this time to the ground. "As you wish, my lord." In his fashion, Sobieslaw left in a hurry to fulfill Mornoc's commands. As he had so many times before, he flew to his chamber, giving word to his guard of the message that was to be sent.

As command gave way to action, Sobieslaw's guard traversed the Black Mountain's desolate courtyard as the day's shadows were reaching their full length. He thought of nothing but his task and the news he carried, looking neither to the right or left; he noticed nothing different. But only yards from the path, the green shoot of a small flower began to rise. Yet unseen behind a large rock, its single bud reached for the sky, boldly displaying the bright red of its pedals.

CHAPTER 17

As shadows in the Lowlands grew long in the setting sun, the stride of a large creature carried on untiring. Its immense power drove every step, pounding the earth relentlessly. On the back of this horse-like beast rode a man dressed in black, his cloak flying behind him in the wind. His features were sharp and his skin pale, standing out against his dark hair. Strapped to his back was a pouch of short spears, more closely resembling large arrows. The tension in his face spoke of the nature of his mission and the long sword hanging from his waist revealed its significance.

Behind him three more hargus drummed their rhythmic gallop, each with its own rider. On the right and left were men dressed the same as the first: a pouch of spears, dark dress, and a stony countenance. In between these two rode an old man dressed in ordinary clothing, the one in the party against his will. With no coat to keep him warm, he gripped the mane of his mount, trying to hide from the wind. Despite his efforts it pulled at his shirt, long white hair, and his very strength. His once long white beard had been shorn off and his wrists were tied tightly with cords, cutting into his skin. A cut across his cheek and battered hands were signs of his resistance, but it had not been enough.

His head was still tender from some of the blows he had received two nights before, when he had awakened to a band of scouts entering his cabin. Before he could reach for his sword or even cry for help, they had thrown him to the ground, leaving him with little to do but gasp for air. All that night he had fought, breaking free once, but to no avail. His every attempt at freedom earned him some new stripe and worse treatment than he would have received if he had been compliant.

Creedus was at last looking and feeling the part of his age, worn to the core. The one thing that remained the same was the look in his eyes. In them could still be found a glimmer of hope. Even though his captor, Selcor now carried the Sword of Homsoloc, a prize that he had sworn to lose his life to protect, he did not wear the face of despair; something far greater than the Sword filled his thoughts now. He knew that Wellman had withstood the attack, and that Casimir was dead. It was because of these events that he was being so desperately rushed toward Mornoc's keep.

Creedus had seen it even in his captor's cold eyes: the fear of one greater than the wicked captain he had once served. Creedus' initial suspicions of such a thing had been openly confirmed by the stammering speech of one of the scouts in his escort. Dragged from his cell in the crevices of the Bryn Mountains, Creedus had watched in awe as many of the scouts that had returned were without weapons and scared witless.

There was talk of the one who had slain Casimir, a man who shone as bright as the sun in battle. It was almost more than Creedus could contain, for he knew of only one who could have accomplished this: the promised champion, sent by the King. *Could this at long last be him?* He whispered to himself. And so Creedus was sustained within, though his outward strength was failing him.

Selcor hadn't stopped pressing the pace since they had left the southernmost part of the Bryn Mountains hours before, and Creedus knew they were not likely to stop anytime soon. The hargus was nearly twice as large as a horse and could run nearly twice as far without rest. Lifting his head to look again, Creedus could almost make out what looked to be the beginning of the Plains of Shole to the north. The land opened up more and more the further away from the Bryn Mountains they rode. It would be faster traveling in the open, but a much greater risk of being seen. It was clear that Selcor was leading them to the south to avoid Shole and its surrounding towns.

Trying to maintain his grip on his hargus mane, Creedus lived each moment one at a time. Not only was he suffering from the cold, he had had nothing to eat in over a day. Wanting to communicate with the scout on his right, Creedus turned his head slightly, looking to see whether he might catch his attention. The scout's pale face was riveted on the path ahead, as if he were in a trance. Creedus reached out his right hand, waving it about, hoping to catch the scout's attention.

After a moment the scout caught the motion out of the corner of his eye and turned his head. Glaring at Creedus with disapproval he returned to watching Selcor's lead.

Creedus tried again, waving his hand and holding it then to his mouth. Moving his lips, no sound came out of his dry throat. When he tried again, he could barely hear his own words. "I need bread. Do you have any food?"

The scout shook his head without really giving any acknowledgement that he understood Creedus' requests.

Giving up after a few more tries, Creedus accepted that suffering would be his place in this journey. Hugging again the back of his hargus, he buried his face in its mane and shut the wind out of his mind. When his stomach cramped, he told it to be patient. When fear began to creep into his thoughts, he remembered what the scouts had said about the battle of Wellman. When anger toward his captors threatened his peace of mind, he recounted the Promise, knowing that they hated because they had no hope.

Into the night Creedus held onto his remaining strength, stealing glimpses at the stars and what the moonlight would allow him to see. He had to keep his mind active. The cold was setting deep into his limbs, making it hard to stay awake. A fall from the hargus could be fatal at the speed they were moving. He could not let go. Though a prisoner, he was still a leader of his people. Since the hour of his capture, he had thought of Corred, wondering how he was faring without him. Creedus knew that Corred was not ready for the leadership he had been thrust into, and especially without the Sword. But it was too late now. Many things should have happened differently.

"A champion has come," Creedus whispered to himself. "A champion has come . . . as surely as the brightest star still shines in the sky." Creedus looked up yet again; the brightest stars were shining. He continued, whispering to himself, ". . . a deliverer from the West to bring an end to exile, for the hope of every heart and the life of every soul. He will come swiftly to crush our enemies and to make a way of return to the home of our father . . . the City of Amilum." Even as he finished he noticed the speed of his hargus lessening. Looking ahead he saw his captor pulling up on the reins of his ride.

Leading them into a cluster of trees, Selcor slid from his hargus to the ground and tied it immediately to one of the lower branches. In one motion he drew from his supplies a very large bag of feed and poured it on the ground for the hargus to eat. His fellow scouts did the same, sure to feed the animals right away to keep them calm. They were beasts of fierce emotion and had to be handled just right.

Creedus could only try to make out what was taking place in the darkness around him. He couldn't feel his limbs. Laboring to sit up straight, his mount began to paw the earth restlessly, seeing that the others were being fed. His vision began to swim. Hugging the side of the beast, he tried to slide to the ground, but with little success. He fell with a heavy thud, knocking the wind from his lungs. Rolling to his hands and knees, he waited for the air to return. Pain shot through his body like a thousand needles as the blood began to flow more freely into his arms and legs.

"Help him up. I'll take his mount," a deep voice said.

Creedus rolled onto his back and closed his eyes, trying to relax as he waited for a breath. The scout taking orders bent over him, grabbed his arms and pulled him to his feet.

"His arms are colder than my hands," the scout said with some surprise in his voice.

With a long, loud gasp, Creedus used his first few breaths to groan as his muscles began to burn. He could do nothing to help in the process. As soon as he was lifted to his feet, he collapsed back to the earth.

"Make a fire, quickly. I will give him my cloak for now.

Our lord will not be pleased if he dies before we complete our journey." The third voice stood out from the others as coming from the one who was in charge. Creedus could hardly feel the cloak as it was laid around his shoulders. Struggling to now calm his breathing, he began to convulse with cold. Every joint in his body screamed. "Water!" he gasped. "Water, please, give me some water." Creedus felt like he was yelling but all that came out was a hoarse whisper.

"Here, drink some of this." Selcor handed him a small canteen. Not stopping to question its contents, Creedus brought it to his lips and drank, choking a little on his first mouthful. Creedus' throat felt as if it was on fire. After another mouthful it became clear that it was not water at all. Coughing a little he handed the canteen back in disgust. "What is this?" he rasped. His mouth still felt dry.

Selcor squatted in front of him and took the canteen back. "It's the strongest ale that can be made, so leave some for us, old man. You'll get your water as soon as we can get a fire going." Leaving him there he walked to the edge of the trees to observe the fields to the north.

Creedus' feeling slowly returned to him, arms first, then his legs as he watched the other scouts build a fire before him. His senses grew sharper with every breath, and the fire in the drink coursed through his veins. Puzzled that fermented drink would have such an effect, he pulled the cloak around his body and tried to gather some warmth. As the first flames licked the air, his surroundings became clearer. The scouts who had been accompanying him on either side drew some provisions from their packs and sat down to a meal of cold, dried meat.

Returning from the edges of the trees, Selcor stood by the fire and stared into the flame. The Sword of Homsoloc was still belted to his waist. Resting his hand on its hilt, he turned to look at Creedus with a cold stare. His eyes were hollow from lack of sleep but wide open.

Creedus returned his gaze, calm enough in his weakness for the first time to stop and observe his captor. "May I have some bread?" he asked humbly.

Without a word Selcor returned to his hargus, which was just finishing its own meal. Bringing his pack of supplies back to the fire, Selcor drew a crust of bread and a canteen of water. Tossing them to Creedus he commented, "A prisoner's ration, as that is what you have become."

Creedus nodded, not surprised by his captor's pride. He knew how great a prize the Sword was to the enemy. Turning his attention now to other tactics, he ate his bread silently, watching his captors. His hope of escape had passed as his desire to fight had faded with his strength. Now he would need to wage his war with words, choice words. Searching the scouts for a foothold with which to engage them in conversation, Creedus watched their every move.

For some time no one said a word. At a point, all four of them were quietly watching the flames as they finished their last bit of food and drink. Creedus seized the moment to mumble very softly, "As surely as the brightest star still shines in the sky."

The scouts sitting across from him snapped out of their own thoughts and stared at him. Selcor did not respond at all. Returning their stare, Creedus watched Selcor out of the corner of his eye. He asked them with a tone of surprise, "Have you never heard of such a saying?"

"Save your breath, old man," Selcor jumped on top of the conversation. His tone was sharp. "The stars don't always shine, and fortune can be lost in one night." He glared at Creedus. "A scout of Mornoc carries the Sword of Homsoloc."

Creedus could see his features more clearly when he turned to face him. The flames cast a soft glow on his gaunt cheeks and sharp jaw. "And what scout might that be?" Creedus quickly asked, as if to challenge his captor.

"My name is Selcor, second in command to Casimir, captain of Mornoc," he proudly responded.

"Which makes you first in command, as your mighty captain has been slain by one greater," Creedus said, nearly interrupting him. He pushed the limit to see their response.

The other two scouts glared at him angrily, but Creedus could see the fear in their eyes renewed. Selcor curled his upper lip in anger. Slowly rising to his feet, he drew the Sword of Homsoloc, letting it ring just as Creedus had countless times before.

Creedus watched in amazement as Selcor held the weapon skillfully, as if it fit in his hand. Adjusting his grip, Selcor took a step toward Creedus, continuing the sharp exchange. "Yes, and a worthy loss for a prize as great as the Sword." His voice was more than sinister. Sticking the blade into the glowing coals he locked eyes with Creedus.

The blade shined in the flames, revealing its inscription. Much to Creedus' surprise it was as brilliant in this scout's hand as it had been in his. But he remained calm, knowing the result of this exercise as he had done it before.

After a long and dramatic pause, Selcor drew the sword from the coals and stepped toward Creedus, thrusting the tip at him. But instead of stabbing him, as his fellow scouts had half expected, Selcor turned the blade to rest the flat of it on

Creedus' neck.

Keeping his eyes locked on Selcor's, Creedus did not even flinch. There was no hiss of burning flesh, no cry of pain or even a single hair singed.

Creedus smiled slightly, enjoying the shocked faces of his captives.

Displeased that his treachery had been thwarted, Selcor turned the blade again and cut some of Creedus' hair from below the ear in a quick twist of his wrist. Returning the tip of the sword to his throat, Selcor looked down his arm. "I don't think you respect the power of my position. I am no common soldier of Mornoc." Returning the sword to its sheath, Selcor returned to his seat. In that moment, as Selcor leaned toward the fire Creedus caught a glimpse of something that made his heart skip a beat. Just inside the collar of Selcor's coat, a nasty scar much like the one he'd tried to give Creedus twisted up from his shoulder.

Creedus tried with every ounce of his control to hide his amazement. A hundred memories flooded his mind as he searched for the answer. Faces and names from the past bombarded him so quickly that he felt faint, but he had no doubt as to whom this scout before him was: Androcles.

Selcor turned to glare at him again, but this time, Creedus saw someone else. The slightest hint of his young grandson remained, lying just under the hardened surface of Selcor's face.

ABOUT THE AUTHOR

Born and raised in the suburbs of Philadelphia, Jaffrey Clark was never without a love for story. There are recordings of tale-telling as early as age four. Reading and writing since then, Jaffrey has been working specifically on "The Reaper's Seed" (among other plots) since it first struck his imagination in the Spring of 2003. After a lot of off-and-on again periods of focused writing and failed attempts to find a literary agent for representation, Jaffrey at last decided to publish independently. "The Sword and the Promise" is the first installment of "The Reaper's Seed," which remains a work in progress. Find out more about the book, the series, and the author at www.jaffreyclark.com.